RACHEL MUCHA

BAD PRESS

BAD PRESS

RACHEL MUCHA

CITY OWL
PRESS

BAD PRESS
By Rachel Mucha

CITY OWL PRESS
www.cityowlpress.com

Cover Design by MiblArt. All stock photos licensed appropriately.

Edited by Mary Cain.

For information on subsidiary rights, please contact the publisher at info@cityowlpress.com.

Print Edition ISBN: 978-1-64898-188-3

Digital Edition ISBN: 978-1-64898-187-6

Printed in the United States of America

This one's for the Mucha Squad.

CHAPTER ONE

WHEN ASKED TO DESCRIBE HIS MUSIC, INSTEAD OF AN ADJECTIVE OR *two, Dave Austin just lets out a laugh.*

"It's practically indescribable," he shares with a grin. "People want to stick me in the Country category, but that's not quite right. My songs can be folk-y, but a little rock and roll, too. And some of them have such a stripped-down indie feel. In case you can't tell, I don't like labels."

When pressed for one all-encompassing word, Austin finally takes the bait.

"Unique," he says. "Just completely, one-hundred-percent, uniquely me."

I continued typing up my story, eyes darting to reference my notes, even though local singer/songwriter Dave Austin's interview reads nearly word for word as his peers' I've covered recently.

Just keep typing, Evie.

I tried to banish any cynical thoughts from my head, reminding myself that I was fortunate to have this job — even if writing puff pieces about wannabe country music stars wasn't my first choice. Or second choice. Or sixth choice.

You're lucky to be employed as a writer at all, I thought, more forcefully this time to get the message to stick. I always liked to look on the positive side, but when you write enough of these stories, you just sort of want to scream.

"You okay? You're making that face again."

I looked across my desk at my colleague and best friend, Grace Lee. She knew all too well how soul-crushing I found the Arts and Culture beat.

"How can I be making a face when I'm writing about the *unique* Dave Austin?" I flashed her a grin.

"I heard him at open mic night at The Ranch a few weeks ago," Grace said. "He's unique in the sense that he's not that great, but still lands gigs."

"What are you working on? Something more exciting?"

"Eh, the hardware store down the street got into the habit of not paying people overtime, and they just settled a pretty big lawsuit," she said. "The details are boring, though."

"I'd kill to write about that," I said, slumping in my chair. Grace covered the business beat, which had been my third choice—hypothetically, of course. I didn't get a vote in my assigned beat. It was either Arts and Culture, or no job—and man, did I need a job.

I opened my mouth to ask Grace if she wanted to procrastinate our assignments by grabbing an early lunch, but shouting from our editor's office made both our heads snap towards it.

"...is *unbelievable*," Shelly yelled. She brought her voice down a tick, but I managed to catch an additional, "...should absolutely know better!"

I looked back to Grace, eyes wide. "What's that all about? Who's in there?"

Looking just as bewildered as me, she quickly surveyed the newsroom, noting whose desk was empty. "Jeff?"

Grace's suspicion was confirmed a few seconds later when Jeff Borelli burst out of Shelly's office, swinging the door open with so much force it collided with the wall. Every reporter's eyes followed his movements as he marched to his desk and began tossing various possessions inside the cardboard box he carried.

"Whoa," Grace murmured as we all continued to watch him. Another minute later, a security guard I didn't even know we had wandered over to Jeff's desk, hands on his hips, legs widened into an intimidating stance.

"Seriously?" Jeff yelled over his shoulder towards Shelly's office.

"Sir, you need to leave," the guard said, voice deep as the ocean. "You can't take anything except personal effects."

"This is *bullshit*," Jeff muttered not-so-quietly. He tossed two framed photos into his box, the surface of his desk cluttered with folders and legal pads he had to leave behind.

"Well, show's over, folks!" Jeff said, already halfway to the door.

The security guard brought up the rear, disappearing with Jeff into the hallway.

The hush amongst us all remained for a solid thirty seconds.

"*What* just happened?" It had all gone down so quickly, I needed verbal confirmation everyone else had seen it too.

"It's about time," Maggie shouted from across the office. "I never liked him."

"It's gotta be porn," Phil chimed in. "When that happens, it's always porn."

"Did you hear what the guard said about not taking anything?" Alyssa asked. "Was Jeff stealing stuff from here?"

"What's there to steal?" Grace gave her monitor a hearty smack. "My nine-year-old nephew has a nicer computer than I do."

Murmurs of agreement filled the newsroom, and more people shouted out wild theories about what Jeff could've done.

"Wait," I said to Grace, tearing her attention away from the gossip. "Wasn't Jeff working on an update on the serial rapist?"

"I think he was."

"Well, who's going to write it now?" I asked.

She shrugged. "Beats me. Something tells me this firing wasn't planned."

I turned once more towards Shelly's office, wondering if she'd thought this through yet. She couldn't just not have someone covering the crime beat. Surely, she'd be reassigning it soon—and if I pounced now, I could throw my hat in the ring.

I sprung out of my chair.

"Shelly?"

Lingering outside her office, I gently knocked on her half-open door. She held a phone receiver to her ear, but when she noticed me, she whispered something quickly and hung up.

"Evie, now's not a good time," she said. "I have to meet with HR in a few minutes. I'll answer your questions about Jeff as soon as I can."

"Well, I actually wanted to ask about Jeff's story." I dared to step inside. "His piece on the serial rapist."

"Oh, *shit*." Shelly closed her eyes and massaged her temples. "That was supposed to run tomorrow."

"I know." I took a breath. "I was going to offer to finish it up."

Shelly stared at me like I'd spoken a different language. "But you have your own assignments already."

"I'm almost done the Austin piece," I said, even though I'd only just started. "I could spend the rest of the afternoon on Jeff's story."

"Hmm." Shelly drummed her fingers on her desk.

"You know," I settled into the seat across from her desk, "I have experience covering the crime beat. I did that in D.C. for two years. I would love to do it again."

I held my breath as Shelly considered this. My kind but tough editor had a really good poker face, and it was impossible to tell which way she was leaning.

"Evie, you know I think you're a very capable writer, but, if I remember correctly, you had some...issues on the crime beat?"

I tried not to sigh. The "issues" she was referring to were a series of ethical missteps that had cost me my job at the *Post* and my professional reputation. The backlash had been so severe I'd had to move six hours away to Podunk, Virginia to find a paper that would take me. Shelly didn't know the details of my slip-up, but my lack of a reference from my previous editor spoke volumes.

I was grateful for this job, but I couldn't help but feel a sense of ownership when it came to the crime beat. It was what I was supposed to do. And now that the opportunity was hanging right in front of me, I couldn't not reach out and grab it.

"That's right, I did have a bit of trouble back there," I said. "But I promise you, I've learned my lesson. I always do everything completely by the book now. You've never had one complaint about my work."

Shelly's mouth quirked to the side. "It's just, with what happened with Jeff, we can't afford to have any more scandals—especially with our crime reporter. It's an important section to get right."

Even more curiosity gnawed at me about what scandalous thing Jeff had done, but I forced myself to focus on the task at hand.

"Absolutely." I paused before continuing. "Why don't you let me just try this one story? And if you're satisfied with it, maybe I could take on the beat on a more permanent basis?"

"Okay." She gave me a weak smile. "I'm in a bind here, so if you deliver on this, we can talk."

"Thank you," I said, leaping out of my chair. "Don't worry. I'm on it."

Shelly had already turned back to her phone, too distracted to bask in my victory with me.

I hustled to my desk. "Grace! Shelly says I can do Jeff's story."

"That's great," she said. "But what about Dave Austin?"

"Oh, who cares about Dave Austin!"

Fifteen minutes later, I'd swiped every notepad from Jeff's desk and started poring over his scribblings. The man had atrocious handwriting, but I finally found what I was looking for.

Four attacks now, same M.O., no suspects announced by PD. Call Delaney for quote and update.

My heart slowly began to sink. This wasn't much to go on. I'd been following the story of the serial rapist, of course—what woman in town wouldn't be? But based on previous articles, it appeared little was known about him, and Jeff seemingly had planned to write an entire story based off information from this Delaney person.

A quick Google search brought me to the Bristol PD's website, gifting me Detective Tom Delaney's extension. I eagerly dialed.

"Delaney," a gruff voice answered after three rings.

"Hi," I said, tone chipper. "This is Evie Hartley from *Bristol Daily News*. I was hoping I could talk to you for a few minutes about the serial rapist."

There was a long pause. "What happened to Jeff? I normally talk to him."

"Jeff is...no longer with the paper," I said. "But I'm taking over for him. So would you be able to give me a quick update on the investigation?"

"Look, lady. I don't know you, and I sure as hell don't have time to chat. I've got a case to solve."

With that, Delaney hung up on me. I stared at my receiver for a moment, a little stunned by his shortness. It was true that cops didn't love talking with reporters, but Delaney seemed to be punishing me for the simple crime of not being Jeff.

"Okay..." I refused to let myself get discouraged. I'd been out of the crime game for a bit. I'd forgotten how tough it could be to get sources to spill. Budding country music singers aren't as tight-lipped as cops working a serial rapist case.

Scrolling through Bristol PD's list of officers, I learned our tiny town only had three bona fide detectives, counting Delaney. Two chances left.

I called Nicole Zimmerman next. A female detective would be all too familiar with handling sexism at work—she might throw me a bone.

"Detective Zimmerman."

"Hi, this is Evie Hartley from *Bristol Daily News*. I—"

A loud click cut off my spiel. Again, I was surprised. How was she ruder than Delaney? What happened to girl power?

Starting to panic now, I dialed number three on the list, Marcus Pennington. The call went straight to voicemail, and I didn't bother with a message. I wondered if he wasn't there, or if his colleagues had warned him not to answer. Didn't really matter, either way.

"Everything okay?" Grace asked as she sat, having returned from a fast-food run.

I threw down my pen. "The cops aren't talking, and Jeff left me nothing." I threw down my pen.

She offered me sympathy fries, and I took a few. "Sorry. It's tough coming into it last minute like this. You might need to get creative."

I shoved the fries into my mouth and tried not to panic. Back in D.C. I'd started from scratch as a crime reporter once, with no connections. Sure, I was a little crunched for time this go around, but I could do it again.

Opening a new tab, I brought up Facebook and searched for Delaney, since he was the only one who'd actually talked to me. I easily found his profile and was pleased to see he posted *a lot*. If I could bump into him somewhere, it'd be harder for him to blow me off.

Scrolling through his page, I looked for any usual haunts. A few weeks ago, he "checked into" Last Call, a local dive bar so seedy looking, I'd never set foot inside. I read the comments, an exchange between Delaney and someone named Paul—the owner.

Thanks for stopping by tonight, Tom. Come back soon!

Those wings are KILLER. Glad Marcus dragged me along.

Haha, he should be our poster boy for wing night. Can't remember the last time he missed one.

Marcus. Could that be detective number three, Marcus Pennington? It would make sense. Excitement rushed through me as I realized it was Wing Wednesday. Would Pennington be there tonight? The owner's comment made me think yes.

I did a quick search for Pennington. He had a Facebook page, but his privacy settings were on. All I could see was a thumbnail of his profile picture, which told me two vague things: brown hair, youngish. Showing up at Last Call in the hopes he'd be there was hit or miss, but if I couldn't get in contact with a source soon, it'd be my only option.

I spent the rest of the afternoon alternating between writing more about Dave Austin's *unique* music and trying Bristol's elusive detectives again, getting nothing but voicemails.

Grace was right—it was time to get creative.

CHAPTER TWO

I PULLED INTO LAST CALL'S PARKING LOT JUST AFTER SEVEN, snagging a spot right in front of the establishment. Car idling, I dug through my purse with shaky hands. After locating the lipstick I was after, I held my frozen fingers in front of the vents and let the blasting heat defrost them a bit before attempting makeup. It was only early October, but the day had been chilly and damp. A few stray drops from an earlier storm plopped onto my windshield from the bar's awning.

I yanked down the visor and slid open the mirror, cringing a bit. Some serious touch-ups were in order. I'd been up since seven a.m. and looked it.

Before tackling the makeup situation, a moment of uncertainty made me pause. What I was about to do was a slippery slope, putting me in danger of falling back into old, bad habits—but, God, did I want this. I couldn't just give up and walk back to Shelly a failure, without having tried my hardest. So I pushed the doubt from my mind. No use worrying about it now.

Fingers no longer icicles, I applied a dark rose lipstick (aptly named Dangerous Liaisons) then unleashed my wavy, dirty blonde hair from my signature ponytail. I ran a comb through it and attempted to fluff it up a little, hoping it looked intentionally wild instead of like it hadn't been washed this morning. After reapplying some deodorant and perfume, I examined myself in the tiny mirror again. Better. I'd flirt with me. I turned off the car and sat for another minute, mustering up my courage.

Finally, after deciding at the last minute to undo one more button on my blouse, I got out of the car and hustled into Last Call.

The inside of the bar matched the parking lot—deserted. Not surprising for a dive bar in a small town on a Wednesday night. But I didn't need a lot of people to be here. Just one.

I took a few steps inside, trying to act like I belonged, but my professional blouse and cigarette pants might as well have been a Halloween costume. A couple of beefy guys playing pool shot me some weird looks. Not leers, exactly—more like that cliché question *"What's a girl like her doing in a place like this?"* had popped into their heads.

Rock music played softly over the speakers, and the two TVs at either end of the bar were tuned in to the same baseball game. A man across the room gave a robust "hoot," and I jumped—but he'd just been celebrating hitting the bullseye on the dartboard. His companion rolled his eyes and dug some cash out of his pocket. There wasn't another woman in this place.

Relax, Evie, I told myself as I approached the bar. As a journalist, I'd learned to be bold and annoyingly pushy—but tonight was different. Even though reporters pulled this kind of shit all the time, I hadn't done something like this since my old life. I'd sworn to myself I'd never do it again, and I'd managed to keep that promise while covering the arts.

Unfortunately, due to aforementioned reasons, this questionable, unethical move was necessary.

Here's to hoping I don't get burned this time.

I saw him right away—or who I assumed was him. He was the only guy wearing a tie, and he had the dark hair I knew to look for. I also spied an empty red basket near him, which presumably once contained hot wings. God bless creatures of habit. First major hurdle, cleared.

Now all I had to do was get something out of him. Easier said than done.

I headed in Marcus Pennington's direction and took a seat, leaving one barstool between us. Resting my arms on the sticky bar top, I tried to appear as casual as possible.

"What can I get ya, hon?" A big bearded man asked me.

"I'm so tired I can't even think of what I want," I said with a loud giggle, rubbing my face for effect. I turned to look at my target on my left. "I'll have whatever he's having."

Pennington finished the dregs of his glass in one gulp. "Make that two," he told the bartender with a slight southern twang. He snuck a peek at me, and I offered him a small, friendly smile. He didn't smile back, but he turned to the bartender and said, "You can put hers on my tab."

"Thanks," I told him.

He gave me a nod. "I've already wracked up quite the bill tonight. What's one more?"

So he'd been here a while, drowning his sorrows. That didn't bode well.

The bartender returned and set a clear drink in front of both of us. I picked it up and took a big sip, which I immediately regretted.

"Holy crap," I choked out, coughing a few times. "What the hell is this?"

"Double shot of gin, with just a splash of tonic." A slight smile curved Pennington's lips.

My chest burned and my eyes watered, but I acted like I could drink liquor like this. I took a very small second sip, but still had to stifle a cough.

"You hate it." He cracked a true smile. "We can get you something else."

"No, no," I said, waving my hand. "I played Russian roulette with my drink order and lost. I can accept that."

Pennington shook his head and smiled again. "You mind?" He gestured towards the stool between us.

"Not at all." My heart rate kicked up. It somehow made me queasy that this was going exactly as planned so far—like I was back to my old tricks without ever having skipped a beat.

He got up and reseated himself on the barstool beside me. "I was going to ask if you come here often, even though I know you don't, since I'm here all the time."

"First time. I tend to do most of my drinking at home alone, but that gets kind of depressing after a while."

"Ah," he said. "Drinking at home alone. I know it well." Pennington took an easy sip of his drink, having no trouble downing the gin.

"I wanted to try something different tonight," I went on, "but this might've been a little too different. I feel like I stick out like a sore thumb here." I glanced over my shoulder at the men playing pool, who were still staring at me.

"Not a lot of women who look like you come around. Especially now with the...with everything going on."

Hallelujah! The perfect segue.

"*Oh*," I said. "Right, the rapes. What is it, three now?"

"Four," he corrected me, as I knew he would. "Four in the past six weeks, all random attacks. This guy is sick. You should be careful, especially coming places like this alone."

"Oh, it's okay. I've got my pepper spray." I pulled out my keys to show him the tiny pink tube on the keychain.

"Cute." His tone was unimpressed. He took another sip of his drink. "I'd be happy to walk you to your car when you're ready to leave."

There was a hint of flirtation mixed in with his concern, and my heart rate picked up for a reason other than nerves. Based on his tiny profile picture, I'd guessed he wasn't hideous, but life-sized and in person, he was handsome. "Youngish" had been accurate—I pegged him for thirty-five. He had a strong jaw, and his thick head of dark hair was messy in rugged sort of way. There was a permanent crease between his brows, which led me to believe he did a lot of scowling, but he somehow pulled off this bristly, unfriendly demeanor. He looked tired in the dim bar, but I had the feeling in the bright light of day, Pennington was a hottie.

"That's a nice offer." I risked a flirty smile, leaned in close and lowered my voice to a dramatic whisper. "But how do I know you're not the rapist? That could be the exact line he feeds his victims, pretending to be all gentlemanly and concerned for their safety."

Pennington cocked his head, considering my reasoning. Then, without saying anything else, he reached into his back pocket and pulled out his wallet. He flicked it open and showed me his police shield.

"Wow," I said, trying to react as if I hadn't already known this. "I feel safer already." I reached out and touched the metal, ensuring my fingers brushed his. After taking another sip of the horrendous drink, I added, "Although, that doesn't exactly prove you're not the guy."

"Fair point. That's smart, really—not to be too trusting. Badge could be fake for all you know."

"Well, that makes me feel better," I said dryly.

He extended his hand. "Marcus Pennington." His accent made it sound more like *Pin*nington. "You can look me up if you want. I'm legit."

Oh, buddy, if only you knew how much I've already looked you up.

I shook his big hand, which enveloped mine. "Evie." Hopefully, his colleagues hadn't mentioned the pesky reporter who'd called them earlier. Couldn't risk recognition at this stage.

"Based on the tie, I'm going to guess you're a detective?" I widened my eyes. "Perhaps on these rape cases?"

"Are you sure *you're* not a detective?"

"A writer." The nervous sweat was back as I waited for him to figure out I was a journalist trying to manipulate confidential case information out of him.

"A writer," Pennington repeated, taking another swig of his drink. "What do you write?"

"I do reviews." I attempted to maintain normal eye contact. "Movies and books, mostly." I held my breath, waiting to see if he bought it. This wasn't technically a lie. After my old editor and I decided it'd be mutually beneficial if I left the *Post*, I did some freelancing for online magazines for a few months. That little stint was enough to attract Shelly's attention, who thought I'd be perfect for her Arts and Culture opening.

"Huh," Pennington said. "That sounds fun."

There was a lag in the conversation, and I decided to go for it.

"So how concerned should I really be about this rapist?" I swiveled in my stool so my knee bumped his under the bar ever so gently. I decided to stay like that, leg pressed against his, and Pennington didn't move away.

"Well..." He finished his drink. "You didn't hear this from me, but we've got nothing. No solid leads or suspects. The attacks are random, with no obvious connection between the victims, which means he doesn't have a particular type. So, yeah, you should be careful."

I considered this with a thoughtful nod as the headline formed in my head: *Bristol PD gives update on serial rape cases: "We've got nothing."*

"Surely, you've got something," I pushed on. "DNA, at least? Unless this guy is a considerate rapist who uses a condom?"

Pennington smirked. "Yeah, we've got DNA." He gave me a nudge with his knee. "Doesn't do much good if you don't have any suspects to check it against."

DNA doesn't do much good if you don't have any suspects to check it against. I couldn't have written it better myself. Between the "we've got nothing" headline and this quote, I had a tantalizing new angle about how no woman in Bristol, Virginia—or maybe even in our twin city of Bristol, Tennessee right across the border—should feel safe.

"That's rough," I said. "Can't be easy on you. I'm sure there's a lot of pressure to catch this guy."

"You have no idea." Pennington twirled the melting ice around in his empty glass. "Why do you think I've had three of these?"

"Impressive. I could only manage three sips."

"That does it. We're getting you something else." Pennington grabbed my drink and slid it in front of himself, then waved over the bartender.

"What's your drink?" he asked.

"Rum and coke."

The bartender fixed it and set it in front of me, and I took a few sips. "Much better."

"I don't know why you just didn't order that from the beginning," he said.

"I needed a way to get your attention." I smiled. "And look, it worked."

Pennington cocked his eyebrow and gave me a bemused smile that made my heart flutter a bit. Why was I still flirting with him? I'd somehow managed to get what I needed. I should've been focusing on finishing this drink and making an excuse to get out of there before he got the wrong idea. I felt bad about ditching him so soon after using him for the story. It had nothing to do with his nice face or that adorable hint of a southern accent.

"Trust me," he said. "I would've noticed you."

I took a sip of my drink, not knowing what to say. My heart was still doing its mini gymnastics routine in my chest.

"You're not from around here, are you?" he asked. "You sound like a northerner."

"Born and raised in Richmond, went to college in D.C. After I graduated, I stayed in the city for a few years, but...things didn't work out there," I said. "I thought I'd try something different and move down to the country. Been here almost two years now."

Pennington nodded.

"You must be a local though, right?"

"What gave it away?" he drawled, leaning into his accent.

I laughed, and we finished our drinks.

"Listen..." He lowered his voice. "It's been nice talking to you, but I'm kind of ready to get out of here. Would you maybe want to come back to my place? Have another drink there?"

Whoops. My plan had gone a little too well, it seemed.

"Oh. Uh, it's a tempting offer, but I have to work early tomorrow, and..."

"Oh, God," he mumbled, putting his face in his hands. "I'm sorry. Forget I said anything. I—"

"No, no, it's okay," I said, feeling just as embarrassed as he looked. *Way to torture this perfectly nice man, Evie.* "You didn't offend me. I really do have to get up early, and—"

"I seriously never do this," he said. "I just got divorced, and apparently I've completely forgotten how to speak to women, and..."

"Hey." I put my hand on his arm, and Pennington finally made eye contact again. "Seriously, it's okay."

An awkward silence settled over us, so I pulled out my phone.

"Why don't you give me your number," I said. "And we can get together again some other time."

He stared at my phone. "You're just asking to make me feel better."

Kind of. But also, I wouldn't mind having the personal contact information of a Bristol detective.

"Put it in," I insisted. Pennington grumbled but nevertheless entered his number into my phone.

"I should get going," I said, sliding off the barstool. "Thanks for the drink."

"I am going to insist on walking you to your car, though," Pennington said. "That pepper spray looks like a toy."

"Okay." I didn't mind prolonging our time together a little more. Pennington closed out his tab and got to his feet, stumbling a bit.

"Well, this is me." I pointed to my ancient Honda Civic that was only ten feet from the door. I looked at Pennington, who swayed on his feet.

"Do you want a ride home?" It was the least I could do. "You probably shouldn't drive."

"Oh, I'll just call a cab or something," he said. "I don't want to put you out."

"Where do you live?"

"Green Street."

"That's like two miles from me," I said. "It's no trouble."

Pennington considered this before shrugging. "Okay. Thanks." We settled into my car.

"I guess I didn't freak you out that much if you're giving me a ride," Pennington said when I pulled out of Last Call's lot.

"I told you, it's really okay. Another night I probably would've said yes."

This wasn't that big of a lie. His offer was pretty tempting. I'd been single for so long I was starting to forget what the touch of a man felt like, but I'd learned my lesson back in D.C. the hard way. No more mixing business and pleasure. If I screwed things up in a tiny town like this, I'd really have nowhere else to go.

Not to mention, chances were good that by tomorrow, Pennington would despise me, so it was probably best to keep sex out of the mix.

"I shouldn't have talked so much about the rape investigation," he said. "Nothing kills the mood quite like that."

"Well, true," I said. "But I'm not too squeamish about that kind of stuff. I'm a bit of a crime junkie, actually. I think it's all fascinating."

"Uh oh. I'm starting to wonder who I got into a car with."

"Too late now." I flashed him a devilish grin and hit the locks on the doors.

He burst out laughing before settling deeper into his seat. "At least if you kill me, I won't have to worry about the investigation anymore."

We rode in silence for the rest of the way, and when I peeked over at my drunk detective, his eyes were closed. I wasn't sure how I'd been expecting tonight to go, but definitely not like this.

When I turned onto Green Street, I gave him a little nudge. "Which one's yours?"

"Right there on the corner." He pointed to a white ranch-style house with blue shutters.

I pulled into the driveway.

"Well, thanks, Ellie." Pennington fumbled with his seatbelt until he got it unbuckled.

"Evie," I reminded him automatically, even though it'd be better if he forgot me altogether.

He winced and let out a curse under his breath. "Good thing I'm home now so I can stop putting my foot in my mouth."

"Don't beat yourself up. You've got a lot on your mind."

"You're too kind. You know, you're the first woman I've tried to talk to since my wife," he went on, which sent a fresh jolt of guilt through me. "I wasn't a total disaster, was I?"

I shook my head. "I'd give the attempt a solid B. There were a few stumbles, I'm not gonna lie, but they sort of made me like you more."

And that, unfortunately for the both of us, was the absolute truth. Why'd he have to be so *handsome?* I'd dealt with a lot of sources over the years, and none had looked like him.

"I'm really glad you wandered in tonight, *Evie,*" Pennington said, putting extra emphasis on my name to show me he remembered. He reached for the door handle. "I hope I hear from you again."

I leaned across the center console and planted a kiss on his stubbled cheek. I figured it was partly a preemptive apology for what was to come, and partly because I wanted to.

"You will," I said. Pennington gave me a lopsided grin before stumbling out of the car and slowly making his way to his front door, dropping his keys once as he tried to stick them in the lock.

Most likely though, I'd be hearing from *him*—and he would be livid.

CHAPTER THREE

It took approximately twelve hours for Pennington to track me down. I knew it wouldn't be hard for him to find me, but I figured a detective trying to capture a serial rapist might not have time to yell at a staff writer from the *Bristol Daily News*.

The worst part was, my day had started off so well. Shelly had flipped when she'd read the article I'd finished the night before with the information Pennington had unknowingly given me.

"Oh, I just knew you could do it, Evie!" she'd said with a giant smile. I didn't bother pointing out she'd been extremely hesitant to give me the assignment. Bygones!

Shelly begged me to name the "Bristol detective very close to the investigation," which would add even more credibility to the piece, but I couldn't. I did have at least a shred or two of journalistic ethics left. Putting Pennington's name to this quote could get him in some serious trouble and make me the shitty reporter I refused to believe I was.

"I'm fine with the occasional anonymous source," she said, "as long as you promise it's legit." Shelly leaned forward and lowered her voice. "Jeff was let go for, and I believe the technical term is, making shit up."

"*Whoa.*" Nervous, I cleared my throat. "But uh, don't worry. My stuff is completely accurate."

It was my methods that were a little dicey.

"Wonderful," Shelly said with a big nod. "Well, you earned it, Evie. I'll give you a shot at the crime beat. Why don't you cover it for the next month, and we'll reevaluate then. If all goes well, it's yours permanently."

Goodbye, Dave Austin! Goodbye, next up-and-coming generic local singer—it was nice knowing you!

Back at my desk, the giant, goofy smile I'd had all morning widened as I got a text from my dad:

Nice story, Pumpkin. Glad to see you back on crime!

It's good to be back, I replied, adding a smiley face. It melted my heart that my dad still read every single story I wrote, suffering through years of the cheesy singer profiles without complaint. He was the best.

"Evie, this article is great." Grace scanned her computer screen, finger scrolling the wheel on the mouse. "'With the police no closer to making an arrest six long weeks after the first attack, all Bristol residents can do is stay vigilant and pray this violent criminal doesn't strike again.'"

"I thought that line was a bit much, but Shelly loved it."

"No, it's perfect," Grace said. "It's scaring the shit out of people. You should see all these comments. Your article already has the most hits of the week, and it only went live a few hours ago."

I reclined in my desk chair and folded my arms behind my head, basking in my slam dunk of a story. That rush I hadn't felt since my *Washington Post* days came flooding back, thanks to all the clicks and Grace's praise.

When I'd washed up in Bristol not so long ago, she'd been one of the only good things. Grace had taken me under her wing, bringing me back to life with gossip-filled lunches and embarrassing karaoke happy hours. I'd deemed her the perfect role model for New Evie. Grace was the epitome of a hard-working, dedicated, ethical journalist. She filed her stories *hours* before deadline. She had normal, healthy relationships with sources. She came into work every day, her black hair perfectly straight and shiny, her round, tortoiseshell glasses stylish and smudge-free. This kick-ass story marked me getting one step closer to Grace status.

I couldn't help feeling impressed with myself, considering that before speaking with Pennington at Last Call, I'd been envisioning my epic failure.

"So who's this detective you quoted?" Grace asked. "Yesterday you were panicking because no one would talk."

I opened my mouth to reply, but was drowned out by a loud, furious bellow that came from across the room.

"*Hartley!*"

I tensed in my chair. My back was to the office door, but I didn't have to turn around to know who it was.

"Um, Evie," Grace said, her eyes glued to the person storming to our desks. "Who is that sexy, angry man, and why does he look like he wants to kill you?"

"Oh, man." I winced. Part of me had been expecting this, but not so soon. I wanted to revel in my victory for a little bit longer before Pennington ruined it. I hadn't thought he'd scream at me in front of the entire paper. The man I met last night seemed more soft-spoken.

"Should I call the police?" Grace asked in a hushed tone, her hand hovering over her phone.

"Don't bother. He *is* the police."

"What the hell is this?" Pennington asked, thrusting today's edition on my desk in front of me. Plain as day, there was my dramatic headline on a front-page sidebar: *Bristol PD gives update on serial rape cases: "We've got nothing."*

"Good morning, Detective." I forced a smile. "It's nice to see you again."

Pennington crossed his arms, the crease between his brows extra prominent as he glared at me. "What the hell *is this?*"

"Let's just calm down for a second," I said, and shot a nervous glance towards Shelly's office. I snatched up the paper and grabbed

Pennington's arm, leading him into a nearby empty conference room. Grace watched us the whole time, her hand still poised to pick up the phone and call for help.

I shut the door and turned to him. "Okay." I put my hands up. "I get why you're mad. I do. But you never would've talked to me if I'd been up front about who I was."

"No," Pennington growled, "I wouldn't have." He grabbed the paper again and waved it in front of my face. "Do you realize how bad this makes the department look?"

"I'll admit, it doesn't look great for you guys. But it's the truth. Residents have the right to know what's going on. It's a public safety issue."

Pennington scoffed. "You and I both know that most residents are idiots, *Evelyn*."

Using my full byline name. Ouch. We were a far cry from the flirty, friendly strangers we'd been in that bar last night. Twelve hours ago, I was just Evie (and briefly, Ellie)—but now, I was Evelyn Hartley: seedy, manipulative journalist.

"People *panic*. They'll start calling us over every noise they hear at night. They'll start buying guns they don't know how to use. Do you have any idea how many gun accidents happen in the home?" He balled up the newspaper. "I should slap you with a libel suit."

I crossed my arms, my heart beating out of my chest. If he talked to Shelly, I was done for.

"On what grounds? I didn't print anything that wasn't true. I also didn't name you without your permission," I said.

"Ha!" He smoothed out the paper and referenced it again. "'Bristol detective very close to the investigation.' Newsflash, there's only three of us. It won't be hard at all for my captain to figure out it was me."

"Well, I'm sorry if this gets you in trouble," I said, actually feeling bad. Right now, history was a little too close to repeating itself for my liking. "But maybe you shouldn't have been blabbing about the case to some random woman you met in a bar."

He shook his head again. "I should've known. I should've known you were one of *them*."

"*Them?*" I asked, arching an eyebrow.

"Yeah, *them*," he spat. "A journalist. A *leech*. A manipulator who does whatever it takes to get the goddamn story."

That wasn't exactly fair. All I did was flirt a little. I wouldn't do *anything* like he implied. Well, not anymore at least. That was Old Evie. Either way, I had the feeling that Pennington might have a more personal reason for disliking us "leeches" so much.

"Look, Pennington, I'm sorry I misled you. I didn't mean for us to get off on the wrong foot. I just got assigned the crime beat, and I'd really like for us to be able to have a professional relationship."

Strictly, one-hundred-percent professional, I reminded myself.

He let out a loud bark of humorless laughter. "You've got to be joking."

"Come on." I risked a smile. "You could be my police point man. Tell me stuff off the record if you want. I promise, no more deception. I won't print anything without your permission."

"You're funny," he said. "I plan on never speaking to you again."

"You seemed to feel differently last night."

This reminder was apparently a mistake. His expression darkened, and I could tell he was hurt. Embarrassed. Now I *really* felt bad. I'd been his first foray back into the dating scene, and I'd managed to humiliate him both personally and professionally. I had the urge to clarify that I hadn't completely led him on. I had enjoyed talking with him, and the little kiss had been spur-of-the-moment and not maliciously plotted ahead of time—but I couldn't figure out how to phrase it.

"Goodbye, Evelyn," he said gruffly, reaching for the doorknob.

"You can't get rid of me that easily," I called after him. "I've got your number *and* I know where you live!"

Pennington continued to storm out of the newsroom, every reporter's gaze tracking him, then turning to stare at me.

"Evie," Grace said as I sunk back into my chair. "Who *was* that?"

"My anonymous Bristol detective." I gave her a weak smile. "I might need to find a new source."

The high from my article wore off pretty quickly after that, and not just because of Pennington's outburst.

The rapist had struck again.

That made five attacks now, and everyone was, understandably, on edge. After dark, Bristol resembled a ghost town, no one wanting to be victim number six. As Pennington predicted, gun purchases went up, and local shops sold out of ammo. Comments flooded our site, demanding an update. I'd written a quick piece announcing the fifth attack, but people craved information I simply didn't have.

If there was no action on this case soon, I was screwed. For the past few weeks, I'd been stuck writing dull pieces about hooligans slashing car tires, and one small burglary in which the homeowners weren't even present. The site received fewer and fewer clicks with each passing day, and more importantly, I had the feeling Shelly wouldn't follow through with her promise if I didn't dig something up.

"Evie, I really need another story from you about this rapist," Shelly said after calling me into her office one afternoon. Her Halloween decorations acted as a stark reminder that my trial month on the crime beat was almost up.

"I'd love to give you a piece about it," I told her earnestly. "But there have been no updates. No suspects, no arrests."

"Do you know that for sure? The police might have things they aren't releasing to the public yet. Any chance you can get your department contact to give you anything?"

I wanted to laugh out loud. Ever since our confrontation last month, Pennington had followed through on his threat and hadn't said one word to me. I'd tirelessly attempted to contact him, my strategy ranging from joking to sincere to desperate. He hadn't returned a single phone call, and he'd only typed three words in response to my weeks-long barrage of texts.

STOP TEXTING ME.

"I can try him again, but I think he would've told me if anything new was going on," I lied.

"Do that," Shelly said with a firm nod, making my stomach lurch. "Even the smallest tidbit we could turn into a story, like a potential lead or old evidence they're reexamining. People want an update on this, Evie. We need to show our readers we aren't leaving them hanging."

I nodded, already knowing all of this. Shelly dismissed me and I headed back to my desk to run through my limited options. Pennington wouldn't take my calls, so I'd have to corner him somewhere to get him to talk to me. I couldn't see that going well, but I doubted I'd have better luck with Delaney or Zimmerman. They didn't know me at all. At least I sort of had a relationship with Pennington, however strained it may be.

I'd made him like me once. I could do it again.

Leaving the newsroom around five, I drove down Green Street, passing Pennington's house. No car in the driveway—he must still be at work. I headed to the police station and parked across the street, watching the lot. Sure enough, about fifteen minutes later, he exited the building and got into his car. Not caring I was going into full-creeper mode, I followed.

Our journey wasn't very long. He pulled into Food City right down the road. Perfect. This was much less weird than making a house call. People ran into each other all the time at the grocery store.

I entered the store, hyperaware of my surroundings, not wanting him to see me before I saw him. No sign of Pennington in the produce section. I slowly began making my way through the store, peeking down each aisle.

Finally, I spotted him in the personal care aisle, studying the selection of shaving cream, shopping basket in the crook of his arm. Taking a deep breath, I walked toward him, gently brushing my shoulder against his as I passed.

"Oh, *excuse* me," I said, grasping his arm as if I'd wounded him.

Pennington turned, his facial expression changing from neutral to furious.

"You've *got* to be kidding me."

"Oh, hi!" I put on a big smile. "Wow, what a coincidence. I guess that's a small town for you."

"Yeah, a coincidence," Pennington said flatly. "Stalking is a crime, you know. I could arrest you."

"If you arrested little old me as your stalker, you'd be the laughingstock of the police department. Besides, I'm not stalking you. I'm just doing my shopping."

"I'm sure you needed something from this aisle," he said, voice dripping with sarcasm.

I looked around. We were surrounded by men's hygiene products, not a pink or flower-scented thing in sight.

"Actually, I did," I sassed. I reached out and grabbed the nearest thing off the shelf—Black Spruce deodorant.

"You needed men's deodorant?"

"Yep. Reporting can be sweaty work."

It hit me a second too late that I could've made up a boyfriend instead of implying I had excessive body odor. Either way, I was losing Pennington. He threw the shaving cream into his basket and strode down the aisle.

I hustled to catch up to him, still clutching the deodorant.

"Look, I really am sorry," I said. "Like I said before, I won't pull any crap again. I just need some info for a story. I'd be grateful for the smallest thing."

"Nope." He stopped to snag a loaf of bread from an end cap.

I sighed and tried to sound miserable. "My career is on the line, here. My editor will demote me if I don't get another story on the rapist."

"So I'd never have you bugging me again?" Pennington asked. "Sounds like a win."

Did I set him up for that one, or what? I was off my game. I decided to blame it on Pennington's rolled-up sleeves, which exposed his muscular forearms.

He paused once again to examine the ground beef and selected two packages.

"You shouldn't eat that much red meat," I couldn't help pointing out. "You should put one back and get chicken instead."

That got a laugh out of him, but Pennington didn't take my suggestion. He looked me right in the eye, grabbed a flank steak to add to his dead cow haul, then led us towards the dairy section.

"Look, I have a pretty good mind for this type of stuff. Obviously, you guys are stumped, or you would've caught this sicko by now. Maybe we can talk it out together, shake something loose. It could be a mutually beneficial thing."

After putting a carton of soy milk into his basket, Pennington faced me.

"Evie, we've got our entire police force working this case nonstop. Why on earth do you think *you'd* be the one to figure it out?"

I frowned, trying not to take offense. "I didn't say I could figure it out. I'm just saying I could offer an outside perspective—a non-cop, female perspective."

Pennington exhaled, shook his head, then headed for the self-checkout. I was running out of time.

"Did you know that three out of four rapes aren't even reported?" I asked as he rang up his purchases.

"And these ones were. What's your point?"

"My point is that women don't want to talk to the police about this. Even the ones who report it," I said. "It's uncomfortable and traumatic. There could be stuff the victims are leaving out."

"There's not." Pennington pulled his wallet out of his back pocket and took out a credit card. "They walked us through the entire thing. No one seemed evasive. They included as much detail as they could."

"What kind of details?" I asked innocently.

Pennington opened his mouth, about to respond, but then he

laughed instead. "You almost got me there. You're trouble." Finished paying, he collected his bags and headed for the door.

"Pennington, let me buy you a drink or something," I said, desperate now.

"You really think I'd be dumb enough to fall for that again?"

"We don't even have to talk about the case." I took a few tentative steps towards him and smiled demurely. "It can be an apology drink. I owe you for last time."

If I could *just* get him to sit down with me again, I was positive I'd be able to reignite that spark from night one. Pennington considered my offer for three seconds before he shook his head.

"Will you give it a rest? I've got enough problems at work right now. I don't need any more from you. You want a quote? Here: We're confident we'll catch this criminal soon. Write that."

The automatic doors slid open and Pennington moved through them.

"Wait! If you could just—"

"This woman is trying to shoplift," he said loudly, pointing at me. Two nearby cashiers froze and looked at me, then at the deodorant I still had in my hand. Damn it!

"Ma'am, you need to pay for that," a manager demanded as he power-walked towards me.

"I don't even want this!" Frustrated, I tossed the deodorant onto a nearby conveyor belt and bolted.

I scanned the lot for Pennington, but he was already gone, leaving me, once again, source-less and story-less.

CHAPTER FOUR

"I can't believe it." My vision blurred as I stared at the blank Word document on my computer screen. "I almost had the crime beat, and I let it slip through my fingers."

Grace, being the good friend she was, didn't comment on my melodramatics. "You've still got some time. Shelly's deadline isn't until tomorrow afternoon. You could still get the story."

"It's not going to happen." I folded my arms on the desk and rested my head on them. "I'll be stuck writing about Dave Austins forever. It's my destiny, I guess. I should just accept it."

"Evie, in the two years I've known you, I've never seen you give up," Grace said. "Come on. You wrote for the *Post*. That had to be more stressful and difficult than this."

"Yeah. I just don't know what to do now. I don't think I can fix things with Pennington. Definitely not in time for this story."

"Then go chat up those other two detectives," she said. "It can't possibly go worse, right?"

"If I try to talk to them, and it doesn't work out, *then* will you give me permission to mope?"

"Absolutely."

I drove to the police station and parked across the street. Delaney was my target, since he'd actually spoken a few words to me before hanging up. Not to mention, he'd probably be more susceptible to my womanly charms than Nicole Zimmerman.

Much like the night I met Pennington, I examined myself in the mirror to ensure I was as appealing as possible. It was mid-afternoon, so my hair hadn't yet turned greasy, and my makeup was still pretty fresh. After applying a new coat of mascara, I swiped on some red lipstick and undid *two* blouse buttons. I meant business.

Wishing I could take a shot of something, I crossed the street and entered the police station. I kept peering over my shoulder, convinced Pennington would spot me and forcibly escort me from the building, but after two quick scans of the bullpen, I didn't see him.

"Can I help you?"

Turning, I found myself face to face with a balding man of about fifty. Delaney. I recognized him from his many Facebook photos.

"Hi," I said brightly, extending my hand. "Evie Hartley, *Bristol Daily News*. I was hoping you might be able to help me."

He shook my hand. "Detective Tom Delaney. Evie Hartley...You try to call me before?"

"Guilty," I said with a little laugh. "You didn't have time to talk then, but I'd be so grateful if you had a few minutes now."

At first glance, Delaney hadn't appeared to be a friendly-looking guy, but he continued to smile, and his gaze wandered from my face to my exposed cleavage.

"I think I can spare a few," he said with a grin verging on lecherous.

Twenty minutes later, I was seated by Delaney's desk, where he allowed me to pore over the case files from each rape. I scanned everything lightning fast, knowing this glimpse into the investigation could be yanked away at any moment.

"These poor women." The most recent victim had only been nineteen years old. "To have a stranger break into your home and assault you? It's horrifying."

"He's a real bastard. You want to know the creepiest part?"

Delaney leaned forward, giving me an unpleasant whiff of his coffee breath. "All the victims said the guy was gentle, like he was trying to be romantic. He liked to kiss, which these guys usually don't."

This particular detail sent a shiver down my spine. "That information hasn't been made public."

"I know." He gave me a big wink. "But keep that between us, okay?"

"Of course." My head spun with how I could use that without breaking my word.

"Romantic," I repeated. "Is it possible he's someone the victims all know? A guy they dated? A casual acquaintance?"

"We can't completely rule that out," Delaney said. "But the women have almost nothing in common; different ages, different physical features. They don't have any mutual friends that we know of."

I tried not to react to all this information that had been so easily handed to me. And to think I'd been wasting weeks chasing after Pennington! I could now see what mistake I'd made with Delaney originally. I'd called, so he'd had no idea what I, or my boobs, looked like. Wouldn't be making that mistake again. Delaney could be the answer to all my problems. He was a blabbermouth, and due to his age and appearance, there was no chance I'd end up in bed with him— something I couldn't confidently say about Pennington.

"A stalker, maybe," I offered up. "He spotted the women around town and followed them home, waiting to strike."

Delaney nodded. "That's our theory. Problem is, that means it could be anyone."

"So where does the investigation go from here?"

"Not much we can do." Delaney shrugged. "Not unless he starts to get sloppy, or some new information comes to light."

"That's too bad." This wasn't good news for these victims *or* my career. I'd promised Delaney this was off the record, so I couldn't even write an insider story with all the sordid details he'd given me.

Not that I would. I don't think.

"Delaney, what do you think you're doing?" I'd know that angry voice anywhere. I turned to find Pennington, arms crossed and scowling.

"Hey, Marcus," Delaney said. "Just chatting with Evie here." He reached over and gave me a pat on the knee, but his hand lingered and slid up my thigh a bit.

I pretended it didn't bother me.

Pennington's gaze darted to Delaney's hand, then to my open blouse. I gave him an uneasy smile, but he looked pissed. I didn't blame him. It looked like I was using Delaney, just like I'd used him. It looked like the unflattering pattern I'd been working so hard to break.

"And do you know that *Evie here* is a reporter?" Pennington asked Delaney, ignoring me.

"Yeah, of course," Delaney said easily. "But don't worry. Everything's off the record, right, Evie?"

"Uh-huh." I forced a smile.

Pennington let out a humorless laugh. "I wouldn't bet on it." He grabbed a hold of my arm and yanked me out of my seat.

"What the hell, Marcus?" Delaney looked quite upset his thigh-squeezing had come to an end.

"It's time for Evie to go." Pennington hauled me away from Delaney and towards the door.

"Thanks so much!" I fumbled in my purse for my business card and tossed it in Delaney's direction. "Call if you think of anything else!"

"You're really something, do you know that?" Pennington said as we made it outside the station.

"First of all, ow." I rubbed my upper arm where he'd grabbed me. "And second of all, you gave me no choice! You wouldn't talk to me, and I had to get an update from someone."

"So that someone had to be *Delaney*? Jesus, he was groping you in front of the entire station. Unlike me, Delaney might not take no for an answer after you throw yourself at him."

Startled, I took a step back. "Wait...Is that the real reason you've been shutting me out? Not because of the article, but because I led you on in the bar?"

Pennington crossed his arms and avoided eye contact.

I let out a slow exhale. "Look...Yes, I might've intentionally approached you for case information, but I genuinely had a nice time with you. It wasn't just business."

"Maybe I would've believed you if I didn't catch you at Delaney's desk with your tits out," he said icily.

My jaw dropped, and my face flushed as I raced to redo my blouse buttons, an overwhelming combination of rage and humiliation rushing through me.

"Fuck you," I hissed, then hightailed it down the sidewalk. I kept waiting for him to stop me and apologize, but he didn't.

"I hate him, I hate him, I hate him!" I yelled into my empty apartment as I arrived home. I slammed the door so loudly that my cat, Wally, who'd been peacefully snoozing on the couch, shrieked and jumped two feet into the air.

"Aw, I'm sorry, buddy." I scooped up my disgruntled Russian Blue, who I'd adopted on my second day in Bristol. For a long while, he had been my only friend, and the only creature who offered me any comfort.

I'd barely held Wally for two seconds before I sobbed into his fur. He struggled in my arms, desperate to get away. When he let out a warning hiss, I finally released him. I loved my little menace of a cat, but at times like this, I really wished he'd read the room and let me cuddle him against his will.

Wally scampered off into my bedroom. Meanwhile, I headed for the fridge and pulled out a bottle of chardonnay. I poured a giant glass and downed almost all of it in one go.

Why did Pennington get to me like this? My skin was pretty thick. I was used to people disliking me and hurling insults at me. When Pennington had called me a leech, I didn't bat an eye. But back at the station, he'd managed to touch on my biggest insecurity—that I was a hack, that I whored myself out for my stories. And I hated him for it.

My fatal mistake was assuming the nice guy I'd met at the bar had been the real Pennington. He'd been drunk and trying to get laid. The second he'd found out that wasn't ever going to happen, he turned the charm off. *Way* off.

I was almost through my second fishbowl of chardonnay when I decided he needed to pay, and I'd use my story to get *my* sweet revenge. If this would be the last crime story I ever wrote, I was going down swinging.

I laid on my couch, contemplating all the information Delaney had given me, desperately searching for some kind of loophole in my "off the record" promise, some kind of angle I hadn't considered, but came up empty.

And then, it hit me.

"That's it, Wally!" I sat up. Wally, standing sentinel by his empty food dish, meowed. Perfect. He'd be a captive audience while I opened his can of food.

"My source doesn't have to be a police officer." I scraped out the fish and shrimp Fancy Feast onto his little plate and started chopping it up into small pieces with the fork. "I could talk to the victims. Considering the cops are in danger of never catching this guy, they might be willing to talk. A feature piece on how they're dealing with all of this would be gold."

Wally meowed again and stood on his hind legs, his front paws rubbing my thigh.

"Fine, here you go." I set the food in front of him. He gobbled it up in twenty seconds flat.

I sat back down on the couch and topped off my wine. My story idea was good. It solved the problem of Shelly's looming deadline. Unfortunately, it didn't accomplish my goal of exacting revenge on Pennington.

I still couldn't believe what he'd said. And really, was the stunt I pulled at Last Call that bad? It was hard enough to get authoritative sources to talk to me; so what if I used my natural gifts to my advantage? That's called being resourceful. How would Pennington like it if I watched him do his job and criticized his methods?

That's when I was struck with my second great idea of the evening.

Of *course*. I'd talk to the rape victims about the investigation proceedings and how satisfied, or dissatisfied, they were with the police response. It was perfect. Something told me none of them would be pleased. Not just displeased, but likely highly critical.

I imagined the look on Pennington's face when he read the headline, something along the lines of, *Rape victims say Bristol PD has forgotten about them.*

If he was pissed about the "We've got nothing" headline, this would undoubtedly make him furious.

Just like that, I had my story *and* my revenge plan. Two birds, one stone.

I put down my wine glass and grabbed my laptop to do some quick Google searches. The victims' identities hadn't been made public, but thanks to Delaney, I'd managed to spot two of the women's names before Pennington tossed me out of the station.

Ten minutes later, I had addresses and intended to pay them both visits in the morning.

A brief moment of uncertainty struck me. Was I taking this too far? Were my personal feelings about Pennington clouding my journalistic judgment here?

"Nah," I said to Wally, who'd deemed me unthreatening enough to sit next to again. "The police *are* screwing this up. I'd just be reporting what the victims say."

I'd be reporting the truth.

CHAPTER FIVE

"Who are you?"

Nervous, I stood outside the house of Claire Barone, the first woman I'd decided to visit. I thought I'd been ready. I'd rehearsed my little speech a hundred times, explaining who I was and promising to handle the story with as much sensitivity as possible. I'd dressed in a modest outfit of jeans, boots and a brown turtleneck, to prove to Pennington, and myself, that I could get a story with my chest covered. My hair was back in a ponytail, and I wore very little makeup—the epitome of friendly, trustworthy, and approachable.

But the second Claire Barone answered the door, my confidence evaporated, and I wanted to bolt. It hit me how incredibly intrusive this was—no matter how nice I was or how good my intentions, I was still asking these women to relive their trauma. I didn't have a lot of experience interviewing victims. I'd always stuck to the crimes, the facts. Not the aftermath. There was so much crime in D.C., I'd never had the time to write about lagging investigations growing cold.

"Claire Barone?" My voice came out higher than usual.

She gave me a stiff nod. "Who are you?" she asked again, more rudely this time.

"I'm Evie Hartley." I extended my hand. "I write for *Bristol Daily News,* and I really wanted—"

"Get the hell out of here." She attempted to close the door, but I shoved my boot in between the door and the jamb.

"Please," I said. "Just give me a minute to explain. First, I wanted to say I'm so sorry about what happened to you. And I wanted to talk to you about how the police have been handling your case."

Claire's frown remained, but she let go of the door.

"I promise to keep your identity anonymous," I added. "I just know the police haven't found the man responsible yet, and I wanted to get your thoughts on that."

"My thoughts? What the hell kind of question is that? How would you feel if someone raped *you,* and the police couldn't be bothered to find him?"

"Um..."

"The police are *useless,*" Claire said. "They took my statement once, and that was about it. No one's come back to check on me. No one bothers to update me unless I call. It's a living nightmare. I did everything I was supposed to do, and look where it's gotten me. I wish I'd never even reported it."

So much for Pennington's insistence he had a handle on victim relations.

"I understand your frustration." I cleared my throat. "Can I come inside, and you could tell me more? I want to make sure the police are held accountable."

"I've said all I want to say." When Claire went to slam the door this time, I didn't stop her.

I walked back to my car in a bit of a daze. That hadn't gone great. I felt awful for bothering her in the first place. Claire had given me a few useful tidbits, and she confirmed my suspicions; this investigation was a disaster. There wasn't enough evidence to go on, and the trail was going cold.

My interaction with Claire hadn't been encouraging, but the next visit couldn't possibly go worse, so I drove to victim number two's house.

Holly Lang was the nineteen-year-old, so I figured the middle-aged woman who answered the door was her mother.

"Mrs. Lang?"

She gave me a careful nod. "Yes. Can I help you?"

"Evie Hartley." I reached into my purse and handed her my card, trying a slightly different approach. "I'm doing a story on the Bristol police and how they're handling open cases. I'd really like to speak to your daughter."

"Mom?"

Before Mrs. Lang could respond to me, a brunette girl walked down the hall towards the door. "Mom, who is it?"

"Just a reporter, honey." Mrs. Lang turned back to me. "No, thank you. Holly doesn't want to speak to you."

"Wait," Holly said, squeezing into the doorway next to her mother. "Why do you want to talk?"

"I just want to know about your experience with the detectives assigned to your case," I said. "How good of a job you think they're doing, how thorough they are; things like that." Holly considered this. "You don't need to talk about the attack if you don't want to. And of course, I'll keep your name out of it."

Holly studied me for a while before saying, "I guess I can talk about the detectives."

"Holly..." her mom tried to protest.

"I said, I can talk to her." Holly gave her mother a stop-embarrassing-me look; a stark reminder of her age. She ushered me into the living room. I seated myself on the couch, and Holly sat beside me. Her mom still hovered over us.

"Mom, I don't need you to stay."

Mrs. Lang looked like she wanted to say more, but instead, headed into the kitchen. She'd probably eavesdrop, but I didn't care. After my encounter with Claire, I couldn't believe Holly agreed to talk. A calmness settled over me. I'd have a story to give Shelly. It might not be the one she was expecting, but I still had a shot at salvaging this opportunity.

"My mom won't leave me alone," Holly whispered. "She barely lets me go to the bathroom by myself."

My heart broke for both Holly and her mother, who were navigating this horrible situation the best they could. "I'm sure she's just trying to be there for you."

"I guess. You came at a good time. She was trying to make me go to spin class with her."

I leaned in, voice conspiratorial. "If you want, we could sit here until it's too late to go."

Holly gave me a shy smile, which I took as permission to proceed.

I got my notepad and pen out of my purse. "What was the initial police response when you called them?" I asked gently.

Holly stared down at her hands, first examining her nails, then picking at her cuticles. "Well, right after it happened, I went to the hospital to do the..." The words "rape kit" hung in the air, unspoken. I gave her a nod, letting her know I understood. Holly cleared her throat. "When I was done, two officers were waiting for me. One was old, like my dad's age, and the other was younger. Both men. I can't remember their names, it's all a blur. I have a card somewhere."

Delaney and Pennington, of course.

"They asked me to take them through what happened," Holly continued. "So I did. I told them as much as I could about the guy. They were nice, but it's really hard to talk to the police about something like this." She glanced up at me.

I nodded, noting she'd confirmed the point I tried to make with Pennington at the grocery store. "It must be so difficult to have to talk about it in such a detailed way."

"Yeah. They asked some really specific questions about the attack, which were hard to answer."

"Hard to answer because you didn't know the answers?" I asked. "Or hard to answer because you didn't feel comfortable telling them?"

"The second one," she mumbled.

"Would you have felt more comfortable with a female officer?"

"Maybe." Holly chewed on her lower lip. "It's still hard to tell a complete stranger about this."

"Are there things you left out of your statement?" I asked her cautiously. "Details you didn't feel comfortable sharing?"

Holly tugged at her sleeve and avoided eye contact, which told me I was on the right track. Though my brain was swimming with a thousand questions, I tried to remain calm. Even if Holly withheld the smallest thing, it might be enough to reenergize this investigation.

"Holly, I know it might not seem important, but any tiny detail could be the key to finding this guy." I paused. "If you wanted to tell me, I could make sure the police get the information. I wouldn't even have to tell them it came from you."

She looked up at me. "Really?"

"You have my word."

"There was one thing I left out," Holly said, "because it was too humiliating."

I gripped my pen so tightly it was a wonder it didn't snap. I knew it. Pennington was convinced the victims hadn't withheld information, but my hunch had been right.

"Before he..." Holly took a deep breath. "Before it happened, he made me put on a different pair of underwear."

I furrowed my brow. "Why?"

"I don't know," Holly said. "They were this sexy lace pair I just bought. Still had the tags on them. I guess he didn't like the pair I was wearing."

"Was he going through your drawers?"

"No, they were still in the shopping bag," Holly said. "It was sitting on my dresser. He went right to the bag, almost like he knew what would be in it."

My throat went dry. "Can you show me the bag?"

Holly led me upstairs to her messy room. She dug around in her closet until she produced a small, white paper shopping bag. In pretty, silver script on the front, it said *Passions*. I recognized the name—a lingerie shop downtown that also sold sex toys. I could see why Holly had been too embarrassed to explain this part to Delaney or Pennington. Teenagers wouldn't talk to their parents about lingerie shopping, let alone two police officers.

"I got rid of the underwear. I know I shouldn't have, but I wasn't thinking straight," Holly told me when I looked inside the bag and found it to be empty. "It was just so weird. I bought them a day before it happened. It's like he knew."

"Thank you for telling me, Holly." I tried to keep my voice calm and even. "This is very helpful."

I exited the house as quickly as I could without being rude, all thoughts of revenge on Pennington gone from my mind.

I had gone to Holly hoping for ammunition against the police department, but instead, she might've given me exactly what I needed to solve this case.

CHAPTER SIX

I GOT TO PASSIONS AS QUICKLY AS POSSIBLE, EVEN BREAKING A FEW traffic laws to do so. As I stared at the establishment, I considered calling the police to give them my lead, but if this turned out to be a dead end, I'd just embarrass myself. Besides, I was *not* in the mood to see Pennington.

Bells jingled as I pushed inside the store. Lots of pretty, skimpy bras and underwear decorated the walls. It was a cute little place—not icky or intimidating like some other sex shops. Definitely somewhere women would feel comfortable and let their guard down.

"Good morning," the cashier said. "Anything I can help you find?"

I turned to the young woman, who looked to be in her early twenties. "Um, yeah." My mind was still reeling from this new information. "I guess I'm looking for some sexier bras. Not really sure what kind, though."

"Well, there's lots to choose from." As the cashier approached me, I glimpsed her name tag: Sarah. She surveyed my outfit. "I'm guessing your style is simple and feminine?"

"Sure." I was barely listening. I kept glancing around the store, looking for other employees.

"What about this?" Sarah pointed to a mannequin wearing a sheer pink bra.

"That's pretty."

"I'll grab your size." She opened a drawer below the display. "I'm thinking 34C?"

I blinked. "Thirty-six, actually. But that's impressive."

She let out a little laugh. "After four years here, you become something of a size expert."

"Hey, do any men work here?" I asked as casually as I could. Sarah turned to look at me. "I just mean, that'd be kind of weird for a guy to help women pick out bras and guess their sizes."

"It would," Sarah said. "We sort of have an unofficial policy to only hire women for sales positions. It's what our customers are more comfortable with."

I nodded, slightly disheartened. I'd been hoping the guy would've been an employee here, but he could've simply been a random customer who happened to spot Holly buying the lingerie.

"I guess guys probably don't want to work in a girly place like this anyway."

"Well, we actually do have one male staff member," Sarah said, stopping my heart. "Roger. But he does inventory and stocks shelves after we close. Customers hardly even notice him.

"I pulled these for you, too," Sarah continued, holding up two lacy bras. "Do you want to try them on?"

"Sure," I said, distracted as I took them from her. Sarah led me to the singular fitting room in the back of the store.

I went inside and pulled the curtain shut, hanging the bras on the hook with no intention of trying them on. I stood there, thinking. I needed to see this Roger guy. Though, it's not like I'd be able to tell if he was the rapist by looking at him. He'd worn a ski mask, so the police really had no idea what he looked like. A few victims had mentioned he looked tall. That was it.

What was I thinking? That I'd be able to solve this case just like that because I found out some new information?

Come on, Evie, I thought. *You just* write *about crime. You're a small-town reporter, not Jessica Fletcher.*

Sighing, I smoothed back my hair in the mirror. I'd probably need to buy at least one bra so it didn't look weird. I was examining the giant bags under my eyes and wondering why I hadn't applied more concealer that morning when I noticed it.

I brought my finger to a tiny circle in the mirror, at about eye level. I ran my fingertip across it. Perfectly smooth, as if it had been drilled. It was so small it was almost imperceptible, especially if you were standing far back enough to examine your entire body in the mirror. I tried to peer through it, but only saw darkness.

Hands shaking and hairs on the back of my neck standing, I grabbed the frame of the mirror and lifted. Stumbling a bit beneath the weight, I managed to lower it to the ground, propping it against the wall. My heart stopped.

I stared through a crudely cut hole in the drywall at metal shelving and a dozen boxes waiting to be unpacked. The stockroom. Where Roger spent his time. Gasping, I staggered backward, getting tangled up in the dressing room curtain. I snatched up my purse and marched to the counter, where Sarah was flipping through a magazine.

She glanced up. "Everything okay? Did they not fit?"

"Sarah," I said, my voice low and urgent, "I need you to call the police right now."

Her very arched brows furrowed together. "Huh? Why? What's wrong?"

"Please just do it," I told her, a nervous sweat coming on. Sarah looked at me like I was insane, but hesitantly picked up the store phone and dialed.

"Is Roger here?" I asked. "The storeroom guy?"

"Um, yeah, he should be back there..." She trailed off, and I heard the call connect. "Hello? Yeah, I work at Passions downtown, and this customer asked that I call you."

"Tell them to come right away," I told her. "It's an emergency."

Sarah nodded, repeated the message, then hung up.

"What's going on?" she asked in a hushed tone.

"Roger's been spying on people in the dressing room. From behind the mirror. There's a peephole in it."

"*What?*" Sarah's mouth fell open. "Holy shit." She took another nervous glance towards the back of the store. "You know what, he *has* always given me creepy vibes."

I felt dizzy as it became increasingly clear Roger could be the serial rapist, scoping out his victims from the unsuspecting Passions clientele.

"The police will be here in five minutes," Sarah said. "Should we do anything?"

"No. He'll run if he knows something's up."

The second hand on my watch ticked by painfully slowly. Sarah went back to her magazine, but her eyes didn't move as she stared at the pages.

"Crap," I blurted out. "The mirror."

If Roger noticed his peephole had been discovered, he'd hightail it out of there. Sarah looked at me to ask what I meant, but I scurried back to the dressing room, heart racing. I grabbed the mirror, my hands slick with sweat, and attempted to hang it back up.

When I turned towards the hole, I found myself face to face with a tall, skinny man, his eyes dark and wide.

We stood there for a few seconds, frozen in place. And then he bolted.

"Shit!" I dropped the mirror and darted out of the dressing room. I sprinted towards the storeroom door, having no clue if there was a back exit Roger could've already escaped out of. I needed a weapon. I dug in my purse until I found my keys, and I uncapped the tiny tube of mace Pennington had dismissed.

Before I could raise it and search for Roger, I was shoved against the wall. I cried out as my forehead collided with it, and a wave of dizziness washed over me. A warm trickle of blood ran down my cheek as Roger spun me to face him. He wrapped his hands around my neck, tightly.

I flailed my legs, kicking his shins as hard as I could, but it didn't faze him. He seemed laser-focused on killing the witness who'd discovered his dirty secret. Still clutching the pepper spray, I closed my eyes, aimed, and sprayed. I held the little button down until there was nothing left in the tube.

Roger yelled out in pain and stumbled backwards, coughing and frantically wiping at his eyes. I was experiencing a coughing attack of my own, and my eyes burned as if someone had held a bowl of chopped onions to my face.

Trying to ignore that, I shoved Roger hard. He fell to his knees. I pushed him to the ground and sat on his back as he continued to writhe in pain. Rapid footsteps grew closer. Sarah burst into the storeroom.

"What the—" She gaped at us, looking to Roger and then the cut on my head.

"Do you have something we can restrain him with?" I asked her in a raspy voice.

"Um..." After a second, Sarah's eyes brightened as if a lightbulb had lit up over her head. "Yeah!" She rummaged around in one of the nearby boxes then turned to me, a pair of pink fuzzy handcuffs dangling from her fingers.

I burst out laughing as I imagined the headline, *Serial rapist finally in (fuzzy) handcuffs.* "Those'll work."

Sarah knelt, and we wrestled the cuffs around Roger's wrists. We'd just managed to secure him when two uniformed cops tip-toed into the storeroom, hands resting on their holstered guns.

"I've got your rapist," I told them, still panting. They looked dumbfounded, but one officer grabbed his radio and called for backup.

Five minutes later, I sat on the stool behind the counter, a wad of paper towels pressed to my bleeding head wound. The deafening sound of sirens filled the street as two more cop cars and an ambulance pulled up outside of Passions. Sarah chatted with one of the uniformed officers, giving her statement, and the other cop hauled Roger—now in proper handcuffs—to his squad car. Two men in suits emerged from an unmarked police car and rushed towards the building. I groaned when I saw Pennington and Delaney.

Pennington headed straight for me. He pulled my hand away from my head and examined the wound beneath the paper towels I was clutching. "Jesus, Evie, you're bleeding."

"Thanks, Captain Obvious."

"What were you thinking?" Pennington asked. "Why did you come here alone? Why didn't you call me?"

"Because you're a *jerk*," I shouted, my voice cracking. To my horror, tears sprung to my eyes. "And you would've just ignored me anyway!"

The tears slipped down my cheeks, accompanied by embarrassing whimpering sobs.

"Evie..." Pennington put an awkward hand on my shoulder. "I'm sorry. You were right. I'm an asshole with a bruised ego." He moved his hand down to my forearm and gave it a squeeze, the gesture turning slightly less weird. "It's no fun getting played. I'm sorry."

I nodded and sniffled, wiping my nose with the back of my hand.

"Will you tell me what happened?" He released me. "How did you figure it out?"

"I talked to one of the victims," I said. "She shopped here right before she was attacked, and the rapist made her put on what she bought. I figured he could be an employee here, so I came to check it out. I'd bet all the victims were customers—that's probably why they had nothing else in common."

Pennington's eyes widened. "No one said anything about shopping here."

"Interesting how you couldn't get this crucial bit of information out of five different women, but I got it in ten minutes."

He stared for a second before letting out a chuckle. "You don't need to rub it in. Come on. Let's have EMS check out your head."

After a paramedic had glued my cut closed with liquid stitches and bandaged me up, I sat in the back of the ambulance, legs dangling off the edge. I'd been cleared to go over an hour ago, and I didn't really need any more information for my story—I had a firsthand account of how the serial rapist who'd been terrorizing Bristol had been captured —but I lingered, waiting for Pennington. I wanted an update once he'd interrogated Roger, or at least that's what I was telling myself.

A handful of news reporters stood behind the police barricade, jockeying to be first in line to question the police. My lips crept into a smile. *Bristol Daily News* was going to have the scoop of all scoops. Shelly was going to lose her mind.

And I was going to get the crime beat. It hadn't really sunk in yet.

"Detective, Detective!" Trina Quinn from Channel 9 yelled at Pennington as he walked past the mob. "How was the suspect finally apprehended?"

Pennington ignored her, making his way towards me. He perched onto the back of the ambulance, his thigh touching mine.

"Roger confessed. He said he's been spying on women in the dressing room for a year and couldn't control his impulses anymore. All of the victims paid by credit card, so it wasn't hard for him to find addresses. We'll do a DNA test to be sure, but..." Pennington shook his head. "You got him, Evie. I can't believe it."

"And with my pepper spray you laughed at too." I smirked.

Pennington's face softened. "As grateful as I am, I never want you doing something like this again. Got it?"

"Well, I wouldn't have gone rogue if you'd been a little nicer to me."

He sighed, staring out at the circus of police cars and reporters. "I think...you may have been right. Maybe keeping each other in the loop could be beneficial for both of us."

I couldn't stop the smile spreading across my lips. "What are you saying, Pennington?"

"I'm saying, maybe I could be your point man after all."

"Okay," I said, goofy smile still plastered on my face.

"But we need ground rules. First off, you've got to respect when I say something's off the record."

"Of course."

"No quoting me without explicitly asking." He pointed his finger at me. "And no more of that 'detective close to the investigation' crap either."

"Got it."

"And the most important rule," Pennington continued, "is if you find new evidence or a lead, you *cannot* withhold that from the police. You tell me, right away."

"That would involve you taking my calls," I said.

Pennington took his phone out of his pocket and scrolled through it.

"What are you doing?"

"Unblocking your number."

"Wow!" I hit his arm.

"Don't make me regret this," Pennington grumbled.

"Since this guy could've killed me," I reached into my purse and grabbed my notepad again, "I think the least you can do is give me a quote."

"Alright, fine. Here's your damn quote." Pennington cleared his throat. "The department is thrilled to have this dangerous criminal off the streets, and we couldn't have done it without the courageous, albeit reckless, actions of reporter Evie Hartley. She really does *not* know when to quit."

I snickered as I jotted down some notes.

"How's that?" Pennington asked.

"It's perfect."

CHAPTER SEVEN

"Oh, Jesus Christ."

"Morning, Penn!" I shouted cheerfully from the curb. Since each hand held a hot cup of coffee, I lifted one in way of a greeting. I shifted from foot to foot, both from impatience and the chilly morning air. I'd been standing outside his house for fifteen minutes, hoping to catch him. He was good at avoiding me, so I had to be proactive.

After Roger's arrest, Pennington had warmed up to me a teensy bit and followed through on his promise to give me intel, although he'd done it very begrudgingly. I'd thought we made a huge breakthrough during our little heart-to-heart in the ambulance, but he continued to treat me with mild indifference.

No complaints from me, though. I had my beat and my source. This was better than things were before, and he'd been quite forthcoming with information about Roger's upcoming trial. Besides, I was fairly certain he only pretended I was a giant thorn in his side. I could sense I was growing on him.

He'd grown on me enough that I'd adopted my own nickname for him. Marcus seemed too buddy-buddy, and Pennington was a mouthful—so Penn it was. I liked it. It perfectly walked the line between professional and friendly, which was my goal.

Penn ignored my pleasant greeting and headed for the driveway, opening the passenger's side door of his car and tossing his briefcase inside. It was early December, but he wore no coat; only a shirt and tie, loose around his neck. He had to be freezing.

"I really don't have time for this today," Penn said as I approached. I'd hoped the coffee would butter him up, but either he hadn't noticed it, or he was determined to be as miserable as ever. Seeing as he was a detective, the latter seemed the more likely answer.

"I just had a few questions. Really quick, I swear."

He circled around to the back of his car and stood in front of me, hands on his hips. His expression hadn't softened at all, but he focused on the coffee in my hands.

"For you." With another bright smile, I handed over his cup.

"Does it have—"

"Soy milk instead of cream, because you're suffering from an adult-onset dairy allergy."

Penn grunted in response, snatched the coffee out of my hand, and took a cautious sip.

"Did I get it right?"

"Tastes like shit, so, yeah," he said. "I really miss dairy."

"Anywho, now that I've gone out of my way to be nice to you, will you return the favor?"

Penn shook his head and took another sip of his sad, dairy-free coffee. "First the grocery store, and now my house? This is definitely stalking. I know judges. I could get a restraining order easily."

"Hey, would a stalker be so kind as to bring you your weirdly specific coffee?" I asked. "The soy milk costs extra, you know."

"That's exactly something a stalker would do. You already know my work schedule and where I live. Lord knows how you managed to find out about the dairy allergy." He eyed the cup suspiciously. "I probably shouldn't drink this, in case it's poisoned. Stalkers do that too."

"I would never kill you, Penn," I said. "You're my only friend in the department. How else will I get the big scoop?"

He laughed out loud. "Friend is a very strong word."

I let out an impatient sigh. "Two questions. Please."

He checked his watch. "I'm already late."

"Can't go in like this, though," I said, gesturing to his tie. I set my coffee on Penn's trunk, grabbed both ends of his tie, and made a loop.

"One question. That's my final offer."

I gave him my best smile as I continued to fiddle with his tie. "A little birdie named Delaney told me you might have identified that hit-and-run suspect from the parking garage security footage, and you'll be bringing him in for questioning today."

"Why are you stalking me if you're getting stuff from Delaney?"

"Well, first of all, you're a lot easier on the eyes," I said with a cheeky grin.

He snorted in response.

"Delaney's more interested in chit chat than giving me anything useful. I found out about the dairy allergy from him, by the way. It was a very entertaining story about the two of you getting milkshakes on a stakeout one day, when suddenly—"

"*Stop*," he begged. "Finish with your question, please."

"How sure are you the guy you're bringing in is the one?"

A trace of a smile crept up his lips. "Hundred percent. He's the guy. Some friend came forward and destroyed his alibi. Got an arrest warrant all ready to go. Case'll be closed by the end of the day."

"Nice!" I knotted his tie. It didn't look right, but I kept tugging at it anyway. "Can I quote you on that?"

Penn grabbed my hands to stop my pulling, and I looked up into his deep brown eyes. "Absolutely not," he said with a smug smile.

"Damn it." I abandoned the tie I'd tied completely wrong.

Penn squinted at it. "What the hell?"

"Yeah, turns out I don't really know how to do that." I picked up my coffee again. "Well, thanks for nothing." I turned and headed for the curb where I'd parked my car.

"You'll get the full story at the press conference this afternoon, along with everyone else," Penn called after me.

"But I want the story *before* everyone else! Honestly, why do I bother?"

"I ask myself that every day," Penn shot back. "You're a gnat, Evie. No matter how many times I swat you away, you keep coming back."

"At least I'm a cute gnat!" I flashed him another giant smile.

Penn chuckled as he opened his car door. "Yeah, you're a cute gnat. But that doesn't make you any less annoying."

"Have a nice day, Detective." I waved him off as he backed out of the driveway. Penn raised his soy latte in a silent toast before his tires squealed and sped off down the street.

"Grace," I whispered over the top of my monitor. "I need your help."

"Can't now. On deadline," she answered, focused on her screen. Her manicured nails clacked on the keyboard, the story she was furiously typing reflected on her glasses lenses.

I spun in my chair, staring at the ceiling. I'd already written up the piece about the hit-and-run arrest yesterday, with no help from Penn, I might add. Nothing interesting was going on in Bristol today, and I needed an idea for my blog.

After the Roger incident, I wrote a really kick-ass piece with juicy details about his capture that only someone who was there could know. I stuck to the facts and graciously omitted myself from my own article.

However, Shelly had wanted me to write a thousand-word feature piece from my point of view, detailing exactly how I figured out Roger, stocker at Passions, was the serial rapist terrorizing our community. Now *that* was fun to write, and readers ate it up. We didn't just get local attention, either. The story spread like wildfire on social media, thanks in large part to my own family.

My little girl caught a vicious serial rapist! My dad had proudly proclaimed on Facebook, and it seemed our entire extended family also shared the article.

My sisters, Elise and Emma, had both posted some variation of "my baby sister is a BADASS," and their hundreds of friends couldn't resist clicking either. Our site briefly crashed because the article got so much traffic. This resulted in Shelly bequeathing me my own crime blog called *Evie Investigates*, with a cute little magnifying glass graphic next to the title.

I was tickled by this development. But after blogging a few follow-ups about Roger, I had nothing. How could I possibly top that? It's not like there were a lot of high-profile unsolved crimes in Bristol, just waiting for me to bust them wide open.

I hadn't made a post in a week. My readers wanted more, and more pressingly, Shelly wanted more. She'd been sending me not-so-gentle reminder emails, asking if I had any ideas yet. I had to prove to her that what happened wasn't a fluke, and I could continue to excel on this beat.

"I need to update *Evie Investigates*," I said. "And my mind is blank."

"I'm *busy*," Grace said. "Why don't you ask your sexy detective for help?"

I blew out a sigh. "He's not *my* sexy detective."

"He could be." Grace stayed focused on her screen. "You know, I heard he got divorced not too long ago. You should snatch him up before someone else does. I don't know why he's still single. It can't be his looks."

"It's his personality," I said dryly, trying to dodge the subject. Grace didn't know I'd made a personal policy to never touch another cop again, and I wasn't up for hashing out the details. She grunted at my response and her typing resumed.

"How can I investigate crimes for my readers if there aren't any crimes?" I mused loudly.

Grace sighed and finally looked at me. "If there aren't any new crimes, why don't you write about an old one?"

Huh. That could be interesting. Taking a new angle on an old case residents might not know about. People loved that kind of stuff.

"That's good, Grace." I eagerly typed in a Google search of "Bristol, Virginia famous crimes."

I leaned in close as I scrolled through the results. Six years ago, there was a murder-suicide. Gruesome, but boring. Not much to investigate there.

I continued to sort through the results, skipping over a string of bank robberies back in the nineties and the murder of a pregnant teenager—her boyfriend was the culprit, arrested a mere twenty-four hours after the killing.

Nothing grabbed me. I frowned, about to close out the tab, when the last result on the page caught my eye: *Bristol teen still missing, parents hoping for her safe return.*

Intrigued, I clicked. The story was dated nine years ago.

Bristol, VA—It's been six months since eighteen-year-old Bristol High School senior, Danielle Livingston, went missing, and the police are still no closer to finding out what happened to the teen.

Livingston, a popular girl with a bright future ahead of her, vanished on a cold December night when she failed to return home from a friend's house. The friend, Samantha Davenport, confirmed Livingston left her house safely, and in good spirits. The next morning, Tennessee state troopers discovered Livingston's car abandoned at a bus station right over the border, leading authorities to believe she may have been running away. Livingston's mother shared with Bristol police that she and her daughter had an argument the evening she disappeared, further fueling this theory.

Though there has been no sign of Livingston and her parents have received no contact from their daughter, they're hopeful she will return home unharmed.

If you have any information on the disappearance of Danielle Livingston, please contact the Bristol Police Department.

Alright, this could work. From what I gleaned from a search of Danielle's name, she'd never been found. Every article about her was over five years old. No news outlet cared anymore. The story would be exclusive to us.

Even better, we were coming up on the ten-year anniversary of her disappearance, so I had a timeliness angle too. I clicked on every article I could find about Danielle and hit print.

"Grace." I leapt from my chair. "You are a *genius*."

"Tell me something I don't know."

That evening, I set up shop in my living room, spreading out the printed, highlighted articles about Danielle all over my coffee table, laptop on my lap. Wally kept stepping all over the keyboard, desperately craving my attention because he saw I was busy. I scooped him up with one hand and dropped him onto the floor, then opened Twitter.

We're coming up on the ten-year anniversary of Bristol teen Danielle Livingston's disappearance, I typed. *She still hasn't been found. If you knew Danielle or know anything about her disappearance, send me a DM.*

I hit "tweet" and sat back on the couch, eagerly awaiting replies. I only had about 1,500 Twitter followers, but I wanted to put feelers out. Someone had to know something. Even if it wasn't groundbreaking, it could help shake loose a few new details. As I'd learned from the serial rapist case, the tiniest thing could change everything.

The articles I found painted a decent picture of Danielle Livingston; beautiful, good student, star tennis player. Based on the amount of people who attended a vigil for her, Danielle was quite popular.

The thing nagging at me was the possibility Danielle left on her own, which was what it sounded like the police had believed. I knew nothing about this girl, but I didn't buy it. An eighteen-year-old with a seemingly perfect life disappears and never calls her parents again? She leaves all her friends behind? No way.

Why had the police been so dead set on that theory? Had it been laziness, or unwillingness, to solve the crime? Or was there something they knew that hadn't been made public?

It was time to call my sexy detective.

"What is it?" Penn said upon answering.

"Hey! How's it going?"

"Evie, I know you're only calling because you want something. So just ask."

"That's a pretty rude assumption," I said. "Maybe I was calling to check in on you. Christmas is coming up soon. Got any plans? Traveling at all?"

Penn sighed.

"Okay, I did want to pick your brain for my next blog post."

"Can it wait until tomorrow? I had a really long day."

"Come on," I said. "It's Friday night, old man. Live a little."

"Oh, so you're insulting me. I definitely want to help you out now."

"Meet me for a drink. I'm buying."

"Hmm." Penn was silent as he mulled it over, but was ultimately unable to resist free booze. "Fine, but let's go to The Ranch. I have some unpleasant memories at Last Call."

CHAPTER EIGHT

"This isn't really the best place to talk," I shouted at Penn, even though he was sitting right across from me. "There's live music on Friday nights."

"I know," he yelled back, then grinned. "Why do you think I picked it?"

I gave him an exaggerated eye roll and took a sip of my rum and coke. Since I was picking up the tab, he had taken the liberty of ordering a double shot of pricey bourbon.

"I think you're still trying to get back at me." I meant both the locale and the top shelf liquor.

The grin remained. "Maybe."

The Ranch was a country music bar, stuffed to the gills with tacky western decor. Dozens of cowboy hats had been nailed to the ceiling, blinding fluorescent beer signs featuring busty barmaids crowded the walls, and drunk, hooting patrons took turns riding the mechanical bull in the corner. This was *not* my scene at all, and I'd bet my life it wasn't Penn's, either—he was just torturing me.

We sat at a tiny round table far from the stage where a young guy strummed a guitar, singing woefully about a one-night-stand who'd broken his heart.

I fell in love when you fell in my bed,
but it must've all been in my head.
I fell in love when I held you tight,
but I guess you just loved me for one night.

"I want to write about an old case for my next post," I belted over the awful song.

Penn cupped a hand around his ear. "What?"

I sighed heavily, stood, and scooted my chair over until it touched his. When I sat back down, we were shoulder to shoulder. Penn looked taken aback, like he was fighting the urge to move his chair away. I reveled in his discomfort—two can play *this* game.

I brought my lips to his ear. "I *said*, I want to write about an old case."

Penn leaned in close to me. "Which case?"

"Danielle Livingston. Missing high school student from ten years ago. Do you know it?"

"I know it." A frown formed on his face. I waited for him to elaborate, but he didn't.

"That's it?" I asked. "That's all you've got for me?"

Penn leaned back in. "Wasn't my case. I was just a beat cop back then. From what I remember, they thought she ran away."

His warm breath tickled my ear, and it sent an involuntary shiver down my spine. He looked *good* tonight, and being this close was a bit distracting. Penn must've showered before meeting me. He smelled like fresh soap and aftershave. He'd dressed casually in jeans and a long-sleeved thermal shirt, which was a lot snugger than his typical button-downs. I'd noticed several women eyeing him up, to which he was oblivious. The amount of relief this gave me was alarming.

Ignoring that for now, I turned to him. "I'm not buying it. A girl packs up her whole life and never contacts her friends or family ever again because she had a fight with her mom?" I shook my head.

"Teenage girls fight with their mothers constantly. That's nothing unusual."

"Yeah, but there was no body. And believe me, we searched everywhere for it. Every field, every square mile of woods. There were volunteers, cadaver dogs..." He sipped his drink. "We tried hard to find her."

I sat back in my chair, taking a few swigs from my own drink. I was jolted out of my thoughts when I could suddenly hear again. The music had stopped.

"Hey, everyone, I'm going to take a quick break," the singer announced. "Be back soon!"

There were a few scattered claps as he put the guitar down and got off the stage.

"So what are you going to write about Danielle?" Penn asked at a normal volume, no longer needing to invade my personal space to communicate.

"I'm not sure. Maybe just a ten-year anniversary piece. A reminder that she still hasn't been found. You know, get the word out again, maybe shake something loose."

"That's going to be tough," Penn said, a grim expression on his face. "This case is a decade cold, Evie. People have moved by now or forgotten basic details."

I opened my mouth, but my reply was cut off as a man approached our table.

"Evie?" he asked. "Is that you?"

Penn and I turned, and I nearly knocked over my drink when I saw the terrible singer standing there. Oh, jeez. I hadn't realized while he was singing, but now I recognized my old—very brief—flame, Brent Taylor.

"Oh...hi," I said awkwardly, forcing a smile a few seconds too late. "How's it going? I, uh, didn't recognize you up there."

"Really?" He grinned. "Because I spotted you all the way across the room."

My cheeks had to be scarlet right now. I snuck a look at Penn who had his lips pressed together, surely suppressing laughter.

"You sounded great up there," I lied.

"Thanks."

"How do y'all know each other?" Penn asked Brent.

"Evie wrote a story about my music earlier this year. She'd been doing a bunch of features on local young talent. We really hit it off," he added in an embarrassing tone.

"Really," Penn said, leaning back in his chair, giant smile on his face. "That's fascinating. What a small world, huh?"

I kicked him under the table.

"Young talent," Penn repeated. "Just curious, how old are you?"

I finished my drink in three gulps and motioned to our server for another.

"Twenty-one."

"Wow," Penn said. "Good for you. So successful at such a young age."

"Thanks, man," Brent said, not realizing Penn was making fun of him. He looked to me, his eyes begging for me to acknowledge him.

"Well, we were kind of in the middle of something." I spotted Penn's hand on the table and instinctively grabbed it.

"Oh. Sure. I'll let you get back to your date," Brent said, looking sad.

I relaxed at the prospect of him going away.

"Oh, this isn't a date." Penn detangled his hand from mine. "Strictly business. In fact, I have to get going soon, so you could keep Evie company."

I turned to stare at him, jaw hanging open.

"I would," Brent said, "but I gotta get back up there."

"That's too bad," Penn said.

"Nice seeing you, Evie."

"You too." I plastered on that fake smile. When he'd put enough distance between us, I grabbed Penn by the front of his shirt and pulled him close.

"What is *wrong* with you?"

He laughed, which made me madder. "The real question is, what's wrong with *you*, robbing the cradle like that? Did you check his ID beforehand, just to be safe?"

"God," I moaned, putting my face in my hands as our server plunked a fresh drink in front of me. I glanced up at Penn. "You really couldn't have pretended to be my boyfriend for five minutes?"

"He never would've bought it," he said. "If he's your type, I'm almost fifteen years too old."

There was actual glee in his eyes—a rare sight. He was thoroughly enjoying himself at my expense. I balled up my drink napkin and threw it at him. "It was one time!"

Lord. Brent had been such a mistake, that had come dangerously close to violating my new personal policy. At the time, I'd justified it to myself because Brent wasn't a source, just a subject. Normally, I wouldn't have even looked twice at a guy that young, but I'd still been in my miserable rut about ending up in Bristol in the first place.

"Wait. Evie," Penn said. "His song. It was about you!"

I froze as I remembered the lyrics. Between that and the way he acted just now, it seemed possible our little encounter had meant a lot more to Brent than it had to me—especially considering how many times he'd tried to call me afterwards.

"No," I said, shaking my head rapidly. "No, no, no."

"Jesus," Penn chuckled. "Kind of makes me curious what you did with that kid to make him fall in love with you."

"This is over. I wanted to talk about the case, not be judged for my personal life."

I desperately wanted to get away from the topic of me getting intimate with people I wrote about. Not to mention, Penn's last comment was borderline suggestive, which confused me, since he'd called me things like "leech" and "gnat."

I stood in a dramatic fashion, acting like I was about to put on my coat, though I was bluffing—I still had an entire rum and coke to finish, and I hadn't closed out my tab yet.

"Evie, sit down." Penn grasped my wrist. "I'm just giving you a hard time."

I glared at him, but nevertheless sunk back down in my chair.

"What's your plan of attack, then? Where were you going to start?"

"Well..." I put my smile back on. "I was hoping you could slip me the case file."

Penn laughed. "Dream on."

"Come on." I pouted. "I'd do *anything* to get my hands on it."

He raised an eyebrow. "Are you propositioning me? Because, like I said, I'm really tired tonight."

My heart dropped into my stomach, and a troubling combination of desire and unease washed over me as I visualized the arrangement he suggested.

"Ew!" I blurted out, interrupting my concerning little fantasy.

Penn blinked.

"I mean, not 'ew' about you," I clarified. "'Ew' about that. I don't do that. I'm a respectable journalist."

"You're really going to say that with lover boy right over there?"

I groaned and made a strangling gesture at him. "If you won't get me the case file, then I guess I'll start at the beginning. I'll start with the parents."

Penn's uncharacteristic easy-going expression morphed into his signature grim one. "I don't think that's a good idea."

"Why not? Everyone's forgotten about this girl, Penn. That can't be easy on the parents. Surely, they'd want media attention on their daughter's case again."

"Or they might be trying to move on."

"Why don't you want me to look into this?" I asked, my voice rising. "Worried I'll make the department look bad again? This girl has been missing for a *decade*. What if this were your daughter? Wouldn't you want people to never stop looking for her?"

Penn stood so abruptly he knocked his glass onto the floor. It shattered, but he didn't seem to notice. "If this were my daughter," he hissed, "I wouldn't want some random reporter poking around and resurfacing horrible memories, all to get clicks on her fucking *blog*."

With that, he dug a twenty out of his pocket, slapped it on the table, then turned and bolted for the door. I was too stunned to even attempt to go after him.

"What did I say?" I asked nobody. "What the hell did I say?"

"Back up," Grace said. "What was his tone like when he asked if you were propositioning him? Hopeful? Like he'd definitely take you up on it?"

"Can you focus?" I asked. "Who cares about that part? I need to figure out what I did to make him storm out like that."

"Well, it seems like he has some anger issues. Maybe that's why his wife left him."

"You're not helping." I slumped in my seat. I kept peeking at my phone, willing it to light up with a text from Penn.

The minute I got home from The Ranch, I'd tried to call him. Unsurprisingly, he didn't answer. I'd settled for a text instead.

I'm sorry I upset you.

I waited an hour, but no reply.

Penn, talk to me. Clearly I said something wrong, but I have no idea what.

That was Friday. Now, it was Monday afternoon. Not knowing was driving me crazy. On top of that, I was pissed. These little outbursts of his were getting old, and I couldn't help but feel like I was back to square one. I'd put so much effort into carefully cultivating this relationship with him—if you could even call it that—and one sentence had somehow destroyed it.

It was close to the end of the day when my phone finally buzzed, and my heart leapt into my throat, convinced I'd see Penn's name. It wasn't him, and it wasn't a text, but the name on the email made my heart speed up anyway: Sharon Livingston.

Hi Evie, she wrote.

It's been years since we've had reporters asking about Danielle, so I was surprised to get your email. My husband and I have been thinking about her a lot lately, with the ten-year anniversary coming up. I'm not quite sure what we'll be able to tell you that we haven't already told the press and the police all those years ago, but we'd be happy to talk to you about Danielle.

How's tomorrow morning at 10?

I tried to remain calm as I replied, telling her tomorrow morning was perfect. My email to Sharon had been overly kind, but Penn's voice remained in the back of my head, convincing me I was a terrible person for reaching out to the missing girl's parents. I had the urge to text him and tell him how wrong he'd been, but I refrained. He didn't want to talk? Fine. I could do the silent treatment, too.

Focus on the story, Evie.

So I did. The second I got home, I hunkered down, ordered some Chinese food, and sorted through all the info I had to prepare for my interview.

What did I want to ask them? The fight was number one on my list. I needed to determine how bad of an argument Danielle and her mom had the night she disappeared. If that was the reason Danielle had vanished, it had to have been a real doozy.

Number two...I needed to get a sense of her home life. The articles painted Danielle as a girl with a perfect life, but that didn't mean it was true. Maybe her parents were monsters—monsters who could write polite emails, that is.

The rustling of papers jolted me from my thoughts. My cat had jumped onto the coffee table, disturbing all the articles I had laid out. "Wally!" He bolted, sending one of my printouts to the floor. Grumbling, I bent to retrieve the fallen article.

Local businessman Michael Davenport offers $20,000 for info on missing teen.

Davenport. The last name of Danielle's friend, Samantha. A quick scan of the article told me Michael was her father. Huh. That was a *lot* of dough to shell out for his daughter's friend. I'd ask the Livingstons about that, too.

I was finishing my second egg roll when my phone buzzed. Again, I was hopeful it was Penn, and again, it wasn't. It was a Twitter notification. I had several direct messages waiting for me, all in response to the tweet I'd sent out about Danielle the other night.

I was friends with Danielle in high school! A girl named Kara wrote. *I could tell you all about her. Such a sweet girl. I miss her every day!*

I rolled my eyes. I'd bet Kara barely knew Danielle and just wanted to get her name in the story. I opened the next message, this one from a Brianna.

Hi, I went to high school with Danielle, and I think she ran away. After graduation, I moved to Nashville, and I swear I've spotted her around town a few times. I think she's living in Tennessee now.

Now, this was interesting—a possible sighting. There were probably a lot of young, pretty blond girls walking around Nashville, but it was something to consider.

"Who needs Penn, or that case file?" I asked Wally, who peeked out from behind the kitchen island. "I can get all this info on my own."

Wally stared at me, then started cleaning himself.

I had one final message, but the handle consisted of random letters and numbers, and there was no identifying profile photo. They had zero tweets and zero followers. A throwaway account. This person wanted to remain anonymous, which made their message all the more intriguing—-and chilling.

Everyone thinks Danielle ran away. I think she's dead. She hung around the Davenports too much, and they're BAD NEWS. Do not trust them.

CHAPTER NINE

I GOT TO THE LIVINGSTONS' AT TEN SHARP, NOTES ALL ORGANIZED, ready for anything.

Or at least I'd thought so.

Sharon was the first to greet me, and she looked how I'd expected— a short woman in her mid-fifties, with kind, wrinkled eyes and the same blonde hair as Danielle.

But when I'd stepped inside to see David—a tall, black man with graying hair—walking towards me, I was thrown, despite all my preparation.

"Hi, Evie." He extended his hand. "I'm David."

I blinked a few times. "Hello." I shook his hand, recalling every picture of Danielle I'd seen. "And you're Danielle's...father?"

He let out a small chuckle. "We don't exactly share a familial resemblance, do we?"

"Uh, no." I laughed uncomfortably.

"I'm not Danielle's biological father," David said. "Sharon and I got married when Danielle was three. I adopted her not too long after that."

"Oh." I felt like an idiot for not having known this. "Of course."

Fortunately, Sharon and David weren't hung up on my slip-up and ushered me into the kitchen, where a pot of coffee had already been brewing.

"How do you like your coffee, Evie?" Sharon asked me sweetly.

"Just milk, thanks."

She set a steaming mug of coffee in front of me, along with a cow-shaped cream pitcher. I'd been in her presence for only five minutes but was already convinced she wasn't a secret child abuser.

Come on. *A cow-shaped cream pitcher?*

The three of us were settled around a square, oak kitchen table, everyone's hands cupped around their warm mugs. The Livingstons' house was small but cozy-looking, with natural wood beams lining the ceilings and rustic paintings decorating the walls. Framed photos of Danielle adorned almost every surface available. In one glossy eight-by-ten in the living room, Danielle smiled and posed with a graduation cap on her head—a cap she never got to wear to the ceremony.

"Thank you for talking to me." I tried to stay focused and present, though my brain still raced with possibilities the adoption angle inspired.

What happened to Danielle's biological father? Could he be a potential suspect?

"Is it alright if I record this?" I asked, finger hovering over the button on my phone.

"Sure," Sharon said.

David gave me a nod as well, so I hit record and set my phone in the middle of the table.

"Why don't you start by telling me about your daughter? What she was like, her interests—that kind of thing."

"Danielle was a very sweet girl," Sharon said. "She was funny. Smart. She really wanted to go to the University of Virginia and become a nurse."

"Danielle had a lot of different interests," David chimed in. "She was good at tennis—she was on the high school team, and she and I would play on the weekends. She usually kicked my butt."

I smiled at the sweet detail.

"And she had a lot of friends. The second she got her license she was zipping all over town to hang out with everyone," Sharon said.

"That's also when her little rebellious stage started to kick in." David exchanged a knowing look with his wife. "I guess that's the age when hanging out with Mom and Dad isn't so fun anymore."

"Rebellious stage?"

"Oh, nothing but typical teenage antics," Sharon said. "She'd miss curfew a few times, or say she was going to hang out with a friend, but really be with a boy. Once, she called in the middle of the night and asked David to come get her because she'd gotten drunk at a party."

"At least she didn't try to drive home," David said.

"That's what I mean, though. Even when she did this kind of stuff, for the most part, she was still the good, responsible kid we raised."

I nodded. "Did you like her friends, then?"

"Most of them, yes," Sharon said. "She had a couple of newer friends we never met. But Danielle had been friends with a lot of girls since elementary school, so we knew them well. Like Samantha. We've known her for a long time."

"Right, Samantha Davenport." The anonymous Twitter user's message floated through my memory.

The Davenports are BAD NEWS.

"Samantha was the last person to see Danielle, right?"

Solemn nods from Sharon and David.

"Danielle went to Samantha's house to study for mid-terms." Sharon's gaze fell to her hands. "We were worried when it started to get late, but like we said, Danielle sometimes missed curfew. We just assumed she and Samantha lost track of time."

"Did you know Samantha's parents well? I saw Michael Davenport offered a pretty big reward for information on Danielle when she first went missing."

Sharon's calm expression darkened for a split second at the mention of Michael's name. Her eyes narrowed the tiniest bit, but it was so brief I was almost certain I'd imagined it. Though when Sharon attempted her kind smile again, it didn't look quite the same.

"When the girls were young, David and I were close with the Davenports." Sharon's tone remained polite, but it had lost its warmth. "We even took a few family trips to Virginia Beach together. The Davenports have a house there."

"What about when the girls were older? Were you still friendly with the Davenports?"

Sharon and David exchanged a glance.

"We don't want this in the story," David said, "but we had a falling out with the Davenports when Danielle started high school."

Jackpot.

"Would you mind telling me what happened?" I asked, heart racing. "Off the record, of course. I'm just trying to get a full picture of Danielle's life."

"There was an issue at a sleepover." Sharon pursed her lips. My mind started going to many dark places in the few seconds' pause. "Samantha has an older brother, Hudson. The kids all used to play together when they were little. But when Hudson hit puberty...Let's just say he wasn't only interested in Danielle as a playmate anymore."

"Did Hudson ever do anything inappropriate?"

"The girls caught Hudson spying on them during this sleepover," David said, his face grim. "He'd been hiding in Samantha's closet while the girls were in there. He watched them change into their pajamas. Danielle made a comment when she got home about how creepy Hudson was, and we managed to get the story out of her."

I had a brief flash of discovering Roger's peephole in the Passions dressing room. Roger told Penn he'd started off just peeping—but then it had escalated.

"That's awful," I said. "Did you talk to the parents?"

"Of course," Sharon said firmly. "Michael and Georgina completely brushed it off. Said it was no big deal—a teenage boy being a teenage boy. We were furious. Hudson had always been a troublemaker, and they never disciplined him. We were very worried he'd try something else with Danielle."

Suddenly, Hudson became my number one suspect. Was he so enraged that Danielle never returned his feelings that he'd killed her?

"So Danielle and Samantha were still friends, even after you fell out with her parents?"

"We tried to keep them apart after that. I didn't want her going back over there. But the girls still saw each other behind our backs." David ran his hand over his hair. "So we just had a 'no sleepovers' rule, but once Danielle turned sixteen and got her license, we couldn't really stop her from going to the Davenports'."

"Did Danielle ever mention having issues with Hudson again?" I asked.

"No," Sharon said. "But I imagine she wouldn't tell us, considering how we reacted the last time."

"Right." I needed to find out everything I could about Hudson. The Davenports covering up their son's peeping didn't sound like great parenting at all, and that type of behavior could definitely be described as "bad news." Surely, they had other secrets, too.

"Were you surprised Michael was helping in the search for Danielle, then?" I asked, confused now. "That he offered such a big reward, seeing as how you didn't get along?"

"I'm sure Michael just felt badly." There was a bitter edge to Sharon's voice. "And twenty-thousand dollars might sound like a lot to you or me, but for the Davenports, that's nothing. They have several homes. Large ones."

"I was always convinced it was a publicity stunt." David rolled his eyes, then took a big sip of his coffee. "Michael was about to open a big apartment complex around the time Danielle went missing. He just wanted to look good—get some free press for the apartments out there."

I nodded, devouring this useful information that was far more than I had dared to hope for. I couldn't even be sure Danielle was dead, but Sharon and David had convinced me the Davenports had something to do with her disappearance.

Them, and that ominous, anonymous tweet.

"I think we should get back to Danielle and your story now." The sudden harshness in Sharon's tone startled me. She did *not* like Michael Davenport.

"Of course." I cleared my throat. "What do you two believe happened to Danielle? Do you think she could've run away?"

"It's hard not to have hope she's still alive." Tears formed in Sharon's eyes. "And maybe at eighteen, she would've wanted to get away from us. We had our fair share of fights." She dabbed at her eyes with a napkin. "But there's no way she would've cut us off for ten years, not even letting us know that she was okay. Something must've happened to her."

David rose and disappeared into the living room. He returned and set a photo album on the table in front of me.

I began to page through it.

"Danielle was a happy little girl." The endless photos of a tiny Danielle eating an ice cream cone on the boardwalk and sitting on her dad's shoulders in the ocean appeared to back up David's claim. "We were a close family. Every teenager pushes away their parents at some point."

I nodded and continued to flip through the album, getting to some pre-teen photos of Danielle at a bowling birthday party. "I remember saying some horrible things to my parents when I was in high school," I told them. "But I didn't run away."

"Exactly," Sharon said with a sniffle.

"Could you tell me about the fight you had with Danielle the night she went missing?" I asked gently. "I found an article that mentioned it."

"God," Sharon breathed and closed her eyes. "Sometimes I wish I'd never mentioned that to the police. They took it and ran with it, using it as their justification that she left town. But they didn't *know* Danielle."

I gave her a few seconds.

"About a month or two before she disappeared, Danielle started being more secretive than usual," Sharon said. "We'd ask where she was going, and she'd snap and say it was none of our business. I wondered if maybe she was dating someone she didn't want us to know about."

"Interesting. Is that why you fought the night she disappeared? She wasn't telling you where she was going?"

"Yes. I demanded to know, and it got nastier than usual. Danielle just stormed out. Later, we found out from Samantha that Danielle had gone over there. But it didn't make sense to us. Why would Danielle make a big deal about not telling us if she was just going to see Samantha?"

"That is weird. Do you think Samantha was lying?"

"She told us the same story she told the police." David shrugged. "I don't think she'd lie about that."

Not unless she was covering for Danielle for some reason—like if she was running away with a secret boyfriend.

"The police seem to be under the impression Danielle ran away, which might've led to the case going cold," I said. "What would you like the police and the public to take from this story?"

Sharon exchanged a look with David before replying. "We think our daughter was murdered. We want the case reopened, and we want the police to find out who took her from us."

CHAPTER TEN

"Wally, I'm overwhelmed."

The mess of papers on my coffee table had worsened considerably after my visit with the Livingstons. I'd transcribed my entire interview with them and printed it out, highlighting in different colors the pertinent information.

In yellow was the stuff I put in my article—the ten-year-anniversary piece on Danielle. I'd written that up this afternoon: *Ten years after Bristol teen Danielle Livingston disappeared, parents want investigation reopened.*

"We think our daughter was murdered," Sharon Livingston, mother of Danielle Livingston, said as she wiped her eyes. "We want the police to find out who took her from us."

Shelly adored my rehashing of a decade-old mystery, and was even more floored when I announced my intention to poke around and blog about it on *Evie Investigates.*

That's what the pink highlighter was for—information I needed to dig deeper into. The Livingstons had given me so many threads to follow, it made my head hurt. A lot of this would be easier to look into if I had the case file, but that obviously wasn't going to happen. I was going to end up doing a lot of grunt work the police had already done years ago, but what choice did I have? Penn had shut me out for some unknown reason. I was on my own.

My head was pounding. I put down the transcript and looked at Wally, who napped contently on my lap, sucking up all the body heat I had to offer.

"Excuse me." I gave him a gentle nudge that accomplished nothing. I pushed harder, which resulted in Wally hissing and scampering across the apartment.

"Love you too!" I called after him as I shuffled to the kitchen. I located the Advil, popped two, then filled the kettle for some tea. I'd just set the tea bag in the mug when I heard a knock on my door.

Alarmed, I glanced at the microwave clock. It was after nine. Grace was really the only person who'd stop by, and she never came over unannounced.

"Evie? You there?"

Penn.

This was an interesting development. I took a few steps towards the door before panic set in. I was in cutesy polka dot pajama pants and bright pink fuzzy socks. I had my hair up in a messy ponytail and not a speck of makeup on my face. Not to mention, I was braless. No way was I letting him in.

"Evie?" Penn called again with another knock. "Look, I'm sorry. Can we talk?"

As quietly as I could, I crept up to the door, scarcely daring to breathe. I stood there, frozen, fighting an internal battle. Curiosity gnawed at me—about why he'd flipped out at The Ranch and why he was here now—but part of me was still upset. Maybe I'd ignore *him* now. See how he liked it.

After a few more moments, a loud rustling made me leap backwards—he was shoving something under the door. With a final push, a manila folder slid across the hardwood floor and stopped at my feet. His footsteps receded down the hall.

I stared at the folder wide-eyed before snatching it up. It took me about three seconds to open it and figure out what it was. Grabbing a nearby cardigan and pulling it on over my thin t-shirt, I yanked the door open and poked my head into the hall.

"Hey," I called after Penn, who'd almost reached the stairs. He froze, then turned to face me. I held up the folder. "What made you change your mind?"

He slowly made his way back towards me, hands shoved into his pockets. I felt a bit better about my own appearance as I took in his wrinkled, half-untucked shirt. "I saw your story...I guess Danielle's parents wanted to talk after all."

"Yeah, they did," I said. "They told me a lot of stuff."

Penn and I stood there in uncomfortable silence—me, waiting for an explanation, and him, presumably waiting for an invitation inside.

The whistle from the tea kettle cut through the heavy awkwardness.

"Oh. I made tea." I left the door open as I headed for the stove. Penn continued to linger in the hallway.

"Do you want some?" I shouted from the comically far distance. Apparently, I was still too bitter to ask him in, but not to offer him a beverage.

"Sure. Thanks." Penn deemed that close enough to an invitation and stepped inside, shutting the door behind him.

I focused on fixing the tea, my back to him. It sounded like he settled on the couch.

Wally let out a little chirp, surely alarmed by the strange man in the apartment.

"Oh, hi there," Penn said softly.

Mugs in hand, I turned. "Careful, he's not very friend—"

Wally was in Penn's lap. His front paws rested on Penn's chest and he rubbed his head against Penn's scruffy chin. I could hear Wally purring all the way in the kitchen.

Penn smiled. "I think he likes me."

"What the hell!" I walked over, put the tea down and sat next to Penn. "He doesn't even do that to me."

My traitorous cat gave Penn a few more head bumps before curling into his lap, still purring softly.

"He's seriously the grumpiest cat." I snorted. "Maybe that's why he likes you so much."

Penn shook his head. "I guess I deserve that."

"You gonna tell me what happened the other night?" I asked cautiously before sipping my hot tea.

"I'm sorry I lost it," he murmured, eyes not meeting mine. "This case stirred some things up." Penn cleared his throat, his hand softly stroking Wally's head. "My ex-wife and I...we lost a baby a few years ago. A little girl. She was premature, but she held on for a few weeks. Even the doctors thought she'd make it."

A wave of dizziness washed over me as my words from Friday night flitted back into my mind.

What if this were your daughter?

"Oh, Penn..." I put down my mug, and tears pricked at my eyes at the thought of this big, grumpy man still grieving the loss of his baby girl. "I'm so sorry."

He gave me a shrug. "You didn't know. I shouldn't have yelled at you like that."

"Still," I said. "I understand your reaction. I probably sounded like some heartless monster, trying to exploit a family tragedy. I get so wrapped up in these stories sometimes that I forget the other side of things."

Penn finally looked at me and gave me a small smile. "You're not a monster, Evie."

"A gnat, then," I suggested. "Or maybe a leech."

"I was so against you doing the story because I only looked at it from my perspective," Penn said, ignoring my joke. "But unlike me, Danielle's parents never got any closure. It sounds like they're in agony. It's kind of against the rules, but if they want the case reopened, I figured there's no harm in making some copies for you. An extra set of eyes couldn't hurt."

I picked up the case file. "You did it again."

"What?"

"Just when I'm about to write you off as the world's biggest jerk, you find the perfect way to make it up to me."

"I don't mean to be," Penn said. "I know it's not an excuse, but between the baby and the divorce...I'm having a hard time with it."

"Of course," I said softly. The awkward silence returned. I assumed Penn's divorce was a direct result of the death of their child. A lot of couples struggled to survive that. It amazed me that Danielle's parents managed to stay married after what happened—though maybe the faint hope of her return was the glue holding them together.

"I know you're dying to look through that file." Penn nodded towards the folder.

"Just a little bit." I leaned forward and grabbed the interview transcript and handed it to him. "Here, you read this. Pay attention to the stuff in pink."

Penn pretended to struggle to lift the hefty stack of papers. "This is a *lot*."

"What? Do you have some place to be?"

"No."

Penn and I sipped our tea and paged through our respective documents. Eventually, Wally got bored and hopped off Penn's lap, going to check his food bowl even though he'd already had dinner hours ago.

It was bizarre, us curled up together like this, me in my jammies and Penn in his crumpled work clothes. We probably looked like an exhausted married couple who collapsed onto the couch after a long day. I'd been walking on eggshells around Penn for so long, the comfort level I suddenly felt was jarring.

I risked a few up-close glances of him in this more intimate setting, taking in his seemingly permanent five o'clock shadow, and the way he had one piece of unruly hair that curled over his forehead when he looked down. I had the urge to brush it back for him and run my fingers through his thick hair. Watching a bit more intently, I noticed the crease between his brows deepening as he read certain parts of the interview. My eyes skimmed to his chest, where two shirt buttons were undone. The glimpse of skin this afforded me was tan and dusted with dark hair. I briefly wondered what he'd look like with no shirt at all, which sent a rush of heat to my cheeks. *Dangerous thinking, Evie.* I averted my gaze and went back to the case file.

After about a half hour, I broke the silence. "Not that I'm complaining, but I kind of expected there to be more in here."

There were statements from Sharon and David, Samantha, and a few other people who knew Danielle—but there wasn't much there I didn't already know. My interest had been piqued when I got to a series of black-and-white photos of Danielle's abandoned car, but nothing stood out. The cops had found a bunch of different sets of fingerprints, including Samantha's, but no one's who shouldn't be in there.

"Lots of good stuff here, though," Penn said. "Any particular reason you wrote 'psycho stalker killer' next to Hudson Davenport's name?"

"Well, he's my prime suspect, of course." I blushed slightly. I'd forgotten about the little notes I'd added.

"Why?"

I made a face. "Are you joking? Because he's a major creep. Sharon said he had a thing for Danielle. He got caught spying on her, and his parents did nothing—essentially encouraging his behavior. It could've escalated. And with Danielle and Samantha being best friends, he would have easy access to her."

"Hey, no arguments from me. He's been brought into the station a few times over the years—small-time stuff, always had the best lawyer so he got off. But, yeah, he's just another messed up rich kid." Penn paused. "Well, not a kid anymore, I guess. He'd be about your age now."

"I have so many leads to look into." I leaned back into the couch. "Did you know that David Livingston isn't Danielle's biological father?"

"No," Penn said. "Who's her real dad?"

"No idea. But David adopted Danielle, meaning the bio dad isn't in the picture. That could be significant. Sharon also thought Danielle might've had a secret boyfriend right before her disappearance. Another potential suspect."

"You're really thinking murder, aren't you?"

"How can you not?" I flipped to the pictures of Danielle's car. "If you were running away and had a car that could take you anywhere, why on earth would you ditch it to take the bus?"

"It's a good question," he said. "It's not a leap to assume someone else dumped it there. But you have to consider everything. Maybe she ditched the car because she was getting picked up by someone—the secret boyfriend, let's say—and the bus station was just the meeting place."

"Oh." My heart sunk. "Right."

Penn let out a small laugh. "You can't expect to solve every case you get your hands on, Evie."

I raised an eyebrow. "Are you saying the rapist was just beginner's luck?"

"Based on your tone, I'm thinking the correct answer is 'no,'" Penn said. "But you have to remember, this case went cold for a reason. I don't want you to get your hopes up."

"I'm not," I lied. "I just want to do what I can for the Livingstons. And I want to do the story justice."

"You will. You're a good writer. Your blog is great."

I blinked, taken aback by his compliment. "You read my stuff?"

"Well, sure. How else can I make sure you haven't wildly misquoted me?"

I laughed. "Fair enough." I closed the folder and held it tightly to my chest. "Thanks for this, Penn. I really appreciate it."

"I'm going to push for the case to be reopened," he said. "But it'll be a hard sell without new evidence."

"Oh, don't you worry. I'm going to dig up something."

"I believe it," he said with a grin. "What's your next move?"

"Samantha," I said. "She'll know if there was a boyfriend, and I can get some more info about Hudson from her. I want dirt on that whole family, actually. Something feels off about them."

Penn's brow furrowed. "Just because of Hudson's peeping?"

I grabbed my phone and brought up Twitter, finding the anonymous message.

"Hmm," Penn said when I showed him.

"*Hmm?* That's your reaction?"

"A completely anonymous account sent you a creepy, vague message," Penn said. "Evie, someone's messing with you."

"What happened to considering every possibility? They might have a good reason to be anonymous."

"If that were true, they would've given you more information." Penn squared his shoulders, in lecture-mode now. "Something more useful than 'don't trust them.'"

"Must you poke holes in *all* my theories?" I collected our empty mugs and stood. "You're seriously one of the most frustrating people I've ever met."

"Funny, I was thinking the same thing about you." The corners of his mouth curled up as he gave me a once-over, getting the full effect of my cardigan-and-pajama combo.

I glared at him, because otherwise it would've seemed like flirting.

Penn glanced at his watch. "Shit, it's almost midnight."

Shocked, I turned to the microwave clock, which confirmed it was 11:38. He'd been here for two-and-a-half hours.

Penn stood from the couch and stretched. "I need to get going. Thanks for the tea."

"Thanks for going down the rabbit hole with me." I walked him to the door, but he barely made it two steps outside before turning back.

"Oh, and Evie?"

I paused before closing the door. "Yeah?"

"If you do happen to find the murderer, call for backup this time, okay?"

CHAPTER ELEVEN

Hi! Me again, I wrote, cringing. I just wanted to circle back and make sure you got my last message. I'd really like to set something up soon to discuss Danielle's disappearance. Even if you just had fifteen minutes, that would be so helpful. Appreciate it, thanks!

I closed my eyes and hit send before I could chicken out. Sometimes, being a gnat got old. This was my third attempt in as many days to contact Samantha Davenport, and so far she'd given me zilch. After my successful visit with the Livingstons, Samantha's radio silence surprised me.

"Do you think Samantha's hiding something?" I asked Grace. "And that's why she won't talk to me?"

DON'T TRUST THE DAVENPORTS!

"Maybe she just doesn't want to talk to a reporter about her missing friend." Grace, as always, kept typing away. Her ability to multitask was unparalleled.

"I *need* to talk to her." I flopped back in my chair. "And Michael Davenport. I think the key to all of this lies with them."

"And *I* think you might be letting this Twitter message cloud your judgment a bit," Grace said.

I groaned. "You sound like Penn."

"How are things with him? Still fighting?"

"Nah. He came over the other night, and we worked it out."

Grace's keyboard clacking came to a halt. "Worked it out...in the bedroom?"

I scoffed. "Will you give that a rest? I'm not interested."

"Why not? You haven't had any action since that Brent guy. I don't see the harm in taking Pennington for a spin. He's tall and has a great set of shoulders, and as a bonus, he's always got some handcuffs on him for fun times."

"Keep it down," I hissed, then glanced around to see if anyone was eavesdropping.

"Don't even try to tell me you haven't thought about him that way."

"Okay, sure, he'd probably be a dream in bed," I whispered. "He has dark, smoldering eyes I could stare into for hours, and these nice, big hands..."

Grace smirked and raised her eyebrows, waiting for me to continue.

It was tempting to come clean about why nothing could happen with Penn. I hated talking about it, but once Grace set her mind to something, she couldn't be stopped—and apparently, her latest mission was to push Penn and me together.

"Grace, I just can't. I got involved with a source back in D.C. and things got...messy. It's a huge conflict of interest. I don't want to jeopardize my job for a hookup."

She gave me a bemused smile. "Oh, Evie, sometimes I forget you're a big-city girl from a world-renowned paper. Down here, we've got a different set of rules."

I scrunched my eyebrows together. "What do you mean?"

"In a town this small, everyone knows everyone. It'd be impossible to cover local stories and not have the occasional conflict of interest. Just last week I interviewed my old high school boyfriend. And Wendy, who had the crime beat before Jeff, was *married* to a Bristol PD officer. As long as the piece is good, Shelly doesn't care."

"Huh." Shelly's attitude on the matter was certainly much different than my old editor's at the *Post*. Though, in all fairness, I hadn't been pushed out the door because I screwed a cop—it'd been because I screwed *over* a cop. Maybe Penn wouldn't be out of the question if I handled things a bit better this time around...

"It'd be a disaster," I said, stopping my train of thought dead in its tracks. "Penn's pretty messed up from the divorce, and I'm not looking for a project. I tried to fix enough guys in my twenties."

"Is he still hung up on the ex?"

"I have no idea," I said. "I don't even know her name."

"Hold on." Grace clicked her mouse a few times, then typed something. "Found her."

I bolted upright in my chair. "*Her,* her?" I knew learning the identity of Penn's ex-wife had only been a Google search away, but every time the thought crossed my mind, I managed to stop myself. Cyber-stalking the ex-wife of a man I wasn't even dating sounded crazy.

But I was dying of curiosity. And hey, Grace did the search, not me. No harm in a quick look.

I got up and walked around to Grace's desk, hunching over the screen.

"Audrey Pennington," Grace said, clicking on an image of a beautiful, smiling woman with auburn hair and blue eyes. "Looks like she kept his name. Oh." Grace found another photo, a group one, of several women huddled together in a classroom. "She's an English teacher at the high school."

"Interesting." I perched on the edge of Grace's desk. It felt strange to suddenly have a face and a name to go with this mysterious, blank image I'd had in my head. Now, when I thought about a devastated Penn in the hospital after the death of his daughter, I would picture him with this woman.

I'd been lost in my thoughts and hadn't been paying attention to what Grace was doing, but when she gasped, my head snapped back towards her.

"What?"

"Evie, you are not going to believe this," Grace said, eyes wide. "When I Googled Audrey, an old article popped up about *Danielle*."

I squinted, not understanding the connection.

"Danielle was her student! I'll send you the article. Audrey talked about what a great student Danielle was, and how she wanted to go to UVA. It sounds like they were close."

"Wow." Penn hadn't mentioned any of this when I'd first brought up Danielle—though it appeared that when it came to personal matters, his go-to coping method was to keep everything bottled up until he exploded.

"You should talk to her," Grace said. "Maybe Danielle confided in her about stuff she didn't tell her parents. It's worth a shot, especially since Samantha's not replying."

My jaw dropped. "I cannot go talk to Penn's ex-wife! Are you crazy?"

"Evie, it's business," Grace said easily. "It's not like you're going to scope her out. Though, you might as well while you're there. Maybe get a sense if there's any chance of reconciliation."

"I'm not talking to her. It's a bad idea."

"Why is it a bad idea?" A smirk crept across her lips. "Could it be because you *are* actually into him?"

I made some sputtering sounds. I'd meant to tell her no, but all my brain could think about was how Penn had looked all sexy and relaxed on my couch the other night.

"That's what I thought."

I groaned and circled back to my own desk.

Grace started furiously typing again, back to work. The business beat was a bit more hopping than the crime one lately.

After a few silent minutes, she announced, "Done. You'll thank me later."

My heart stopped. "Grace...what did you do?"

"I may have pretended to be your assistant and emailed Audrey to set up an interview."

"Grace Anna Lee," I said through clenched teeth. "You did not."

Her computer dinged. "Oh, that was fast!" Grace clicked and her eyes scanned the email. "Great news, Evie. She wants to talk to you."

"Grace!" I leapt from my chair and darted towards her, though I had no clue what I intended to do. Strangling her would be no use. The damage was done.

"Wait, wait, wait." She put her hands up. "Before you kill me, at least read what she wrote. She really might have something for you."

I glared at Grace, but nevertheless turned my attention to Audrey's message on the screen. And as much as I'd wanted to murder my best friend for her meddling, as I read the email, my rage vanished.

Hi Grace, I'd be happy to talk to Evie. Danielle's disappearance never sat right with me. She'd been having some personal troubles that I don't think the police ever looked into.

Evie can stop by the school either today or tomorrow, between 3:00 and 5:00.

I blew out a long exhale, trying to slow my racing heart. "Personal troubles. Danielle's parents didn't say anything about that. They said it was just typical teen antics."

Grace gave me a knowing nod, silently telling me, "I told you so."

"Oh, Grace, you pesky, meddling genius." I shrugged into my coat and grabbed my keys. "If I wasn't so mad at you, I'd kiss you."

I paced the empty school hallway, staring at red lockers and generic winter decorations all over the walls, the words "Merry Christmas" intentionally absent. I was outside "Ms. Pennington's" classroom, and that identifier alone made me start to sweat.

Should I have given Penn a heads up about this? I didn't know how much contact he and Audrey had, and it'd be terrible if he heard about this interview from his ex instead of me. Visions of our fragile relationship once again crashing down like a house of cards filled my head.

Smoothing my visitor's pass sticker one more time, I knocked on the polished oak door.

"Come in," a voice called from inside.

I took a deep breath and entered.

"Audrey?" I flashed a nervous smile.

"You must be Evie." She rose from her desk and closed the distance, then extended her hand, a cheerful smile on her face. "It's nice to meet you."

"You too." I tried to prevent any disappointment from clouding my expression. Audrey was prettier in person than she'd been in the photos. I guessed she was the same age as Penn. Her auburn hair was pulled back in a loose bun, showing off her high cheekbones. Her blue eyes were warm and kind, and her sweater and black slacks accentuated her trim figure. I couldn't help but feel a tiny pang of jealousy. She looked so put together. Something told me she didn't drink too much wine, communicate an unhealthy amount with a cat, or need to occasionally show some cleavage to excel at her job.

"Thanks for seeing me so quickly," I added as she moved some books off a chair for me.

"I should be thanking you. I desperately needed a break from all this essay grading." We settled into our seats.

"I'm not sure how much Grace told you," I began, "but I'm looking into Danielle's disappearance, hoping to find some information that could get the police to reopen the case."

Audrey nodded. "I saw your story the other day. The interview with her parents. You handled it really well."

"Oh. Thanks."

"I've read some of your other stories, too." Audrey's smile faded a little. "You quote my ex-husband quite a bit."

Lord. I hadn't anticipated Penn coming up this soon. She'd said it in a light tone, but I couldn't help but take it as an accusation. Was this the real reason Audrey had been so eager to talk with me?

"Uh, yeah," I said with a shaky laugh. "He's the only Bristol detective who'll give me the time of day."

Audrey pursed her lips and gave me a small nod. She took her time choosing her next words. "How is he?"

I cleared my throat and shifted in my chair. "He's okay." I wasn't about to tell Penn's ex how much he was still struggling. "We're not... we only have a professional relationship. I don't know him very well."

Audrey frowned slightly. "I see."

"I mean, he's kind of a stick in the mud, and he gets pissed off easily, but I don't know if that's normal or not."

Audrey let out a sudden laugh. "That's pretty normal for Marcus."

Another few seconds of silence passed, and I wasn't sure if I should say something else about Penn. Luckily, Audrey solved the issue.

"So what would you like to know about Danielle?" She put the friendly smile back on.

"Right." I pulled out my phone and hit record. "In your email you seemed to suggest that you don't think she ran away. Why is that?"

"UVA was Danielle's dream," Audrey said. "Her grades weren't fantastic her freshman and sophomore years, but once she decided UVA was where she wanted to go, she worked so hard to get them up."

I nodded.

"At the beginning of her senior year, Danielle's grades were almost there. She had a good shot at getting in, so she asked me to help her write a great admissions essay." Audrey leaned in a little, like she was about to tell me a secret. "Danielle finished the essay and submitted her UVA application the day she disappeared."

A chill went up my spine. The timing was absurd—seemingly disproving the police's theory. "Who would run away after putting in all that work?"

"That's why it never made sense to me. I told Marcus at the time, and he tried to talk to the detectives on Danielle's case, but no one took him seriously. He was still a rookie cop, and I was just a young teacher. They didn't listen to us."

I let out a heavy sigh and shook my head. "It sounds like these cops' minds were already made up. They just focused on Danielle's fight with her mom and the car at the bus station, then ignored everything else."

"You mentioned that fight in your story."

"Mrs. Livingston seems to think it was no big deal. Typical teenage stuff." I noted the grim expression on Audrey's face. "Is that not true?"

"Well, I have no way of knowing what their fight was about," Audrey said. "But I have a good guess."

I leaned forward. "Do you know something? Did Danielle have a boyfriend? That's what Mrs. Livingston thinks."

Audrey tilted her head. "I don't know anything about a boyfriend. But Danielle and her mom were fighting a *lot* before her disappearance."

"About what?" My voice was a whisper.

"Her real father," Audrey said. "Danielle was trying to find out who her biological father was right before she disappeared."

"Wow." I leaned back in my chair. "Did she find out?"

"I'm not sure," she said. "If she did, she didn't tell me. But that's what her college essay was all about—identity, and how blood doesn't make a family. When she was drafting the paper, she'd wanted to include a section about what meeting her father was like, but Danielle didn't end up putting it in."

"She probably didn't find him, then."

"That, or the meeting didn't go the way she thought it would." Audrey's comment made it all too obvious she was once married to a detective. "Danielle and her mom fought a lot about her biological father. Mrs. Livingston wouldn't give up his name, and she wanted Danielle to stop looking for him. If I had to guess, I'd say that's what they were fighting about the night she disappeared."

"Hmm." I frowned. "Mrs. Livingston didn't mention any of that."

My mind raced to come up with why. Her deception appeared suspicious, but there were plenty of reasons Sharon wouldn't be forthcoming about Danielle's father. For one, her husband had been with us the entire time. Maybe it was a touchy subject for them. I was also a total stranger; why would she reveal this personal secret to me?

But why try so hard to hide it from Danielle? Didn't she have the right to know?

"I can see the wheels turning," Audrey said when I hadn't spoken for a while.

I laughed. "I just keep stumbling onto all this information. Every time I'm about to sit down and do this jigsaw puzzle, hundreds of new pieces get added to the box."

"Sorry to make your job harder." She flashed a tiny smile.

"No, this was so helpful." I paused. "You don't happen to still have Danielle's essay, do you?"

"Normally, I wouldn't." Audrey swiveled her chair closer to her computer. "But Danielle's essay turned out so well, I held onto it as an example to show my students. I could print you a copy."

My heart felt like it leapt out of my chest. "That would be great."

Audrey located the essay, then the printer started to whir.

"I really hope you keep digging, Evie." Audrey retrieved the pages and paper-clipped them together for me. "I'm still so sick over what happened to Danielle."

"Were you close?"

"We were." Audrey's eyes shone with emotion. "When you're teaching at twenty-four, a lot of students see you more as a friend than a teacher."

"Right."

"Danielle and her friend Samantha used to hang out in my classroom after school all the time," Audrey went on. "Just chatting and doing their homework."

"Samantha Davenport?" My voice rose an octave.

"Uh-huh," Audrey said. "Samantha and I still keep in touch, meet for dinner or a drink every now and then."

I took a deep breath, my body practically vibrating with excitement over this development. I stood and slid Danielle's essay into my purse.

"Audrey, would you maybe want to help me do some more digging?"

CHAPTER TWELVE

THE COFFEE TABLE PILE HAD GOTTEN SO OUT OF HAND, I resorted to taping and pinning things to the wall, kissing my security deposit goodbye. I'd also stopped at the craft store and purchased a giant white board, which I had propped against my TV.

I sat on my couch, legs crossed, typing up a post for *Evie Investigates*, but my eyes kept darting to the table where I'd set Danielle's essay. Shelly's deadline took priority, so any potential clues to Danielle's paternity had to wait. While eager to finish my post, I also dreaded it, because before I could press publish, I had to warn Penn that my latest update would feature his ex-wife. And surely he'd be furious with me. Again.

"Wally, how do I always get myself into these situations?" I asked.

He hopped up onto the coffee table and stared at me, offering no answer, before plopping down right on top of Danielle's essay.

"It'd be more helpful if you could read it instead of sitting on it."

I refocused on my post, finishing up the final paragraph.

Ms. Pennington has doubts her former student would have run away after putting so much work into her college application. Mr. and Mrs. Livingston also can't imagine any reason their daughter would've left in this way—for this long. With every person I speak to who really knew Danielle, Bristol PD's theory, in my opinion, grows weaker. And if there's even the slightest chance foul play was involved in Danielle's disappearance, this case needs to be officially reopened.

One of the many reasons I preferred writing for my blog versus stories for the paper—I could boldly declare things like this, as if I were some clever investigator.

I couldn't put off calling Penn any longer. I grabbed my phone.

"Hey," he answered, an improvement from his typical what-do-you-want? greeting.

"Hi." I was too nervous to say anything else.

"Uh oh," Penn said. "What's wrong?"

"Why do you assume something's wrong?"

"Because you skipped the small talk, and you don't sound as annoyingly chipper as usual."

I chewed on my thumbnail. "I just don't want you to get mad at me again."

"I'm not...going to get mad at you," Penn said.

"Try saying it like you mean it."

"*Evie.*"

Ugh. Time to rip off the band-aid. "Well, I'm about to update my blog."

"Okay..."

"And I didn't want to blindside you..."

"Evie, spit it out!"

"I talked to Audrey for the story," I blurted, before I could change my mind.

Dead silence on his end.

"Penn?"

"Audrey," he finally repeated. "*My* Audrey?"

His Audrey. That alone made me want to shove my face into one of the couch pillows and scream.

"Um, yes," I said, face burning. "I found out she was Danielle's teacher. And she was really eager to talk about her, and..." I trailed off, no idea what to say.

Penn was silent for a few beats, presumably waiting for me to finish my sentence.

"Go ahead, yell at me," I said. "It's weird I did this; it's weird I didn't tell you."

"You know what? I can't even yell. This is my fault for thinking I could keep one aspect of my life private from you. I should know by now that it's pointless."

I wasn't sure what to make of this. He sounded upset, but not in the way I'd thought.

"Penn, I'm not purposely trying to poke around in your business. I just want to find out all I can about Danielle," I said. "Audrey said they were close. You could've told me. I wouldn't have made a big deal about it."

"Gee, maybe I just didn't feel like talking about the ex-wife I don't even speak to."

"I'm sorry. I wanted you to hear it from me before the story got published."

Penn exhaled loudly. "How is she?"

My heart twisted. Two exes not speaking, but still caring enough to want to know how the other is doing.

"She asked the same thing about you," I said. "She seems good. Maybe you should give her a call."

If Grace were here, she'd smack me upside the head for saying this, but I couldn't help myself. It seemed so sad that two people who loved each other weren't together because of a terrible tragedy. Besides, if Penn got back with Audrey, any temptation would be gone, thus allowing me to stick to my no-touching-sources policy.

"Well, you told me," Penn said gruffly, ignoring my suggestion. "Anything else?"

This had gone better than expected, but his harshness still stung. "Uh, I guess not. Just assembling my giant murder board over here. You're welcome to join me."

"Not tonight," he said, voice flat. Ouch. It felt like I had dreamt up the other night when he sat next to me on the couch for hours.

"Okay. Bye, then."

Penn hung up without saying goodbye. I couldn't blame him. Look how uncomfortable I was when Penn had chatted with Brent at The Ranch—and Brent meant nothing to me. What I did with Audrey was that times a hundred.

Well, I felt plain awful now. And as if the universe sensed how much I was beating myself up, my phone buzzed with a text from Audrey.

Good news. Samantha's in for drinks tomorrow night. She's supposed to meet me at 7:30 at The Ranch, so I'd suggest "bumping into us" closer to 8:00.

A grateful smile spread across my cheeks as I typed my thanks. After I'd told her Samantha had been skirting my emails, she'd been more than happy to help plan an ambush.

"Samantha will be much more likely to spill if I'm there," she'd said. "Especially if we get a few drinks in her."

Audrey was kind of awesome. Damn it. Surely Penn still loved her.

I opened Twitter to promote the new *Evie Investigates* post that would go live in the morning, but I found myself clicking on my messages instead. The anonymous warning I'd received stared me down like Wally did when I was late with his breakfast. I opened it and began to type.

Why shouldn't I trust the Davenports?

My heart raced the second I pressed send. Engaging with this potential lunatic was a bad idea, but I couldn't get their warning out of my head. And if I was going to get the chance to talk to Samantha, I should know if she was a compulsive liar, right?

I stared at my screen for a few minutes, willing the person to reply, but they didn't. I put my phone down with a sigh and set my sights on Danielle's essay. Wally was still warming it. I grabbed a corner of the paper and tugged, dragging him across the table before he growled and jumped to the floor.

Settling back into the couch, I began to read.

My entire life, I've felt like something was missing. I don't know why; I had two loving parents, lots of friends, and a happy childhood. That's more than a lot of kids get. But I still felt somehow cheated, as this one giant question hung over my head: Who's my real father?

I was probably about five years old when I first noticed that my dad's skin color didn't match mine. Even with this observation, I didn't understand what it meant until the second grade, when a classmate saw my dad drop me off at school and teased me about being adopted.

I went home from school that day in tears, but my mom quickly soothed me by insisting she did in fact give birth to me, and she had the hospital pictures to prove it. Then my dad sat me down and explained that while we might not be related by blood, he still loved me as if we were. At seven years old, this made complete sense to me, and I didn't even realize this meant that if he wasn't my actual father, someone else was.

A few years later, when the question finally popped in my head, it stuck there. I couldn't get it out, and I became obsessed with finding the answer. I thought it'd be easy to find out; I'd just ask my mom. But she brushed me off, claiming she'd tell me when I was older. But with every passing birthday, she seemed less and less willing to give up his name.

Danielle continued to write about her attempts to find the identity of her biological father over the years and how much it consumed her. It led to increasing tension between her and Sharon, which reached an all-time high after Danielle turned eighteen. She figured that finally, as a legal adult, her mom wouldn't lie to her any longer.

What was the big deal? Danielle wrote. *Why couldn't she just give me the name?*

I put down the essay for a minute, pondering this very question. Why wouldn't Sharon just tell Danielle? Surely it would be worth it to finally end all the arguments between the two. Even something as simple as, "Your dad was a random one-night stand whose name I've forgotten," might've sufficed. But Sharon wouldn't budge at all—which meant Danielle's dad wasn't someone random. He could've been someone Sharon was scared of.

And maybe Danielle had found him. Right before she went missing.

I hopped off the couch and walked over to my whiteboard. In my suspects column, I had written *Hudson Davenport* and *secret boyfriend* (?), and now I quickly scribbled *biological father* there too.

I had a column for Danielle's activities right before her disappearance: *Applying for college, working on essay, fighting with mom, going out and not telling parents where, obsessed with figuring out her biological father.*

I stared at the board for a bit before finishing up the essay. The sudden tone change was almost jarring.

I'd put so much of my energy into figuring this out, but one morning I woke up and asked myself: Why? Why did I need to know so badly? It wouldn't change anything. I didn't want a relationship with this man—I already had a dad.

I always thought this information was like the last missing puzzle piece to knowing who I really was, but finding it wouldn't make me feel any more whole. I'd still be just as confused as any normal eighteen-year-old who knew who both her parents were. And I realized that was alright with me. I have my whole life to figure out who I am.

Brows furrowed, I paged through the essay again. The entire paper, Danielle had been determined to discover the identity of her father, and then in the last few paragraphs, she suddenly decided it wasn't important. It made a great conclusion for the essay. It showed growth, but based on everything I knew about Danielle, it didn't make any sense. Waking up one day and deciding to just drop it? After all the grief she gave Sharon? No. The only thing that would make Danielle abandon her mission so suddenly is if...

"She figured it out," I said aloud. "Danielle figured out who her father was."

And she must've not liked the answer.

My phone let out an angry buzz, and I yelped, heart racing at the intrusion. I put down the essay with a shaking hand and retrieved my phone. I had a new Twitter message. My mouth went dry.

They're liars. All of them.

That's all my anonymous pal had wrote. I tipped my head back and exhaled. Maybe Penn was right. This person was messing with me.

Why should I believe you? I don't even know who you are. I typed back. *You're going to have to give me more information.*

The typing dots appeared almost immediately. And when the mysterious informant pressed send, the message made me toss my phone across the couch.

Let's meet.

CHAPTER THIRTEEN

"Evie, do I have a surprise for you."

I looked up from my computer and groaned as Grace walked towards me, big smile on her face.

"No way," I said. "I can't handle any more surprises after yesterday."

"I thought you said that went well." Grace dumped her purse onto her chair.

"I mean, it did. But Penn's pissed at me again."

Grace rolled her eyes. "When is he not?"

"What's my surprise?" I asked, already cringing.

"As you know, I'm working on a story about the giant new apartment complex going in downtown," Grace started, her fingernails drumming on her desk.

"Yes, of course, the apartment complex," I said weakly. I'd been a little too wrapped up in Danielle World to pay much attention to Grace's recent assignments.

"Since you're not lighting up with glee already, I'm going to assume you haven't read any of my previous articles about it," Grace said with a pointed eyebrow raise.

I grimaced. "Sorry. You know how obsessive I've been about this case."

"I know. Which is why I'm helping you despite your being a terrible friend."

"The suspense is killing me, Grace."

"The builder of said apartment complex?" Grace asked. "Davenport Properties. Owned and operated by none other than Michael Davenport himself." She paused for dramatic effect. "And guess who just scored an interview with him today?"

I let out a gasp and stood. "No."

"Yes."

"And you're telling me this because..." I could barely contain my excitement.

"Get your coat."

Grace and I sat in a small waiting area outside of Michael Davenport's office, the constant ring of his administrative assistant's phone the only sound in the room.

"I'm sure he won't be much longer," she told us with a nervous smile.

Grace and I gave her polite nods before exchanging a glance with each other. Michael was almost thirty minutes late for Grace's interview.

I shifted in my chair, crossing and uncrossing my right leg, then trying the left. Nothing felt comfortable. I was nervous enough about grilling Michael about Danielle, and I felt this golden opportunity slipping away with every minute that ticked by. What if he was so crunched for time he could only answer Grace's questions? What if he cancelled altogether?

"Here he is!" The administrative assistant finally announced, looking immensely relieved.

The sound of two men talking preceded Michael's grand entrance.

Grace and I stood, and I smoothed out the front of my sweater dress. A younger man had walked into the room with Michael, but when he saw us, he lingered in the background.

"I'm so sorry, my meeting with my property manager ran late," Michael said, an apologetic smile on his face as he approached us. "As you can imagine, we have a lot to get done if we want to be ready for move-in by January first."

"It's no problem." Grace extended her hand. "Grace Lee."

"*Very* nice to meet you, Grace," Michael said, charm on full blast.

"This is my colleague, Evie Hartley." She gestured to me. "Evie is working on a different story and hoped she could have a few minutes of your time when we're done."

Michael set his ice-blue gaze on me. Beneath his bushy salt-and-pepper eyebrows, his eyes looked wolfish. "Unfortunately, my schedule is very tight today, but I'll do my best to squeeze you in."

"Thank you." I forced a smile.

Michael was a decent-looking man for his age, though wrinkles marred his face, and his thinning hair was steel gray. But you could tell with one look he was loaded. He wore an immaculately-tailored suit, a crisp shirt, and his cologne smelled expensive.

"Grace, right this way," Michael said, ushering her towards his office door.

She and Michael disappeared, and I sat back down.

"He's going to blow you off."

I turned to find the source of the voice—the young man who'd walked in with Michael.

"Yeah, I kind of got that impression too," I said.

The man approached and sat in the chair Grace had occupied.

"So if you're not interested in hearing Mr. Davenport's rehearsed spiel about the apartments," the man said, "what are you here for?"

I paused, not wanting word about Danielle getting back to Michael too soon. When I spoke to him, I didn't want a carefully crafted answer —I wanted his genuine, unfiltered reaction.

While I thought about how to respond, I paid attention to the man's appearance. This did nothing to help my jitters, because he was gorgeous. He looked to be about thirty and had bright green eyes and close-cropped sandy hair. His body was lean, but muscled—I could tell as I subtly examined his upper arms, his biceps practically busting the seams of his fitted blue dress shirt. He smelled just as expensive as Michael.

"Well, I cover the crime beat," I answered cautiously.

The man's eyes lit up. "Crime? This is getting interesting. What has Mr. Davenport done now?"

I raised my eyebrows. "What do you mean by 'now'? Does Mr. Davenport often commit crimes?"

The man chuckled and relaxed into his chair, crossing his legs. "Even if he did, I'm sworn to secrecy."

"Corporate lawyer?" He sounded polished, educated—barely a trace of the accent I was used to hearing from Bristol locals.

"I'm flattered. Executive assistant. I'm not certain of the exact terms of my contract, but I'm pretty sure Davenport Properties owns my soul." He leaned in close. "I think if he kills someone, I *have* to help him dispose of the body."

The statement sent a shiver down my spine. He was joking, of course, but it made me realize that speaking to Michael's colleagues could be as beneficial as speaking to Michael himself. His inner circle would know a lot.

"Those *are* typical executive assistant duties," I said gravely. "How long have you worked for Mr. Davenport?"

"On and off for eight years. I keep trying to get away, but he always finds a way to reel me back in."

I frowned, and he picked up on my disappointment.

"Was that not the answer you were looking for?"

"I was hoping you'd been here ten years ago," I admitted. "I'm writing about something that happened way back then."

"Curiouser and curiouser. And this 'something' involves my boss?"

"Possibly, yes," I said. "A girl went missing, and he offered a pretty big reward for whoever found her. I'd like to know why."

"Hmm. I'd pump you for more details, but this mysterious reporter vibe you have going on is incredibly sexy. I don't want to ruin it."

My cheeks got warm, so I deflected by smirking and tapping my chin. "Yes, I'm very mysterious, but so are you. You've implied Mr. Davenport is a violent criminal, *and* I don't even know your name."

The man grinned, and his pupils widened. He was enjoying our banter. He was about to respond, but the door to Michael's office opened.

"Thank you so much for your time, Mr. Davenport," Grace said.

"I'm looking forward to seeing the story. Jessica will be able to send you some pictures of the site we've taken recently." Michael glanced to the overwhelmed admin and she quickly turned to her computer and began typing.

"Now's your chance," the man whispered into my ear.

I gave him a nod and hurried over to Grace and Michael.

"Mr. Davenport?" I asked hopefully.

He frowned. "Evie, I'm sorry, but I'm already late for my next appointment. If you talk to Jessica, we might be able to set something up in the new year."

Next *year*? Dear God.

"I'm doing a story on the disappearance of Danielle Livingston," I blurted out.

Michael's features twisted with shock—and maybe a touch of anger —before he regained his composure.

"The police are considering reopening the case, and anything you can recall about the time of her disappearance would be so helpful."

Michael glanced at his watch. "I'm sorry, but I really don't have the time. It's a tragedy what happened to Danielle. She was my daughter's best friend. I helped with the search as much as I could."

"If we could talk soon, even over the phone—"

"I don't think so," Michael said sharply, his polite facade slipping. "I have no interest in discussing the past."

Before I could respond, Michael went barreling past Grace and me, heading for the door. He paused, and for a brief moment, I thought he might've reconsidered.

But he'd been looking for his executive assistant.

"Hudson, let's *go*," Michael barked.

My jaw dropped as I watched the man I'd spoken to casually get out of his chair and walk towards his boss. Towards his father.

Michael stormed out, and before Hudson followed, he looked over his shoulder and winked at me.

Grace kept trying to get my attention, even tugging on my arm to get us out of there, but I was rooted to the spot, in complete disbelief that I'd been chatting the entire time with Hudson Davenport—my prime suspect.

"I still can't believe that was Hudson." Grace had spent the day finishing up her story on the Davenport apartments, and I'd spent the day replaying my entire conversation with Hudson over and over.

"He purposely misled me about who he was." I scoffed and shook my head. "And when I mentioned the missing girl, he *had* to have known I meant Danielle. Yet he acted like he had no clue what I was talking about."

"Don't trust the Davenports," Grace recited. "And did you see Michael's face when you brought up Danielle? Dude is hiding something."

My heart leapt. "So you're finally on my side about the Twitter tipster?"

"I didn't say that. After ten minutes with the Davenports, I think anyone would be wary of them. Doesn't exactly add credibility."

They're all liars, the tipster had said. And so far, that had been accurate. I grabbed my phone and brought up Twitter, staring at the unanswered message from the night before.

Let's meet.

"It'd be crazy to meet up with this person, right?" I asked Grace, even though I already knew the answer.

"Evie, I swear, if you try to do this, I'm calling Pennington."

I pouted, trying to look wounded. "Grace, you're supposed to be my friend and support me."

"I *am* your friend," she said. "Which is why I don't want you to get murdered by some rando from the internet."

As she continued to lecture me, I composed a response.

You're right. The Davenports are liars. They aren't talking.

After an anxious five minutes, my phone buzzed.

Let's meet, they insisted.

If I meet you, it's going to be a VERY public place.

That's fine. How's tomorrow night at Last Call? 9:00?

"...not to mention, it could just be some bored person completely wasting your time, and—"

"Grace, enough." I held up my hand. "I got it. I won't do it."

See you tomorrow, I wrote.

CHAPTER FOURTEEN

I GOT TO THE RANCH OBSCENELY EARLY, THINKING THAT WOULD help ease my nerves. It didn't. After my encounters with Michael and Hudson, it didn't seem like approaching another Davenport would go well. What would Samantha be like? Defensive and evasive like her father? Or lying and manipulative like her brother?

My car clock read 7:35, and a few flurries started to land on my windshield. At the sight of them, I bumped up the heat a few degrees. I had a bit to wait before I could bump into Audrey and Samantha. I stared at my Twitter messages again, still a little stunned I'd agreed to meet the tipster. Of course, I hadn't made up my mind about going yet —I could very well stand them up. That'd be the smart thing to do.

But they knew something. They'd sent their original message before I was even suspicious of the Davenports. The tipster had to be close to Danielle and this case. How else would they have known to warn me?

After killing time playing Candy Crush, I couldn't stand the wait anymore. I burst out of my car, trying to slow my racing heart. I had to look nice and casual when I not-so-accidentally ran into Audrey.

A blast of heat and music hit me as I entered the bar. It was a weeknight, but my eyes darted towards the empty stage anyway. Phew. No Brent.

There was a low hum of chatter and country-rock music blaring over the speakers. As I approached the bar and ordered a coke (hold the rum), I surveyed The Ranch. A few heavyset men occupied barstools, and smaller groups crowded around the high-tops. A loud woman in a crop top clung to the mechanical bull for dear life.

I came up empty after my first scan of the bar and started to panic, but sure enough, I spied Audrey at the same corner table Penn and I had occupied not too long ago. A blond woman who had to be Samantha sat next to her. Go time.

The table wasn't far from the ladies' room, so I headed in that direction. I reached the door and looked over my shoulder, shooting Audrey a glance.

She looked up at me, lips still moving as she spoke to Samantha, and suddenly put on a big smile. "Evie?" Audrey put up her hand. "I thought that was you!"

"Hey, Audrey," I shouted over the music, making my way to the table. "What are you doing here?"

"Just catching up with an old friend." Audrey looked at Samantha. "Sam, this is my friend, Evie. Evie, this is Samantha."

"Hi," I said. She gave me a generic smile, but after a few seconds, recognition flickered in her eyes.

"Evie...Why does that sound familiar?"

"Evie's a reporter for *Bristol Daily News*. You've probably seen her articles."

"*Oh.*" Samantha broke eye contact awkwardly. "You, uh, sent me some emails, I think? Sorry I didn't get back to you yet, I've just been *so* busy..."

Sure. So busy you could meet your old teacher for a last-minute happy hour, but not talk to me for twenty minutes.

"Oh, don't worry about it, I totally get it," I said with a nod.

"Well, we were just catching up," Audrey told me. She turned to

Samantha. "Maybe Evie could join us for a little bit, and she could talk to you about the story she's working on?"

Samantha looked a bit uncomfortable, but said, "Okay, sure."

Thank goodness for Audrey and peer pressure.

I gratefully took the empty seat at the table, getting my first good look at Samantha. She looked just as pretty as she had in her yearbook photo. Samantha had the same green eyes as her brother, and I assumed her hair was the same shade of sand—though she'd chosen to highlight it to a bleach blond. Her sparkly cocktail dress was far too fancy for The Ranch, but the Chanel bag hooked on the back of her chair told me Samantha probably didn't know how to dress down.

"Evie's writing about Danielle," Audrey said to Samantha.

"I'm hoping to get the police to reopen the case," I added.

Samantha's eyes got big. "I mean, I skimmed your emails and knew you wanted to talk about Danielle, but why?" I tilted my head, and Samantha clarified. "I mean, why now? It's been so long."

"Cold cases are really difficult to investigate." I took a sip of my coke. "But I just couldn't believe it's been ten years and still, nobody knows what happened to her. It's been so hard on her parents. They need closure. I figured it couldn't hurt if I start asking around."

Samantha bowed her head. "I still think about her, even after all this time."

I waited for her to elaborate, and when she didn't, I pushed harder. "What do you think happened to Danielle?"

She cleared her throat and finished her drink. "I know it seems unlikely that she'd just vanish on her own, but I think it's possible."

I couldn't help but exchange a quick glance with Audrey, who scrunched up her face.

"Would Danielle really have left without a word?" I asked. "And never contact you, or her parents, ever again?"

"You know what, I think I want to get another one of these." Samantha picked up her empty wine glass and began to stand.

"I could use another too," Audrey said quickly, taking Samantha's glass before she could head to the bar. "Evie, you good?"

"Fine, thanks," I said with a grateful smile. Audrey vanished, leaving Samantha and me alone.

She sunk back into her chair, her escape route blocked. "Things with Danielle were kind of rocky right before she went missing."

"How so?" I asked, leaning forward.

"She was being a really shitty friend," Samantha said in a burst of anger. I raised an eyebrow, and she cleared her throat. "Sorry, I didn't mean it like that. But Danielle was acting so weird. She started bailing on plans, and when I asked her why, I could tell she was lying. We always told each other everything; it didn't make sense."

"Danielle's mother thinks she had a secret boyfriend," I said as Audrey rejoined us with fresh drinks. "Do you think that's who she was with?"

"I guess it's possible." Samantha took a few big gulps of her wine. "Like I said, she was being secretive." She paused, and her voice turned bitter. "There was *one* guy she was hanging out with a lot, which caused some of our problems."

"Who?" I asked eagerly.

"My brother, Hudson." Samantha wrinkled her button nose.

I sat back in my chair, shocked. "Danielle and Hudson? I thought she wasn't interested in him."

"So did I," Samantha said. "He was embarrassingly creepy around her, and Danielle was completely grossed out. Hudson and I would fight about it all the time—I'd tell him to stay the hell away from my friends. And Danielle never gave him the time of day until a few months before she disappeared."

"What changed?"

"I really don't know," Samantha admitted. "I was relieved junior year when Hudson went off to college. But then around September or October of our senior year, I found out Danielle and Hudson were texting. She told me it was just about UVA—she was asking him how he liked it." She shook her head. "I never bought that. And then when he came home for Thanksgiving break, they actually hung out. Several times. So weird."

"Was Hudson home?" I asked, my throat dry. "When Danielle went missing, was he here or at school?"

"He'd just gotten home for winter break," Samantha said. "They hung out then too. I got mad at her because she'd claim she wanted to come over and do something with me, but then she'd wander off and find Hudson."

"Huh." I was truly dumbfounded. From all accounts, Hudson sounded like a stalker with unrequited feelings for Danielle all these years. What changed her mind about him? And if Danielle was into Hudson, that gave him *less* of a motive to kill her.

"Did you ever catch them..."

"Doing the no-pants dance?" Samantha asked.

I nodded.

"No, but come on. Why the secrecy? What else could they have been doing?"

I didn't have an answer for that.

"Yeah, so Danielle and I were kind of fighting before she left," Samantha said with a shrug. "That's why I'm not surprised I haven't heard from her."

"Wouldn't she have contacted her parents, at least?"

"She was fighting with them too," Samantha said. "I'm telling you, she was going through something weird. That's why her disappearance wasn't that shocking to me."

"Do you know what they were fighting about? Danielle and her mom had a fight the night she went missing."

"No idea," Samantha said. "Maybe Hudson. Her parents hated him, ever since he got caught spying on her at our house. Maybe Danielle told them they were together."

My head began to hurt as I struggled to make sense of all this information coming from different sources. The Livingstons said the fight was about Danielle not telling them where she was going. Audrey thought they could've fought about the identity of Danielle's birth father. And now, Samantha had thrown out a brand-new possibility involving her brother.

"Okay, say your brother and Danielle were together," I said, trying not to let my frustration come through in my voice. "Would she leave town without him? Wouldn't she contact him?"

"You're assuming Hudson would tell us." Samantha raised an eyebrow. "He's a troublemaker. Always has been. It wouldn't surprise me at all if he knows where Danielle is and hasn't said shit."

Samantha finished her wine in a gulp and set down the glass with a clatter. "I'm sorry, but I have to get going," she said, not looking the least bit apologetic. She grabbed her Chanel bag. "Have a late-night meeting with my dad. Lots going on right now with the new apartments."

I couldn't hide my surprise. "You work for your dad too?"

She laughed. "If you're a Davenport, you work for Davenport Properties." Samantha leaned down and hugged Audrey. "It was nice seeing you."

"You too," Audrey said with a smile.

"Wow," was all I said after Samantha had left.

"She was in a hurry to get out of here, wasn't she?"

"I didn't even get to ask her about the night Danielle disappeared," I complained. "And something tells me it's going to be tough to get her to talk again."

Audrey leaned forward. "Did you notice how she didn't even entertain the possibility that Danielle is dead?"

"I sure did. You don't think..."

"That Samantha killed Danielle?" Audrey laughed. "No. But I think she knows more than she's saying. She might be protecting someone."

"I can't get over the Hudson information. What was Danielle doing hanging out with him? Why the sudden interest?"

"Sounds like you're going to have to talk to Hudson," Audrey said.

I took a swig of my drink, remembering too late it contained no alcohol. "I stopped by Davenport Properties today, and getting information out of them is easier said than done."

"I guess being a reporter can only get you so far."

"Not a lot of people enjoy talking to us leeches, as your ex-husband has so kindly called me."

I hadn't even meant to bring up Penn, but it just came out.

"He's always hated journalists," Audrey said with a wry smile. "His dad was a reporter and a complete workaholic. He was never home—for a lot of other reasons too. But Marcus always blamed the job for it."

"Oh." I was stunned by yet another personal tidbit about Penn. Every time I found one, I filed it away for later reference, to help me better understand whenever he acted like an ass. "I guess him hating me isn't personal then."

Audrey tilted her head and arched an eyebrow, amused. "Trust me, Evie, he wouldn't be giving you anything at all if he hated you."

I had no idea how to respond, so I defaulted to sabotaging myself again.

"You know, I told him we talked," I said. "And I really got the sense he missed you, and maybe you should give him a call..."

"Evie, I'm going to stop you right there," Audrey said. "That's sweet of you to say, but Marcus and I didn't get divorced on a whim. I still care about him, but there were problems we just couldn't work out."

My cheeks burned. "Sorry, I shouldn't have said anything."

"It's okay." Audrey gave my arm a nudge. "And if you brought this up because you're interested in Marcus, you have nothing to worry about from me. Go for it. He's a good man."

"Oh, no, I..." I made some more awkward sputtering sounds to let Audrey know her proposition was absurd, but she gave me the same look Grace does whenever I deny being into Penn.

"I should get going," I told her. "I have a lot of new theories to sort through. And another blog post to write."

"I really think you could be on to something, Evie. Don't stop digging, no matter what."

CHAPTER FIFTEEN

I'VE SPENT THIS ENTIRE INVESTIGATION CONVINCED DANIELLE *must've been murdered,* I wrote on *Evie Investigates.*

But after speaking with a friend of Danielle's, I was reminded that you never truly know what's going on inside another person's head. None of us could say what Danielle was thinking in those final hours before she vanished. Tunnel-vision and assumptions are the enemy of the truth. And, as a wise detective once told me, we have to consider every possibility. So, for the sake of fairness, I will look into the possibility that Danielle could have left on her own—and may not want to be found.

My fourth blog entry about Danielle, done. I was adjusting my style with each one, getting more comfortable with the tone—more daring with my theorizing. Readers loved when I did that, and they'd comment their own wild theories right back. Shelly was in heaven.

"Okay, Grace, I'm heading out," I said a little after five. "You coming?"

"I'm still trying to tweak this apartment story to make it at least semi-interesting. Michael didn't give either of us *anything* yesterday."

"What was your impression of him when you got him alone?" I asked as I pulled on my coat.

"He's a total politician," Grace said. "He's got the plastered-on smile and canned responses down. Every quote he gave me was perfectly rehearsed."

"That's what I was afraid of. Even if I managed to get him to speak about Danielle, he wouldn't level with me."

Grace's computer dinged with a new email, and as she scanned the message, I could tell she was fighting a smile.

I tilted my head. "What?"

"Nothing," she said quickly. "My brother just sent me a cute picture of Timmy."

"Aw, let me see." I moved towards her computer. Grace's new baby nephew was adorable, and his chubby cheeks always managed to cheer me up.

"Sorry, but I really should get back to this story." Grace hit a button on her keyboard lightning fast, then resuming her typing.

I blinked, taken aback.

"Have a good night, Evie." She attempted a normal smile and failed. Something was up. I didn't know what, but that email definitely wasn't from her brother.

It was weird, but I was too antsy about my evening plans to press her. Using Grace's distracted state to my advantage, I scurried out of the office before she somehow sensed I was hours away from doing the very thing she forbade me to do. I was so focused on getting out of the *Daily News* building that my ringing phone made me drop my bag on the staircase landing. You could've knocked me over with a feather when I saw the name on the screen.

"Well, this is a historic moment," I answered. "I'm going to have to write this down in my diary."

"How's it historic?"

"This is the first time you've called me first," I said. "It's nice. Makes me feel like less of a nuisance."

"I heard you've roped my ex-wife into your little investigation," Penn said. I strained my ears for any hint of annoyance, but I heard none. It appeared Penn wasn't angry. That was new.

I continued down the stairs.

"I did no roping. Audrey volunteered to help. She was the mastermind." I paused. "How'd you even know?"

"She called me," he said simply.

"Wow." I was shocked that she took me up on my suggestion. "How'd that go?"

"It was...It was kind of nice, actually. We hadn't spoken since we signed the papers a few months ago."

"Oh." My heart did this weird, sinking thing. "Good for you." I couldn't think of what else to say. Why was he telling me this? I suddenly got nervous Audrey might've given him her blessing to start something with me, as she'd done with me last night, which would be mortifying.

"When she told me about your chat with Samantha, I got a little jealous."

I made a face as I opened the door and was greeted with a wallop of cold air. "Jealous?"

"Well, yeah, I realized my ex-wife knows more about your investigation than I do. What's up with that?" His tone was almost teasing.

"There's a lot you don't know." I tried to convey an air of mystery. "Like that I managed to meet both Michael and Hudson Davenport yesterday."

Penn let out a low whistle. "You've been busy."

I had almost made it to my car. "I have been. I have so many theories I'm dying to tell you about."

"Can I stop by later?"

Thrown, I froze in place. "Uh, well, I sort of have plans tonight. I'm not sure how late I'll be. Can I call you after?"

"Ooh, you got a date? Are you giving that kid singer another chance after all?"

"No! I have to go. I'll talk to you later."

Penn laughed. "Bye."

Relieved, I hung up and slid into my car, frozen hands fumbling with the keys. When I got it going and blasted the heat, I looked up through the windshield. A piece of paper was tucked under my wipers, rustling gently in the wind. Confused, I got out of my car and grabbed the note, and the five words typed on it sent shivers all the way to my toes.

Stop asking questions, or else.

I taped the note to my crime board; I didn't know what else to do with it. In an attempt to ease my terror, I scribbled a list of every possible person it could've been from—every person I'd asked questions: *Sharon, David, Audrey, Michael, Hudson, Samantha.*

I was positive it wasn't from any of the first three. That left the last three.

Don't trust the Davenports!

After ten minutes of frantic pacing, I realized the note didn't even have to be from someone I'd spoken to. I'd been blogging about this entire investigative experience. It could've been from any reader.

It could've been from anyone.

I was shaken. The note wasn't explicitly a death threat, but the "or else" covered a lot of ground. What would they do if I didn't stop? Ransack my apartment? Do something to my car? I shot a nervous glance at Wally, who was scarfing down his dinner. What if I'd put my cat in danger?

This was not the emotional state I wanted to meet my tipster in. Changing my clothes and freshening up my face only made me feel the tiniest bit better. I chose a casual V-neck sweater which showed an appropriate amount of cleavage, and my unruly hair went into my usual ponytail. I wasn't certain of the gender of my Twitter friend, but it wouldn't hurt to put a bit of effort in, so I swiped on some dark lipstick at the last minute.

I had my hand on the doorknob when Grace's voice popped into my head, reminding me this was an awful idea. What if I really was about to get murdered by an internet rando? The internal debate continued for a few more moments, then I pulled out my phone.

"I wasn't expecting you to call until later," Penn said.

"I need to tell you about my plans." I braced myself as if I were about to defuse a bomb.

"Your date?"

"I told you, it's not a date!" I took a deep breath. "Remember how you told me to call for backup if I found a murderer?"

I couldn't see Penn's face, but I somehow knew he was scowling. "Evie, what's going on?"

"I'm about to meet up with that person who sent the anonymous Twitter message. We'll be at Last Call. Just thought you should know in case it goes terribly wrong, and I get murdered. Bye now."

"*Jesus*, Evie, what the f—"

I hung up before he could yell at me more and rushed out of my apartment. Okay, I could relax a bit. I'd told Penn. At least if I was kidnapped or killed, someone would know where to start looking.

My hands shook on the wheel as I drove to the bar. When I made it into a spot, I pulled out my phone. Ignoring the two missed calls and five texts from Penn consisting mostly of profanity, I opened Twitter.

I'm outside, I wrote. *Are you here yet? What do you look like?*

Their response was immediate.

Find a table where it's quiet. I'll come to you.

Oh, boy. This didn't bode well. Reminding myself this was a public place, and I'd be safe, I hurried inside. My eyes darted around the room like crazy, convinced I could identify the tipster on the spot. No one stood out. Two couples played darts. Three men and one woman sat at the bar, eyes glazed over as they stared at the TV screens. None of the tables were occupied.

Still trembling, I sat at a high-top by the pool table. After a minute, I scanned the room again, craning my neck to spot anyone I might've missed. Anxiety replaced fear as I became nervous that I was being stood up, that I'd been played, and this was all some elaborate prank. Wouldn't that be just perfect?

But then I heard a door opening not too far behind me. The bathrooms. I froze, not daring to look as the footsteps got closer. And then I sensed the person right behind me. I could feel the body heat radiating off them.

Finally, they stood in front of me. And when I tilted my head up to watch them sit, my jaw hit the floor.

CHAPTER SIXTEEN

"Hᴉ, Eᴠɪᴇ." Hᴜᴅꜱᴏɴ Dᴀᴠᴇɴᴘᴏʀᴛ ɢʀɪɴɴᴇᴅ ꜰʀᴏᴍ ᴇᴀʀ ᴛᴏ ᴇᴀʀ, reveling in my utter shock.

"Are you shitting me?"

His green eyes danced in the dim bar lighting. "It's nice to see you again—and looking just as cute as yesterday too."

I sat back in my chair, mouth hanging open, unable to do anything but shake my head in disbelief. The nerves dissipated, replaced with shock and mild disgust.

"You're unbelievable," I finally managed.

"I'll take that as a compliment. You want something to drink?"

I scoffed. "No! I want to know what the hell is up with the cloak and dagger routine. Why didn't you just tell me who you were?"

"All in good time, Evie," Hudson said easily. "I'll get you something."

He wandered to the bar and leaned against it, his jeans snug across his nice butt. I was gawking, but I couldn't help it. He emanated this effortlessly-cool vibe, his light hair styled just so, his leather jacket slung over his shoulder as he ordered our drinks. Hudson didn't look like the psycho stalker killer I'd added to my suspects column; he looked like a suave, gorgeous guy whose only crime was breaking hearts.

While Hudson was occupied, I considered bolting, but I couldn't go through with it. I was still dumbfounded Hudson was my tipster. Everything I knew about him kept swirling through my mind, and the longer I thought about it, I only became more confused.

Hudson returned and set a dark mixed drink down in front of me.

I eyed it, suspicious.

"Rum and coke, right?" He took a long sip from some imported beer.

"How'd you know that?"

"Come on, I did my research. I read your blog," Hudson said. "Picked up a lot about you from there. The personal details you put in your stories are a nice touch. Makes your readers feel like they know you."

Hudson continued to drink his beer while I refused to touch my drink.

"What?" He raised his eyebrows. "You think I'm trying to roofie you?"

I gave him a look indicating I very much thought that.

Hudson sighed, grabbed it, and took a few gulps.

"See?" He slid the glass back to me. "Perfectly safe."

Glaring, I took a tiny sip.

"I'm surprised, Evie," Hudson said. "I figured you'd have a thousand questions for me."

"I do, but why bother asking them when I can't trust a word that comes out of your mouth? The Davenports are all liars, right?"

Hudson let out a bark of laughter. "Every last one of us."

I couldn't contain myself anymore. "What do you know about Danielle?"

"I saw your post from today," Hudson said.

My hand clenched around my glass. I could tell I wasn't going to get one straight answer out of him.

"That friend of Danielle's you mentioned was my sister, right?"

I paused before giving him a nod.

Hudson scoffed. "Figures. I can't believe she still has the nerve to peddle that crap after all these years."

"You don't believe Danielle ran away?"

Hudson's smug expression finally disappeared, and his gaze grew intense. "She's dead, Evie. I know she is."

My heart stopped. My eyes darted towards the door, and I was prepared to run, just in case Hudson was about to confess to murder.

"How do you know that?" I asked, voice low.

"I didn't see a body, if that's what you're asking." He put down his beer bottle and leaned in closer. "But Danielle wouldn't have disappeared like that. She wouldn't have disappeared on me."

I exhaled and took a sip of my drink. "So you two *were* together."

The serious moment passed, and Hudson's smirk returned. "Is that what Samantha told you? Of course, that's where her mind went. She always was the jealous type. Never liked sharing when we were kids."

I let out a frustrated sigh. "Hudson, if you're just going to jerk me around—"

"Okay, okay," he said, putting his hands up in surrender. "Excuse me for enjoying your company and wanting to draw out the evening a little."

"I'd enjoy *your* company a lot more if you'd just be straight with me."

"To answer your question, no. Danielle and I were not together. I didn't like her like that."

"That's funny," I said, "because I heard about a certain peeping incident at a sleepover."

He waved his hand dismissively. "Give me a break, I was a horny sixteen-year-old boy. I looked; I didn't touch." He drained his beer. "Trust me, nothing kills the attraction more than finding out you might be related."

I inhaled sharply. "Might be?"

"Yep. Danielle thought my dear old dad may not have been entirely faithful to my mother."

Michael Davenport, Danielle's father? If that were true, it would certainly give him reason to want Danielle out of the picture. A long-lost love child would be detrimental for his image—and his marriage.

"Why did Danielle think that?" I asked. "Did she have proof?"

"She found a letter," Hudson said. "Of the lovey-dovey variety between her mom and my dad. It was dated not too long before Danielle was born."

"And she confided in *you* about this?"

"I'm an excellent listener," Hudson said, waggling his eyebrows.

"Why wouldn't she tell her best friend that they might be half sisters? Why *you*, Samantha's peeping Tom of a brother who was away at school?"

"Ouch." Hudson's eyes wandered over my shoulder. "Hey, you wanna play pool?"

"What?" I watched in disbelief as Hudson got up and wandered over to the table. I swigged the rest of my drink and trailed after him. Hudson was toying with me. Every word out of his mouth was likely a lie. But why was he doing this? What did this accomplish?

I grabbed a pool cue while Hudson racked the balls. "You want to break?"

"I want *answers*, Hudson."

"Come on, play with me," he said with a grin. "I don't get out much."

Everything in me wanted to refuse, but a game of pool was a small price to pay for Hudson's side of the story.

"I'll break." I lined up my shot, hyper aware of Hudson's eyes on the neckline of my sweater as I bent over the table. With a loud clack, the balls went flying in all directions across the felt. I managed to sink one striped.

"Nice shot."

"Why did Danielle confide in you?" I asked through gritted teeth as I poised behind the cue ball again. Hudson hovered over me, his hand pressed against the wood of the table, the tendons in his forearm tight.

"There was some trouble in paradise between the gals," he said lazily. Unable to focus on my shot with him staring at me so close, I hit the cue ball with barely any force, and it slowly rolled into the corner pocket. Damn.

"You're holding it wrong." Hudson fished out the cue ball and set it back on the table. Without warning, he got behind me and grabbed my arms, guiding me into position. "Aim right for the middle of the ball." His right hand was clasped over mine, his chin tucked over my left shoulder.

I turned my head slightly. "Why were Danielle and Samantha fighting?"

His sage-green eyes bored into mine. Hudson moved his hand, forcing me to take the shot without looking. The cue ball *clacked* against another. "So close," he said with a smile, releasing me.

"Their priorities weren't the same anymore." He moved across the table to set up his shot. "Danielle was focused on studying and getting her college applications in. Samantha couldn't care less about college. The pressure's not exactly on when you have a cushy job with Daddy waiting in the wings. Sam would get pissed if Danielle blew off plans for school stuff."

Hmm. Samantha told me she didn't know why Danielle was canceling plans. One of the Davenport siblings wasn't telling me the truth. I considered this as I watched Hudson sink one. I hoped he kept up his streak so he wouldn't get any ideas about "teaching" me again.

"So Danielle was upset with Samantha, and didn't want to tell her about this," I said.

"She knew her secret would be safe with me. In case you haven't already noticed, I'm a bit of a black sheep. I'm not that tight with Mom and Dad. Even less so with Samantha."

"Samantha said she saw you and Danielle spending a lot of time together."

Hudson failed to land his second shot. "That's why?"

"Yep," he said. "She needed someone to talk to. And then, she needed some of my DNA."

I'd been lining up my next shot, but I whipped around so quickly I twinged my neck. "*What?*"

"Yeah. Her mom wouldn't fess up, so Danielle took matters into her own hands. She sent both of our DNA to some testing place to see if we had a familial match."

I stared at Hudson, waiting for him to put me out of my misery.

"It's your turn, you know," he said, gesturing towards the table.

I strode over to him until we stood nose to nose. "What did the results say?"

"That's the million-dollar question, isn't it?" he whispered. "You see, the night she went missing, Danielle and I were supposed to open the results together. But by the time I got home, Sam told me Danielle had already come and gone. She stood me up."

I exhaled slowly. "Samantha told the police Danielle left your house that night like nothing was wrong."

"And I'm telling you," Hudson said, "that Danielle wouldn't have gone AWOL without showing me those results."

"So Samantha lied," I said as Hudson turned towards the table and took my turn for me.

"Shocker," he said flatly.

"The Davenports are liars," I repeated like a mantra.

Hudson gave me a knowing eyebrow raise.

"Why should I believe anything you're saying?" I asked him. "You've already lied to me—yesterday, when you misled me about who you were. Not to mention, you're part of the very family you've been warning me about since day one."

"I lied to you yesterday because I wanted to talk to you without you knowing who I was," Hudson said, wandering back to me. "Because I had a little feeling I might be on your suspect list."

"Not only are you on the list, but you're at the top."

Hudson crept closer until I was backed up against the table with nowhere to go.

"You should trust me, because I want justice for Danielle just as much as you do. I cared about her." His breath was warm on my face. "I know my family killed her. I can't prove it, but I know it. So I'm going to help you as much as I can, but I have to be careful about it so the old man doesn't find out, or I'd be out on my ass so fast."

My heart thrummed in my chest for a variety of reasons, my skin burning hot. Hudson leaned in closer, and for one horrifying second, I swore he was going to kiss me—and I might've waited a few seconds before pushing him away. But his full lips went to my ear instead.

"Your turn," he whispered. Face flushed, I gave him a shove and took a few side steps away from him. I tried to focus on my shot, but my mind was racing. It'd be stupid to believe him. But his version of events made the most sense so far.

"You're too tense. You've got to loosen up." Hudson came up behind me, put his hands on my waist, and pressed his hips hard against me while I was bent over the table. Surely this looked incredibly lewd to any onlookers. I was about to elbow him in the abdomen when he let out a yelp and got hauled off me. I spun around in time to witness Penn shoving him up against the wall.

My pool cue fell to the floor with a clatter. "Penn!"

"Aw, come on, Evie, we were just having a little fun," Hudson whined as Penn held him to the wall, fists bunched around the front of his shirt. "You didn't have to sic your boyfriend on me."

"Oh, I'm much worse than a boyfriend." Penn reached into his pocket and whipped out his badge. Hudson's eyes bugged out.

"Jesus," he moaned. "I didn't even do anything."

"Really? Because it looked like sexual assault to me."

Hudson laughed in his face. "Okay, sure, man. Go ahead and arrest me. My lawyer will have me out in an hour."

"Penn." I politely tapped him on the shoulder while he was busy glaring at Hudson. He slowly turned to look at me, like he'd forgotten I was there. "It's fine. Just let him go."

He looked from me back to Hudson before slowly releasing him.

Hudson sidestepped away from Penn while smoothing out his wrinkled t-shirt. He waltzed back to our table and grabbed his jacket.

"Evie, I'm not into threesomes, so call me when we can talk again. Alone," he called, heading for the door.

Penn and I stood in silence long after Hudson made his exit.

"Was that Hudson Davenport?"

"Yeah," I said weakly. "Turns out, he's the Twitter guy."

"Let's go," Penn grumbled. "You're going to tell me everything."

CHAPTER SEVENTEEN

PENN FOLLOWED ME BACK TO MY PLACE, AND I WAS THANKFUL
for the ten minutes for him to decompress on his own. There'd been a
special type of fury in his eyes back at the bar, and I had no idea if it
was because Hudson got gross with me, or because I'd been so stupid.
Most likely, it was a combination of the two.

We made the walk up to my apartment in silence, and the moment
we stepped inside, I bought myself even more time.

"I'm gonna change real quick." I made a beeline for my bedroom.
"Make yourself at home."

Wally was waiting for me on my bed, so I gave him exactly three
belly rubs—any more and I was asking to lose a finger. I stripped off my
jeans, put on my comfiest sweatpants, selected one of my many pairs of
fuzzy socks, then crept back to the living room.

Penn stood with his arms crossed in front of my whiteboard. He
turned. "You've gone full *Beautiful Mind* over here."

"I haven't started drawing on the windows yet."

Penn squinted and took a few steps closer to the board. "What's
this?" He pointed at the threatening note I'd received earlier.

"Oh..." I headed for the kitchen. "Yeah, someone left that on my car at work today."

"Great, just *great*," he said. "You're getting death threats now."

"That isn't exactly a death threat. Just a sort of vague threat." I opened the fridge. "Do you want something to drink?"

"You got anything stronger than tea?" Penn asked.

I surveyed the contents of my barren fridge. "I've got wine...and wine."

"I'll take the wine then."

I grabbed the large bottle of Pinot Grigio and located two glasses.

Penn's eyes were still locked on the board as I plopped down on the couch and poured the wine.

"Come sit down and yell at me," I said after a few minutes. "You know you want to."

"I don't want to yell at you." Penn sat, picked up his glass and took a few sips. "But *damn* it, how could you be so reckless? I mean, meeting up with him was bad enough, but doing it right after getting that threat? Do you actually have a death wish?"

"I *had* to know who sent me those messages. And I'm not going to let one note stop me. The note means I'm onto something!"

"That note was probably left by Hudson," Penn said sternly. "He's playing you, like he did with those Twitter messages."

"That's what I thought at first too. But what he said made a lot of sense." I gave Penn a quick rundown of Hudson's and my entire conversation—the love letter between Sharon and Michael, the DNA test, the results they never got to open, the possibility of Samantha lying.

He remained silent for a while after I finished, draining his wine glass as he processed everything.

I gave him a refill. "Why aren't you freaking out as much as I am?"

"Because I think it's all bullshit. Hudson has no proof of any of this. Does he have this letter he claims Danielle found? Proof Danielle sent their DNA to be tested? Text messages or emails of their plans to get together and open the results?"

I frowned, kicking myself for not asking him. "Well, I'm not sure, but..."

"He told you a really good story, Evie," Penn said. "But that's all it was. He claims his sister lied to us, but based on everything we know, I'm more inclined to believe Samantha."

"But if Hudson had something to do with Danielle's disappearance, why contact me at all?" I could hear the desperation in my voice. Damn it, I wanted to believe Hudson. "Why draw any attention to himself?"

"He could be panicking. Figures gaining your trust and shifting the blame to his sister would get the heat off him. He knows he makes a great suspect." He paused. "If he really wanted to help, he wouldn't have been so cagey with this information. And why didn't he tell us any of this ten years ago?"

I sighed heavily and took a few big sips of my wine. "I want to believe him."

"I know, but Hudson doesn't have a good track record. He's a creep —as he so graciously demonstrated tonight."

"You really didn't have to intervene. I've dealt with guys much worse than him."

"You need to be more careful," Penn chided me like a worried dad.

"You think I can't take care of myself?" I raised an eyebrow.

His eyes bored into mine for a heart-stopping moment. "I think you underestimate the effect you have on men."

The wine seemed to hit me at the exact moment he said that. I had an *effect* on him? My cheeks felt hot as I finished my glass, so I busied myself by pouring more wine, trying not to overanalyze his comment.

"And I'm sure you've never used your looks to help you out at work," I said with an eye roll.

Penn scrunched up his face as if it were news to him that he was hot, but his display of confusion was far too over the top. "What do you mean?"

"Please!" I shook my head. "I bet you've had female suspects and witnesses drooling all over you, dying to spill their secrets."

Penn's furrowed brow relaxed and a smile crept across his lips. "I guess it's been known to happen once or twice. Especially if I turn on the charm."

"You have charm to turn on?" I asked with a laugh. "I've never seen it."

"You couldn't handle my charm, Evie. Imagine how much you'd stalk me if I were nicer to you."

"Shut up!" I gave him a shove, which caused wine to slosh over his glass and onto his shirt. I grimaced. "Oops. At least it wasn't red."

"My fault. I'm not drinking it fast enough." Penn then finished glass number two. As he went to refill it, I noticed his cheeks had turned rosy. This visit was becoming more social by the minute, but I found myself having a pleasant time.

"Your accent gets stronger when you drink."

He gave me a sheepish grin. "Careful, if we keep going, I might start calling you darlin'."

My breath caught in my chest, and my face burned as I imagined us in a much more intimate setting; Penn's face close to mine, his deep voice whispering a honeyed "darlin'" into my ear...

I cleared my throat and took a big gulp of wine.

"Okay, I want to hear your theory now," I said, steering us back to business as I readjusted myself on the couch. I leaned back against the arm and faced Penn, my legs stretched out as much as I could without invading his space. "What happened to Danielle? No cop-speak, no noncommittal statements. Just what you think. Go."

"Alright." Penn leaned back into the couch as well, putting his feet up on the coffee table. "Well, I'll agree with you on one thing—I think she's dead. It's what makes the most sense. If she were alive, she would've contacted someone after all these years." I nodded, urging him to continue. "I still think it was Hudson," Penn said. "He has a bit of a record, and a history of questionable behavior around Danielle. We have both Hudson and Samantha confirming he spent a lot of time with Danielle before she disappeared. Maybe he got his hopes up that she finally returned his feelings, and when he found out it wasn't true, he snapped."

"What about Michael Davenport possibly being Danielle's father?" I asked. "You think Hudson would be into his half sister?"

"I think you're being too quick to assume Michael is her father. All we have is Hudson's word on that. Did Sharon Livingston say anything to indicate it could be Michael?"

"No," I pouted, drinking more wine.

"There you go," he said. "Until we have proof, I'm going to assume Hudson is a liar."

"I don't think you're entirely unbiased here. I think you have it out for Hudson because of what happened at the bar."

Penn's lips twitched. "Maybe."

I shook my head and finished my third glass of wine. I really needed to stop now. We'd made a huge dent in the bottle, and the room was spinning a bit. I looked over at Penn to see if he was as drunk as I was, but I couldn't tell. I didn't want to get caught staring at him, so I followed his gaze to my whiteboard. Together, we surveyed it in silence.

Penn brushed the back of his fingers against my upper arm to get my attention. When I turned to look at him, he was grinning, pointing at my list of death threat suspects. "Do you really think Audrey might've left you that note?"

"No." I struggled to pretend his feather-light touch had zero effect on me. "But a cop friend of mine told me I have to—"

"Consider every possibility, yeah, yeah," Penn finished for me.

I waited for him to tell me that friend was a strong word, like he'd done before, but the clarification never came.

"I really like her." Normally I wouldn't have continued, but the wine loosened my lips. "What happened between you two, exactly? Was it the baby?"

Penn's expression grew more somber, and I scolded myself for ruining our surprisingly fun night. I didn't expect him to answer at all, but it seemed the wine had loosened him up too.

"The baby was the catalyst, but it was a combination of things," he said, breaking eye contact. "We were high school sweethearts, got married too young, didn't have enough of those important conversations beforehand—kids being one of them. Audrey wanted them from the get-go, and I kept putting it off. But when she finally got pregnant, I was excited. I realized I really did want to be a dad." He stared into his glass. "I think I had a harder time with the loss than she did. We managed to get through it okay, but the real problem came a while later, when Audrey wanted to try again."

"Oh."

"I wasn't ready. The thought of going through that again..." He shook his head. "I told her I didn't know if I'd ever be ready, and she told me she wasn't getting any younger..."

"And you couldn't get past that," I said quietly.

"I didn't think it was fair to keep her waiting around, on the off-chance I changed my mind. She should be with someone who wants what she wants."

"That must've been really hard." Tears welled up in my eyes out of nowhere. "I'm sorry I keep calling you grumpy," I choked out.

Penn let out a small laugh. "Evie, it's okay."

"No," I insisted, wiping at my eyes. "I'm horrible."

Penn spotted the box of tissues on the coffee table and handed me one. "So you're a weepy drunk, huh?"

"I'm not drunk," I lied as I dabbed at my eyes.

"Really? Because I am." Penn finished his wine and set the glass down. "Are you sure you're okay?"

"I'm fine," I insisted, tears under control.

"Tell me something about you now," Penn said. "I think it's only fair."

"Ugh. My life is a disaster. You don't want to hear about it."

"I do." His dark eyes had a softness I hadn't seen since the night we met.

Butt asleep and legs cramping, I fluffed up the throw pillow behind me and stretched out my legs, not even fully realizing I'd put my feet in Penn's lap. In my drunk brain, it felt natural. He didn't seem to mind. In fact, after a minute, he rested his hand on my crossed ankles.

"I'm thirty, single, and I have a cat," I said flatly. "That about sums it up."

"I already know all that. I told you about my marriage. Tell me about your last relationship."

"Oh, jeez." I covered my eyes with my hand. My throat tightened at the thought of talking about it. It had been hard enough mentioning it to Grace the other day, and she was my best friend. How could I tell Penn?

"That bad, huh?"

"It's not a nice story," I warned him, trying to buy some time. "It doesn't...It doesn't make me look very good."

He continued to look at me, undeterred. "I won't judge."

I didn't know if it was because we were both a little plastered or because his eyes looked so warm, but I decided to go for it. To get it out of my system. I hadn't told a single soul about my fall from grace.

"Back in D.C., I was a crime reporter for the *Post*." I pretended to pick lint off my sweater so I didn't have to look at him. "I loved it. I was constantly working, but I didn't care. I thrived off the chaos of writing for a giant paper in a city where plenty of bad things happened every day."

Penn made a face. "Then what the hell are you doing in Bristol?"

I snorted. "Getting there." I took a few breaths. "Not to brag, but I was really good at my job. And I had plenty of D.C. officers willing to talk to me for stories."

"Is that a dig at me?"

"I wanted to keep climbing the ladder, keep turning out great stories, so I got a little reckless," I went on, ignoring his comment. "There was this one cop—one of my sources—who I knew liked me. The feeling wasn't really mutual, but I could see the opportunity there, the potential for insider access. So we started sleeping together."

"I think I see where this is going."

"I screwed up. He got attached. He thought it was more than it was. He let his guard down around me and would talk openly about investigations. And one day, he told me something..." I exhaled. "It was too good not to use."

"So you used it," Penn said quietly.

"I'd been so focused on publishing the scoop no one else would have, I didn't think about the consequences. Things fell apart really fast. Metro PD freaked out, and it didn't take long for my editor to figure out what had happened. Essentially, I was fired. My source got kicked off the force too, and he despised me for it. No other decent paper in the city would touch me after word got around." I let out a small laugh. "I was lucky to get a job at the *Daily News*. There was a time when I thought I'd never be able to write again.

"That's how I ended up here, writing about wannabe country music stars. And when my editor gave me a shot at the crime beat...I felt like maybe I could get back to where I was. That I could finally fix what I'd fucked up."

When I stopped speaking, the silence felt unbearably heavy. Did I actually tell him all of that? I hadn't intended to go into so much detail, but I guess I'd wanted to get it out. Penn had promised not to judge me, but I could feel his eyes on me, looking at me in a whole new light.

"I was...not expecting all that."

"I swore I'd never do anything like that again," I said, "which I already screwed up when I tricked you for that first story. I wouldn't blame you for never talking to me again after hearing that."

"Did you name him?" Penn asked. "Your source—did you use his name in the story?"

"Yeah," I said, looking at my lap.

"Well, you didn't use mine. Sounds like growth to me."

I looked up and gave him a cautious smile. "You're being too nice. You had me pegged from day one. I *am* a leech. I'll do anything to get the goddamn story."

"I think you're being a little too hard on yourself. That cop wasn't blameless. He should've known better too." He patted my ankle. "Plus, you don't exactly look that devious in these socks."

I laughed and wiggled my toes. Penn grabbed them, his hands

squeezing my feet. I could feel his warmth all the way through the socks.

I couldn't believe it. I'd told him my secret shame, and instead of being disgusted or offended, he'd actually made me feel better about it.

"I think you secretly like these socks," I teased, wiggling my toes again.

"Oh, yeah. I definitely want a pair for myself."

A silence settled over us as the light moment passed. "I haven't told anyone that. You're a good listener."

Penn absentmindedly kneaded his thumbs against my sole. "Listening's half my job. You'd be amazed how much you can get out of a suspect if you just wait for them to fill the silence."

"Huh," I said thoughtfully. "I'll have to keep that in mind for my future interrogations."

Penn shot me a grin as he continued to work his fingers up my foot, applying the perfect amount of pressure. I leaned my head against the couch and let out a contented sigh.

"That feels incredible." I shut my eyes for a few seconds, but when it hit me that *Penn* was massaging my feet, my eyes snapped open and I burst out laughing.

He gave me a quizzical look.

"I just realized you're the first man to ever give me a foot rub," I said, followed by a few residual giggles.

"That can't be true."

"It really is." I stuck out my lower lip like a pouty child. "How sad."

"Not even your buddy from The Ranch?"

I grabbed a throw pillow and hurled it at his head, though the wine had really affected my aim. Penn didn't even have to duck as it sailed over him and into the kitchen. "I swear, if you mention him one more time..."

"I'm sorry. I'll stop." He snickered to himself, then switched to my left foot.

"A little harder, right in the middle there." He complied. "It's not fair." I settled back into the couch. "I don't know about any of your embarrassing one-night stands to torture you with."

His mouth twitched before he said, "That's because there aren't any."

I scrunched my forehead as I tried to process this. "Huh?"

"There aren't any. There was just Audrey. We started dating in high school, remember?"

"Right," I murmured, my cheeks heating up as it sunk in that Penn had made a rather intimate confession—and an endearing one too. My grumpy, sexy detective, who was apparently really good at foot rubs, had only been with one woman.

"Hang on." I sat up again. "The night we met, you tried to get me to come home with you."

We'd managed to never speak of this, and thanks to the wine, it didn't even occur to me that bringing it up now could be awkward.

"And I told you I never did that."

"I didn't think you were serious!" I shook my head. "I just thought that was something guys say to make the girl feel special."

"Well, it wasn't a line," Penn said. "It was true."

My mind raced, trying to understand the implications. If Penn had never picked up a woman at a bar before me, well...that suggested he'd *really* liked me. Of course, this was probably moot now, considering he'd been interested in non-journalist Evie, but still. It was a wild thing to know. My head hurt more the longer I thought about it.

The foot rub came to a slow halt.

"It's late," Penn said, but made no move to get up.

"I know."

"I just need to wait a little before I can drive. I'll get out of your hair soon."

"You can stay as long as you want." I stood, almost falling back down, from both the wine and the intensity of what we'd just discussed. "I need to get a shower."

Wally hopped onto the couch to keep Penn company while I

showered. By the time I got out, Penn was asleep and snoring softly. I gave him a little nudge.

"Penn?"

Nothing. I grabbed a throw blanket and draped it over him, then fetched a pillow from my room in case he wanted to lie down. I stared at him for a minute. He looked adorable—peaceful, which I'd never seen before. I felt the need to have some sort of evidence of the strange but wonderful evening. Still pretty tipsy despite the shower, I took out my phone and snapped a quick photo of him. I sent it to Grace with the caption "my sleepy detective."

She instantly replied with, *AHHHHHHHHHH! Why is he not in your bed?!*

I ignored her, knowing I needed to go sleep off the wine before I did other silly things.

On the way to my room, I stopped at the whiteboard one more time, eyes focusing on that note.

Stop asking questions, or else.

"Can you believe this, Wally?" I asked. "Someone's trying to scare me away from the case. Well, it's not going to work."

Before I could think it through, I snapped a photo of the note and brought up Twitter.

Someone doesn't want me looking into Danielle's disappearance. Well, guess what? I'm not going to stop until we have #JusticeForDanielle.

"That'll show them I'm not to be trifled with," I told Wally sternly. Then I wandered into my room and passed out on my bed before I could even get under the covers.

CHAPTER EIGHTEEN

THE NEXT MORNING, I AWOKE WITH A POUNDING HEADACHE. I slowly sat up from my sprawled, diagonal position and looked for Wally. He always slept with me, but he was nowhere to be found. That's when I remembered I had a man sleeping in the living room whom Wally seemed to like better.

On tip-toes I crept out there, seeing the folded blanket, the pillow and Wally on the couch—but no Penn. My heart sunk a little. He must've woken up at some point and gone home. Shoving down my disappointment, I turned and headed for the bathroom, but the door swung open when I reached for the handle.

"Ahh!" I jumped, and my hand flew to my racing heart.

Penn took a stumbling step backwards so we didn't collide. "Sorry."

"It's fine," I said, still a bit freaked about him being here. Last night it didn't seem that weird, but in the sober light of day, it felt like a line had been crossed. "I thought you might've gone home."

"No, I was out. Sorry, I didn't mean to stay."

"It's fine," I repeated, trying too hard to sound casual. "I just wasn't prepared for company. It's kind of a mess in there." I nervously peered into the bathroom.

"Yeah, there's like three bras on the door handle," Penn said with an awkward laugh.

"Great." Speaking of bras, I wasn't currently wearing one. I shifted uncomfortably and crossed my arms.

"Well, uh, I guess I'll get going."

Why did this feel so weird? We were behaving like two strangers who'd had a drunken one-night stand—though our drunken heart-to-heart and the foot massage felt just as intimate.

"You don't have to rush out," I said. "I've got coffee, and I can make toast or something."

"Uh..." Penn glanced at his watch.

"Please, stay. We're acting weird. And we have no reason to."

He let out a shaky laugh. "You're right. Okay. I can get the coffee going."

I quickly dressed in jeans, a blouse, and a warm cardigan, and I put on a bit of makeup. The coffee had just finished brewing when I rejoined Penn in the kitchen. I grabbed two mugs.

"Unfortunately, I don't have any soy milk," I said.

"I'd be alarmed if you did. Black is fine."

As I stuck some bread in the toaster, I heard the staccato buzzing of a phone. "Is that you?"

"No, it's you." Penn grabbed my phone off the table. "You've got a ton of Twitter notifications."

Confused, I took my phone from Penn and opened Twitter.

That's when I remembered.

"Oh, no." I frantically scrolled through the notifications, new ones popping up every few seconds. "*Oh*, no."

"What?" Penn asked.

I looked at him, eyes wide, lips pressed together. "I did something stupid after you fell asleep last night."

Penn set his coffee cup down with a *thunk*. "What?"

I said nothing, but clicked on my tweet and handed the phone back to him.

He scanned it for two seconds before he let out a frustrated, "*Evie!*"

"I know!" The toast popped up, and I put it on a plate. "I'm bad with my phone when I drink. I'll text exes or send crazy work emails, or apparently taunt the person who's threatening me." I reached into the fridge and grabbed the butter before remembering Penn's allergy. I took the strawberry jam instead, brought everything to the table and sat down, a little out of breath.

Penn shook his head at me.

"Don't look at me like that. You were drunk too!"

"Yeah, and all I did was fall asleep," he said dryly.

I thought about pointing out he also rubbed my feet and told me a *lot* of personal stuff, but I didn't want to bring back the weirdness. We'd settled back into our comfortable dynamic of me doing something frustrating and Penn getting annoyed. Things were safer this way.

"Well, I deleted it." He shoved my phone back to me. "But a lot of people already saw it. You got over two hundred retweets."

"A new record," I said weakly.

Penn responded by aggressively putting jam on his toast, the knife scraping against the bread.

"At least I got more buzz going about the case," I said after a few silent moments of us crunching on our toast.

"You people really don't understand how delicate investigations are. Your instinct is to get as much information out there as you can without ever asking if all that information *should* be out there."

"You people?" I said with disgust. "I'm back to being '*you people*'?"

"You can play detective all you want, Evie, but you don't know the first thing about being one."

"If you're so good at your job, how come I'm the one who caught the rapist?" I shot back.

"Dumb luck."

I scoffed at him and snatched his plate away, even though he had a few bites of toast left. "I need to get to work. Which means you have to go."

"Fine," he said in a similarly irritated tone, draining the rest of his coffee. Penn stood, the chair scraping loudly against the floor.

Wally's ears went flat against his head at the sound. We both continued to stomp around and gather our things.

I fumed as I pulled on my scarf and coat. Just when I thought there might be a sweet, sensitive guy in there somewhere, he proved me wrong. And to think I'd actually felt something between us last night.

It was temporary insanity, I told myself. *And all the wine.*

We ignored each other as we made our way down to the parking lot. I stopped when we reached his car.

"Well, goodbye." I crossed my arms. The wind blew my hair into my face, wisps getting caught in my lip gloss. Having to pull away the sticky strands was really ruining my dramatic exit.

"Try not to do anything to put your life in danger today," Penn said. "I know that might be tough."

"What do you care?" I rolled my eyes and marched towards my car a few spaces away.

I'd been so focused on getting into my car that my ears barely registered the sound of a revving engine. It grew louder, which made me look up. Some asshole in a black car was flying through the parking lot. I walked to the back of my car, determined to get the plate off this reckless driver. As they approached, they slowed, and the passenger side window rolled down halfway.

Confused, I stood there and stared—until I heard the first bang. I jumped out of my skin when my taillight shattered. My heart flew into overdrive as I realized what was happening, but I was frozen in place.

"Evie! Get down!"

I barely heard Penn over the sound of my blood pumping in my ears. I wasn't sure what came next, the second gunshot or Penn tackling me to the ground. It all happened so fast. But a few seconds later, I was lying on the cold asphalt with the wind knocked out of me, Penn shielding me with his body. I heard one more bullet sink into my car before the shooter sped off, tires squealing as they peeled onto the main road. I managed to catch an M and a 7 off the plate.

I wheezed, struggling to get air into my lungs again.

"Oh, fuck," Penn moaned. He slowly rolled off me, and he cried out in pain when he landed on his back.

I lifted my hands in front of my face and saw blood smeared on the right one. I gasped as I sat up.

"Penn?" My voice was sharp and urgent. I knelt over him and saw a bright red stain blooming on his left shoulder.

"Oh God. You've been shot!"

"I know."

"Oh God."

"Evie, I really need you not to panic right now," he said, jaw clenched.

"What do I do?" I asked, tears welling up.

"Well, calling for help would be good," he said slowly, as if speaking to a child.

"Right!" I whipped out my phone and dialed 9-1-1 with shaky fingers. "Hi! Yes, I need an ambulance at the Bristol Hills apartment complex. We're in the parking lot. There was a drive-by shooting. Detective Marcus Pennington was shot." I paused as the operator asked me follow-up questions. "It's in his shoulder. That's not that bad, right? There's just a lot of blood." The woman instructed me to put pressure on the wound until EMS arrived.

"Okay, five minutes," I told him when I got off the phone. I pulled off my scarf, folded it, then placed it over the wound. With both hands, I pushed against it.

"OW!"

"She told me to do this!" I looked at his face, twisted in pain, and the tears came back. "Oh, this is all my fault!"

"It could've been worse." Penn winced. "If I weren't here, you'd be dead right now. Who just stands there as they're getting shot at? Do you have zero survival instincts?"

"I was in shock!" I took a few deep breaths and tried not to look too closely at all the blood. The reality of what just happened started to sink in.

"Penn, you saved my life!" I leaned over him and planted kisses all over his face.

"Thank you, thank you, thank you," I said between kisses, my lips traveling from his stubbly cheeks up to his furrowed forehead. Penn looked like he was being attacked by a swarm of bees.

"Are you serious?" I asked when I noticed his lackluster reaction. "You know, most guys would love to get kissed by a beautiful woman on their deathbed."

"I'm not on my deathbed. Besides, you didn't even give me a real kiss."

I stared at him, taken aback by his statement. Was he actually suggesting I plant a big wet one on him? As he lay bleeding in my parking lot, after we'd been fighting five minutes ago? The wail of the ambulance siren cut through the chilly morning air, solving the dilemma for me.

The ambulance screeched to a halt and two paramedics jumped out.

I quickly got out of their way.

"Evie," Penn called, voice weak, after the paramedics got him on the stretcher and were wheeling him away. "Come with me."

My heart lurched. "Of course!" I scurried after them. "Don't worry, Penn, I won't leave your side." I climbed into the back of the ambulance once they got him loaded in.

"I meant so you can give your statement at the hospital," he said flatly.

"Oh."

"Miss? There's a Detective Delaney asking for you."

A nurse stood in front of me, and I looked up from my phone. It was warm from all the use. I'd had to call Shelly to let her know I might not make it in. And then I called my father, because if he somehow heard about this from anyone else, he'd drop everything, hop in his car, and show up at my door unannounced.

Mere minutes after I'd hung up with him, my phone exploded with texts from the group chat I had with my sisters.

Evie, WTF, who's trying to kill you?!

DAD SAID YOU GOT SHOT? WHAT?

Wait, sorry, shot at, not shot. But still!! What is going on?!

He said your cop friend saved you. Is he the cute one you mentioned before? Tell him thanks for us ;)

I'd attempted to reply to them and give Grace a brief summary at the same time. Once Grace knew we were okay, she was more interested in how Penn ended up spending the night instead of what had transpired in the parking lot.

The nurse led me back into the ER towards a bed with the curtain drawn around it. I could hear Penn and Delaney talking. I cleared my throat before parting the curtain and stepping inside.

"Evie! It's nice to see you again." Delaney smiled big as he turned to greet me.

"Uh, hi, Tom," I managed to get out after a few seconds. I was a bit tongue-tied as my attention wandered elsewhere.

Penn was perched on the edge of the bed as a doctor threaded stitches into his shoulder. I could see a bloody, crumpled piece of metal in a small bowl next to him. Glad I'd missed the bullet extraction. What I hadn't missed, however, was seeing Penn without his shirt on. I couldn't help but gawk at him in all his half-naked glory—his chest and abdomen toned, his biceps bigger than I'd expected. A dusting of dark hair covered his pecs, with a nice little trail leading tantalizingly below his waistband. As I stared, warmth flooded my entire body, and a tingling sensation settled low in my belly.

"...anything about the car?"

I tore my eyes away from Penn to look at Delaney, fighting the urge to fan myself. "Huh?"

"I said, do you remember anything about the car? Marcus says it was a black sedan. Did you see the plate at all?"

"I'm pretty sure I saw an M and a seven. It happened so fast. The engine was really loud, though."

Delaney nodded and made a note in his notepad. "And this happened around seven forty-five?"

"That sounds right." I looked at my watch. It was nearly ten now.

"Wait, Marcus, what time did you get there?" Delaney turned to Penn. "Before Evie came down, did you notice anyone idling in the parking lot?"

Penn's eyebrows went up a little, and my face started to get warm again.

"I, um..." Penn cleared his throat. "We came downstairs together."

Delaney stared at Penn, stumped. "So you got there earlier than seven forty-five?"

Another throat clearing. "I...got there last night. I, uh, stayed over."

"*Oh*," he said before he broke out into a giant smirk. "*Gotcha.*"

My face was on fire now. "It's not what you think," I blurted out. They both looked at me. "We just had a lot to drink last night, and..."

"A tale as old as time." Delaney chuckled. "Say no more."

Penn shot me a look, silently scolding me for making it worse, but I couldn't stop talking. It was imperative word didn't get around the police department that Penn and I were sleeping together.

"No, you don't get it," I said. "Nothing happened. He slept on the couch. Wait, I have a picture!" I began to pull out my phone, so pleased with having evidence that I didn't realize how insane that sounded.

"You what?" Penn squinted at me, an abrupt reminder that it wasn't normal to take photos of people while they were sleeping. I wanted to ask the doctor if it were possible to die of embarrassment.

"Um, nothing, never mind." I jammed my phone back into my purse.

Delaney's pen had stopped moving minutes ago, and he had a vague look on his face, his opinion on what had gone down last night clearly unchanged. Damn it. I'd worked so hard to stay squeaky clean here. I hadn't even touched Penn, but my reputation was out the window. How was that fair?

"Oh, Marcus, you got a little lipstick..." Delaney gestured at Penn's cheek, smirk widening on his lips.

Alarmed, Penn roughly rubbed at his face with the heel of his hand. I slumped against the wall and almost started laughing hysterically at how this just kept getting *worse*.

"Okay, you're all set." The doctor had finished stitching up Penn and slapped a bandage on him. Even he looked amused by the embarrassing situation unfolding. "Keep it clean and dry, and change the bandage twice a day."

"Thanks," Penn said before the doctor departed.

Delaney pulled a small plastic baggie out of his pocket and dumped the bullet into it. "Do you have any guesses on who might've done this?" he asked me, back to business.

I shifted uncomfortably. "Well, I sort of got an anonymous threat yesterday..."

"Marcus mentioned that," Delaney said. "He also told me you might've poked the bear with a tweet last night."

I turned to Penn. "I'm *sorry*." I looked back at Delaney. "I have a list of all the people I've talked to about Danielle, but really it could've been anyone who's reading my stories."

"I know who it was," Penn said as he slowly pulled his shirt back on, struggling to get his injured arm into the sleeve. I stepped forward to help him. He allowed me to support his arm, and I carefully guided it through the sleeve, having to remind myself several times not to squeeze his rock-hard bicep. "It was Hudson Davenport."

"Penn," I said, "you have no proof. You just don't like him."

"Damn right I don't like him." He turned to Delaney. "Not only is Hudson the prime suspect in Danielle's disappearance, but I had to haul him off of Evie at Last Call last night. He might've been trying to get her to leave with him. When that didn't work, he decided to take a different route."

"I would *not* have gone home with him," I said. "Stop talking about me like I'm not here!"

"Sounds like motive to me," Delaney said, ignoring me. "We'll bring him in."

I stood there, dazed, as Penn and Delaney discussed logistics. I hadn't thought about it, but what if Penn was right? Had Hudson been trying to seduce me last night? Reel me in with juicy details about Danielle and take me home, all so he could kill me? I shuddered.

"Well, at least one good thing came from this," Penn said as he got to his feet.

"What's that?"

"We've got enough to officially reopen Danielle's case now."

CHAPTER NINETEEN

"My client does not have to answer that."

I crossed my arms and let out a sigh, free to make all the irritated expressions I wanted behind the safety of the two-way mirror. Penn and Delaney didn't have that luxury and needed to have more control over their faces, but after a half hour of getting nothing from Hudson, I could tell their—well, Penn's—patience was wearing thin.

"If your client hasn't done anything *wrong*," Penn said, "it'd be in his best interest to answer."

Hudson just sat there, smirking. He hadn't opened his mouth once, choosing to let his lawyer speak for him. I shouldn't have been surprised —Hudson clearly thrived on withholding information, then doling it out at his discretion. But I thought he'd at least give Penn and Delaney a quick denial at my attempted murder. I chewed on my lower lip, worried Penn's suspicions about Hudson were spot on.

"Mr. Davenport did not try to kill Miss Hartley this morning," Hudson's lawyer repeated for the third time. "He was on his way to work at the time of the shooting. He arrived at the office minutes later. He wouldn't have had time to drive by Miss Hartley's apartment and still make it to work on time. Not to mention, my client drives a red car, not a black one."

Penn glared at the lawyer, fury in his eyes. I understood his frustration. Hudson's lawyer was right; the math didn't add up. To make matters worse, there had allegedly been security camera footage showing Hudson strolling down the hallways of Davenport Properties right after Penn got shot. An airtight alibi.

But Penn wasn't ready to release his new nemesis yet. "Miss Hartley received an anonymous threat yesterday. I'm sure your client wouldn't know anything about that either."

"Of course not," the lawyer said quickly.

"And the fact that your *client* made unwanted advances towards Miss Hartley the night before this incident is just a coincidence?"

"Jonathan, I think we might have to file a harassment lawsuit against the department." Hudson finally spoke, smirk still in place. "Detective Pennington seems to have a personal vendetta against me because I took his girl out for a drink last night."

Penn let out a humorless laugh. "If I have a vendetta against you, it's because you murdered Danielle Livingston."

"*Marcus,*" Delaney hissed, but it was too late.

"That's it." Hudson's lawyer got to his feet. "We've cooperated, we've answered your questions about the shooting. I will not allow you to hurl absurd accusations. If you want to speak to my client further, you'll need an arrest warrant."

The lawyer looked expectantly at Hudson, but he remained seated. I could see his green eyes dancing all the way from behind the mirror.

"It's a real shame you weren't nicer to me, Detective." Hudson examined his nails, tone thick with boredom. "Because I might have some information on who could be behind the shooting this morning, but now, I don't really feel like sharing."

"Withholding information from the police is a crime," Penn said through gritted teeth. "One I will gladly arrest you for."

"I meant I'm not sharing with *you,*" Hudson clarified. "But something tells me you've got Evie back there." He pointed to the mirror. "I'll talk to her. Alone."

"Absolutely not," Penn said. "Doesn't work that way."

I rolled my eyes and rapped my knuckles against the mirror.

Hudson's eyes lit up. "I think that means yes."

Penn's jaw clenched again, but he said nothing more as he stormed out of the interrogation room. I could feel him seething the minute he walked through the door.

"I don't want you talking to him again," Penn said, his hands balled into fists.

"Why not? He can't do anything here. I'll be perfectly safe."

Penn's jaw and hands refused to relax.

"Penn, he's got an alibi," I said. "I'm sorry, but he's not the one after me. He didn't shoot you."

"Just because he didn't pull the trigger doesn't mean he wasn't behind it," he grumbled.

"Let me go in there. What's the worst that could happen?"

Penn threw his head back, but nevertheless gestured for me to follow him towards the interrogation room. He went in first to extract Delaney, but stopped again on his way out.

"Don't even think about printing anything Hudson might tell you," he said, voice low.

"Are *you* threatening me now, Detective?"

It almost made Penn smile. "I would, but I don't think it'd make any difference."

"You're not as scary as you think you are," I said, giving him a pat on the cheek before entering. Hudson sat up straighter at the sound of the door closing, and as our eyes locked, that devilish smile from last night reappeared.

"Jonathan, you can go," Hudson told his lawyer casually.

He balked at his client. "Hudson, please. You know it's in your best interest for me to—"

"It's fine. She's a friend."

I wanted to correct Hudson that we definitely weren't friends, but it seemed to be the only way to appease the lawyer. With one more uncertain look, he left Hudson and me alone.

"I'm glad you didn't get hurt this morning, Evie." Hudson's tone was borderline sincere.

"Are you?"

"Of course. You don't really think I had something to do with it, do you?"

"Your alibi clears you."

"That's not what I asked," Hudson said.

"You said you might know who's responsible," I said, ignoring his question.

"I have theories," Hudson said, just as coy as he'd been last night.

"Hudson, cut the crap. Someone tried to *kill* me. A cop got *shot*. I'd really like to figure this out before they try again."

He frowned. "I realize how serious this is. But I think you can understand my reaction to being hauled in here, just because your boyfriend doesn't like me."

"Make him like you, then, Hudson. Cooperate. Give us something useful. Please."

"Well, since you asked so nicely." Hudson leaned across the table, voice low and intimate. "I don't have any proof, but it's got to be someone from my family."

"Is that so?"

"Who else would want to stop you from digging?"

"Because they had something to do with Danielle's disappearance," I said slowly.

Hudson nodded. "I wish I could narrow it down more, but any one of them could've done it. Maybe they all did it together, who knows. But Mom, Dad, and Samantha all know what happened."

"How can that be? How do they all know, but you're in the dark? What, did you miss the family meeting when they discussed where to hide the body?"

"Evie, if this is going to work, you're going to have to start trusting me a little more," Hudson said. "I told you last night, I'm the black sheep. Why do you think after eight years of working for Davenport Properties, I'm still just Dad's executive assistant? I'm a burden—a liability. They wouldn't have clued me in to their little murder plan. I would've run right to the police."

"Sure." I eyed him doubtfully.

Hudson gave a dramatic sigh. "You've got to keep an open mind. Isn't that what reporters are supposed to do? Be objective?"

"Fine," I said. "Who shot at me this morning, then? Mom, Dad, or sister?"

"Well, I'd bet my life none of them have an alibi as good as mine," he said with a head tilt. "Mom would've still been sleeping, which we all know is the world's worst alibi. Samantha comes into work late, because she always has some hot yoga class or facial to get to; I'm sure she could've squeezed a drive-by shooting into her lax schedule." Hudson paused for effect. "And Dad, usually an early riser, was late to work today. As far as I know, all of my beloved family members were unaccounted for this morning."

I shot a quick glance at the mirror, wishing I could see what Penn thought about this. Again, I wanted to believe Hudson, but it seemed a little too convenient he was the only Davenport with an alibi.

Michael though...That was interesting. I hadn't even met Georgina Davenport, but my instincts told me neither she nor Samantha would be shooting at me from that dark car. It was a man's vehicle—loud and sporty.

And out of all the Davenports, Michael had the most to lose if Danielle turned out to be his secret love child. Danielle would've been conceived right around the same time as Samantha. Surely he wouldn't want the public, or his wife, to find out.

"I can see it in your eyes, Evie," Hudson said with a grin. "You're considering a suspect who isn't me."

"If it was one of them," I said, swallowing hard, "do they really want me dead? Or was this just to scare me?"

"I wish I could say. I would imagine if you keep poking around, they might try again." A smirk spread across his lips. "Something tells me you're not going to let this scare you off the trail, though."

I remained silent for a few minutes. No, I wasn't going to drop the story, but I certainly didn't want a repeat of this morning. I'd gotten lucky, but Penn wasn't always going to be around to push me out of a bullet's way. Whoever did this knew where I lived, where I worked, what my car looked like...

A memory from last night flashed into my mind. Hudson had known my drink order.

I did my research. Hudson had implied he discovered my taste for rum and coke from my blog, but I'd gone back and double-checked. I'd never mentioned it.

"Here," Hudson said, interrupting my thoughts. He reached into his pocket and pulled out his phone, pushing it towards me. "Give me your number. I'll let you know if anyone at home's acting squirrelly. Try to give you a heads up if I think they might come after you again."

I hesitated before entering my contact information into Hudson's phone. Liar or not, it'd be a good idea to keep in touch with him—let him think we were on the same side.

"One more thing," I added, knowing Penn could put an end to this at any moment. "You don't happen to know what became of those DNA test results you never got to see, do you?"

"Wish I did," Hudson said with an exaggerated, clown-like frown.

"And the love letter Danielle found, between your dad and her mom?"

Hudson threw his head back, tapping his chin as he pretended to think. I had the urge to smack him—he seemed to believe he was a guest star on a crime show instead of an actual suspect. "Sleep on it. Maybe the answer will come to you in a dream."

I rolled my eyes. "Riddles, now?"

That must've been the final straw for Penn. He burst into the room, wordlessly concluding our faux interrogation.

"I guess that's my cue," Hudson said as he stood. "Evie, it's been a pleasure." He walked towards the door. "Detective Pennington, not so much."

And then he left.

"I really hate that guy," Penn said.

"Well, now you've got three new suspects to go talk to."

"Yeah, and they're going to lawyer up and not say shit. We need something else. The car, the gun, or at least a clear motive."

"Sounds like you've got your work cut out for you," I said. "Speaking of work, I need to get there. Can you drop me off?"

"Until we make an arrest, consider me your personal chauffeur." Penn strode towards the parking lot before I could even protest.

"Oh, Evie!" Grace rushed me with a hug before I could even put my things down at my desk.

"I'm fine, I'm fine," I said, even though I'd been nauseous since the shooting.

She stepped back and looked me up and down. "And Pennington's okay?"

"Yeah, he got shot in the shoulder. He's already back to work."

"That must've been terrifying," Grace said, sinking back down into her chair.

"This is all my fault." I put my face in my hands and moaned. "I cannot believe he took a bullet for me."

"I can. You'd just spent the night together. He obviously has feelings for you."

I let out an incredulous laugh. "Slow your roll. Nothing happened last night. We were just discussing the case, he had a little too much to drink, and he fell asleep on the couch. End of story. Him jumping in front of the shooter was just his cop instincts in action." Or at least, that was what I was telling myself. Penn's comment about a "real kiss" still swirled around in my head.

Grace smiled like she knew something I didn't. "Evie, trust me. He's into you."

"How do you know?" I asked, suspicious now. "You've never even formally met him."

Eyes wide and lips pressed together, Grace looked like she was bursting to tell me something. "Okay, do not tell him I told you this." She lowered her voice and leaned across her desk. "But Pennington wants to ask you out. He reached out to me to get a feel for if you'd say yes or not. I guess he doesn't want to put you in a weird spot. Kind of sweet, right?"

I stared at Grace, dumbfounded. "That...doesn't sound like him. I mean, sure, we've had a couple of little moments, but I..." I tried to make this make sense in my mind, but couldn't. Even if Penn liked me like that—which, I had to admit was possible—contacting my best friend, who he didn't even know, didn't seem like his style.

"Evie, I know it's been a while, but don't act so surprised a man is interested in you." Grace pulled something up on her computer. "I've got the emails to prove it. Here."

After a few seconds, my computer dinged with Grace's forwarded messages. Still doubtful, my eyes skimmed the handful of emails.

...wanted to take Evie on a date, do you know if she's interested?

What would she like—dinner, drinks, or a movie?

What time does she usually get to work? I wanted to surprise her with breakfast...

My scrunched-up forehead didn't relax as I studied the emails. "When did these start?"

"A few days ago." Ah. The mystery of Grace's weirdness over the email from her "brother" yesterday had been solved.

I recalled the events of the past few days—my conversation with Audrey, her contacting Penn. Could that have spurred him on to pursue me? Had he finally gotten the closure from her that he needed? Penn *had* gotten pretty territorial with Hudson at Last Call. Huh. Could it be true?

"Why does your face still look like that?" Grace asked. "This is good news!"

"I guess." I shook my head. "This just doesn't sound like him, Grace."

Her pursed lips told me she was losing her patience. "Look at the email. That's him, right?" My eyes darted to the sender field and saw Penn's email—the same one I'd used for months. It was definitely him.

"Yeah," I said.

"I wonder when he's gonna ask you," Grace gushed. "Probably not until things calm down a little, I guess. Hopefully they find whoever shot at you fast."

She continued to babble on, going as far as discussing the possibility of a late summer wedding, as I distractedly tried to write up a story on the drive-by shooting. Uneasy feeling still deep in my belly, all I could come up with was: *Bristol detective shot, all idiotic reporter's fault.*

CHAPTER TWENTY

"WOW, YOU WEREN'T KIDDING ABOUT THE CHAUFFEUR THING."

When I'd emerged from the *Daily News* building a little after five, Penn was idling in the parking lot.

"Yeah, well, I'd hoped we would've made an arrest by now," Penn said as I climbed into the passenger's seat. "Things didn't go well with the other Davenports today." He winced as he secured his seatbelt.

I frowned. "Arm's hurting pretty bad?"

"It's fine," he said flatly, though he steered with only his right hand, his left resting on his lap.

"So you didn't have any luck today?" I asked as he pulled onto the main road.

"Turns out, Hudson's the talkative one. His family was even less cooperative. None of them volunteered alibis, but we can't really do anything else without a warrant."

"And you don't have enough for a warrant."

Penn gave me a stiff nod.

"If it's not Hudson, it's gotta be Michael. He killed his love child because she stumbled upon the big secret, and now, he's trying to do the same thing to me."

"Alleged love child," Penn corrected me.

Here we go again.

"If I found proof, or if I could get Sharon Livingston to confirm Michael was Danielle's father, would that be enough to bring him in?" I asked.

"It'd be a really good start. We could start building a case, get a warrant to search for the gun from the shooting."

I pondered this as Penn pulled into my apartment complex. "Well, thanks for the ride. You really don't have to drive me." I waited for Penn to pull up to the door, but he eased the car into a parking space instead. "What are you doing?"

"I'm going to walk you up."

"Don't you think you're going a little overboard?" I asked as we headed into my building.

"I'm sorry, but did I imagine a drive-by shooting this morning?"

I rolled my eyes, even though he was behind me on the stairs and couldn't see.

"Okay, I made it," I announced when we reached my door. "You can rest easy now."

"Open up. Let me take a quick look around."

I considered arguing, but the crazy day had drained me, and it would be easier to let him inside. I stood in my entryway as Penn methodically moved through the apartment, poking his head into closets and checking that all the windows were locked. Wally, intrigued by the security search, stood on the coffee table, his big yellow eyes following Penn's every move. On the way back, Penn gave him a few head scratches.

"Everything looks normal, but don't be afraid to call if you notice anything off."

A warmth spread through my chest. No way did he do this for every crime victim he encountered. I thought back to what had happened between us the night before, and Grace's emails.

"Well, thanks," I said as he slipped into the hallway. "And, uh, just so you know...if you had something you wanted to ask me, that'd be okay."

Penn turned to face me, head cocked and brow furrowed. "Ask you what?"

My cheeks flushed. "Oh, just...you know. Never mind. I guess now's not the best time anyway."

His confusion transformed to bemusement. "I have no idea what you're talking about. Try to stay put, okay?"

Penn gave me a small smile, brushed the back of his hand against my jaw, then disappeared down the hallway, leaving me a little stunned by the casual, comforting touch. Despite his *confusion*, he seemed to be sending me a clear message.

Smooth move, Evie. He obviously wasn't ready yet and was trying to play it cool. At least I'd put the vibe out there. Considering how, up until today, I had no clue he was interested, I could wait a bit. It might be a bad idea to get involved with a cop again, but the idea of a do-over was appealing. We'd take things slow. I could start getting intel from Delaney to prevent conflicts of interest. Everything would be perfectly above board. The new Evie Hartley could be an ethical reporter *and* be in a mature relationship.

"Wally," I whispered as I plopped down on the couch, and he climbed onto my lap. "A boy likes me."

"Ah!"

Exhausted from a night of restless sleep, I nearly had a heart attack when I opened my door and saw a man waiting for me.

"Jesus," I said. "I thought you were here to kill me."

"It's not fun having someone just show up at your house, is it?" Penn asked.

"Yeah, well, you've never had a death threat out on you all the times I've shown up at your place." I locked the door and glanced at my watch. "Jeez, what time did you get here? I'm almost positive you have more important things to do than babysit me."

"I do," he confirmed as we walked downstairs, "but I won't be able to do any of them if I'm worrying about you."

"And here I thought I just frustrated the hell out of you."

"The two aren't mutually exclusive."

When we got to Penn's car, I found a coffee and a Danish waiting for me in the passenger's seat. My heart leapt a little. Was this the surprise breakfast he'd referenced in his email to Grace?

Penn and I exchanged minor chit chat on the drive, then he dumped me at the newsroom, waiting until I made it far into the building before speeding off. When I got to my desk, I found Grace standing by the window.

"Did Pennington drop you off again?" she asked, eyes wide.

I held up the coffee and the last bite of Danish I had. "Yep. And he brought me treats."

Grace squealed.

"You know, I really had a hard time believing those emails," I told her as I settled at my desk, "but it looks like this is really happening."

"Of course, it is. You'll have to give me a special shout-out at the wedding for encouraging this from the beginning."

I shook my head at her, even though I felt giddy. As much as Penn and I clashed, as much as he drove me crazy, I couldn't deny the strong attraction there. Tons of relationships started off in much weirder ways than ours, anyway.

"What are you up to today?" I asked. "Are you on deadline?"

"Nah, I wrapped up my piece last night. Why?"

"Do you want to take a field trip?"

"Thanks so much for seeing us, Mrs. Livingston," I said as Sharon ushered Grace and me inside her home. "I know I should've called first."

"Not at all, I'm so glad to see you," Sharon said, eyes wide and bright. "I just heard yesterday that the police are reopening Danielle's case. I know we have you to thank for that."

I smiled. "I'm just glad I could help." I gestured to Grace. "This is my colleague, Grace Lee." Sharon and Grace shook hands. "I was hoping we could talk more about your reaction to the case being reopened."

"Of course," Sharon said. "David's not here, though, he's at work. Is that alright?"

I breathed a sigh of relief and told her that was fine. I'd been banking on him being gone. Something told me Sharon would be more likely to talk about the biological father of her child without her husband hanging around.

"So, Mrs. Livingston, the two detectives now assigned to Danielle's case seem to be leaning in the direction of murder," I said.

She gave me a solemn nod. "I heard. It's tough to swallow—hearing that word. But part of me is so relieved they're finally taking it seriously."

"Do you have any suspects in mind?" I asked. "I know we talked about Hudson Davenport last time I was here…"

"He's the first name that comes to mind, but I can't be sure he had something to do with it."

"Mrs. Livingston," Grace said, "are you aware that Danielle was spending time with Hudson before her disappearance?"

Sharon blinked at Grace a few times. "N-no…She what?"

"You mentioned you thought Danielle had been sneaking out to meet a boy," I added. "I think that might've been Hudson. Both he and Samantha confirmed Danielle was seeing him."

Terror flashed into Sharon's eyes, which could definitely be interpreted as silent confirmation that Hudson and Danielle were half siblings. "They were…*seeing* each other?"

"Not like that. Just spending time together." I took a deep breath before continuing. "I'm sorry if this is a sensitive subject, but it's important. Is Michael Davenport Danielle's biological father?"

Sharon tried not to react, but the muscle in her jaw tightened. "Excuse me?"

"We know Danielle was trying to find out who her father was before her disappearance," I said. "According to Hudson, Danielle thought it was Michael."

"That's ridiculous." For the second time, she didn't outright deny it.

"She was pretty convinced," Grace added gently. "Convinced enough to send out her DNA and Hudson's to see if they shared a family match."

"She *what*?" Sharon looked from Grace to me, mouth agape. "Well, what did the results say?"

I exchanged a quick look with Grace. "Mrs. Livingston...shouldn't you already know what the results would say?"

She stared at me for a second or two before huffily stating, "Of course the results would be negative. Michael Davenport is *not* Danielle's father."

She was lying—I was almost positive. Sharon had gambled we didn't have the DNA results, and she'd been right.

"Then who is Danielle's father?" Grace asked. "If he found out Danielle was looking for him, and he didn't want her to, he could be a suspect."

Sharon looked up for a moment, as if she hadn't considered this. Then she quickly shook her head. "That's not possible. Danielle's father was just an old boyfriend of mine. He was irresponsible, and a drunk. He didn't want a child, so we went our separate ways. I heard that he passed away a few years back."

More lies. Sharon gave no name, and him being dead was awfully convenient. But I couldn't press her anymore—not without risking upsetting her for good and losing access.

"I'm sorry for prying," I said. "I just want to find out who did this."

"I know," she murmured.

"Mrs. Livingston," I prayed I wasn't pushing my luck, "would it be okay if we looked through some of Danielle's things?"

"I don't know..." She shifted in her seat. "The police already went through her room ten years ago."

"Then it wouldn't hurt for us to have a quick look, right?" Grace asked with a sweet smile.

"I guess not," Sharon said. "Let me know if you want to take anything."

"Of course."

Sharon led Grace and me upstairs towards the only room with a closed door. She opened it a few inches before departing back down the stairs. I couldn't help but let out a tiny gasp as we stepped inside an almost perfectly preserved teenage girl's room.

The air was thick from the lack of ventilation and a layer of dust coated everything, but otherwise, it looked like Danielle would be back any minute, ready to resume her high school career.

Colorful folders and notebooks were strewn across the desk by the window, backpack dangling off the back of the chair. A cork-board full of photos hung above Danielle's white-and-pink striped duvet-covered bed.

"Cute room," Grace said. "I assume we're looking for something in particular?"

"Yes," I whispered, on the off-chance Sharon was listening. "She's lying about Michael not being the father."

"Obviously."

"I'm not sure why she is, but either way, she won't be any help." I approached the desk and began flipping through the folders and notebooks. "Hudson claims a love letter exists, proving Michael and Sharon had a relationship. He says Danielle found it before her disappearance. I'm hoping it'll still be here."

"Good thinking. Michael being Danielle's father is the perfect motive for murder."

"Exactly." I surveyed the room. "Look anywhere that might be a good hiding spot. We probably don't have much time."

Grace and I set to work, quickly and quietly rifling through Danielle's dusty things. The folders were a dead end—just school papers and notes. Grace took a peek under the bed, but only found several pairs of shoes, a tennis racquet, and a bunch of tween books Danielle outgrew. After twenty minutes, I started to panic.

"It's going to look weird if we stay much longer," Grace said.

I nodded, wracking my brain for anything that might help. I replayed Hudson's and my interview from the day before. I'd asked him where the letter was, and Hudson had said...

Sleep on it.

Adrenaline slammed through my body. Hudson hadn't just been a smart-ass for no reason—it'd been a clue after all.

"Grace," I hissed. "I think it's in the bed somewhere."

We approached opposite sides of the bed and grabbed the pillows, shoving our hands into the shams and pillowcases, fingers desperately reaching for anything that shouldn't be there. Coming up empty with the pillows, Grace and I flipped the duvet up and lifted the mattress, hands feeling for paper.

"Evie."

I looked across the bed. Grace's eyes had gone wide. She lowered the mattress, and I dropped my end and hastily fixed the covers, my heart racing as I saw the wrinkled envelope in Grace's hand.

"Girls?" Sharon called, followed by the sound of her ascending the stairs. "I don't mean to rush you, but I need to run some errands soon..."

I darted towards Grace and grabbed the envelope, shoving it down the back of my jeans.

"No problem," I said, forcing a smile as Sharon opened the door. "Thanks for everything."

"You're welcome." Sharon surveyed the room, looking for signs of us breaking our agreement not to take anything. I had to remind myself to walk, when instinct told me to sprint. Grace and I grabbed our coats and purses and continued the agonizing walk to the car.

I drove us a few blocks away before pulling over. My hands shook as I pulled the letter from my pants.

"I sure hope this is it, because no way will she let us look again," Grace said as I opened the envelope.

My eyes wildly scanned the yellowed piece of paper. The ink had faded a bit and the handwriting wasn't the most legible, but the short letter was exactly what we hoped it'd be.

Sharon,

I wanted to apologize. We both know that how I acted the other night wasn't me. I understand this is stressful for you, but I hope you realize the tough predicament this puts me in. I wish things didn't have to end this way, but they do. I'll give you as much money you want. All I ask in return is your silence. I want you to know I loved every minute we spent together. Truly.

Yours,

M

CHAPTER TWENTY-ONE

"Hold onto your hat, Penn, because I've got news for you," I yelled across the police station the second I spotted him at his desk, halfway through his lunch. I was too far away, but I was pretty sure I heard him sigh.

"Unless someone tried to kill you again, this can wait."

Ignoring him, I sunk down in the chair beside his desk and eyed the steak sandwich in front of him. "That looks good."

"It's a cheesesteak without the cheese. I can assure you, it's not."

"Sorry to interrupt your moping, but I've got something big." I reached into my purse and pulled out the envelope. Penn looked at me expectantly, but all I said was, "Open it."

Eyes narrowed, he wiped his hands on a crumpled napkin and grabbed the envelope.

I sat on my jittery hands as he pulled out the letter and read it, almost too excited to contain myself. Penn's eyes scanned the entire letter, stopped, then started at the beginning again.

I huffed. *"Well?"*

"Where did you get this?"

"Danielle Livingston's bedroom. Hidden under her mattress." I gave him a wide-eyed, excited look, but his frown refused to budge.

"Why aren't you more excited? This proves that Michael Davenport had a relationship with Sharon—and likely fathered her daughter."

"No," Penn said, looking up at me. "It proves Sharon had a relationship with someone named 'M.'"

"Oh, come *on!*" I reached out my hands and pretended I wanted to strangle him.

"Evie, I'm just telling you what his lawyer's gonna say," Penn said. "Yes, this seems to support your theory, but it's far from a smoking gun. Lots of names start with M. Hell, I could be 'M.'"

I rolled my eyes. "You were seven years old when Danielle was born."

"I'm just making a point. Did you get Sharon to confirm Michael was Danielle's father?"

I broke eye contact. "Uh, well, not exactly..." I felt Penn staring at me, waiting for me to continue. "Fine. I straight-up asked her, and she denied it. But I could tell she was lying!"

He shook his head. "Now that's *really* not going to hold up in court."

I exhaled and slumped back in my chair, deflated like a balloon. "You just love bringing me down, don't you?"

Penn gave me a shrug and took another bite of his sandwich.

"You're my Scully," I continued.

"Your what?"

"From *The X-Files*. You're Dana Scully, certified skeptic and lover of hard facts. I'm Fox Mulder, the steadfast believer. Scully was always poking holes in Mulder's theories."

"I know. I watched the show. I had a big crush on Scully."

I cracked a smile. "And I loved Mulder."

"Looks like we're finally on the same page about something."

Yes, we are, I thought, recalling the cute emails to Grace. I was ready. This couldn't wait any longer.

"Oh, just go ahead and ask me now," I told him. "I'll say yes, so you don't even have to worry."

Penn sipped his soda, and the same confused expression he'd made the night before moved across his face. "This again? Evie, I don't know what you mean. What am I supposed to ask you?"

He really had a good poker face. I guess that's a detective prerequisite.

"Grace spilled the beans about your emails. I know she wasn't supposed to, but give her a break, she's my best friend and she got excited."

Penn parted his lips, then closed them before finally managing, "Grace?"

Now I was getting a little annoyed. "You can drop the act. I know you've been talking to Grace about the best way to ask me out, and I'm telling you to just—"

He choked on his soda, coughing so violently a fellow cop strolled over and gave him a few slaps on the back. I sat there in shock, both at the choking fit and his reaction to the idea of us going out.

When he finally got a hold of himself, Penn looked me dead in the eye. "I have no idea who Grace is."

I frowned, a faint shiver of unease working its way down my back. "She's my friend at the paper. And of course you know who she is! You've been emailing her." His eyes remained confused and vacant. "You asked her about my schedule, what I liked, if she thought I'd want to..." I trailed off as the unease morphed into a tight feeling in my chest. Penn looked at me as if I were insane.

"Uh oh." I dug my phone out of my purse and pulled up the messages she'd forwarded to me. I thrust my phone at him.

"They're from *you*," I insisted, my voice high. "That's your email, I checked."

Penn scrolled through the emails, his eyebrows furrowing deeper by the second. When he glanced up again, he looked positively freaked out.

"Evie," he said slowly, "I swear, I didn't send any of these."

"I feel like the biggest idiot in the world."

I gave Grace a sympathetic look, because I, too, felt like the biggest idiot in the world. Of course the emails weren't from Penn. My gut had told me that from the beginning, but just like the Mulder I was, *I wanted to believe.*

I snuck a peek at Penn, who was hunched over his computer with the tech guy, occupied with figuring out who had hacked him. I was thankful he was so distracted—it meant we couldn't discuss the embarrassing fact that I'd admitted I wanted to go out with him, and as far as I knew, the feeling wasn't mutual.

"I'm so sorry, Evie," Grace said for the third time. "I feel like the shooting is all my fault now. I told some random person what time you'd be leaving for work. They knew exactly when to wait for you."

"It's okay, Grace. The emails looked legit."

Penn got up from his desk and wandered to the table where Grace and I sat. "He's tracing the IP address right now. A few days ago, I got one of those notices that my account was accessed from an unknown device, but it went to spam—I didn't see it." He let out a slow exhale. "Whoever did this had all of Grace's emails auto-forwarded to a special folder, so they never popped into my inbox. I didn't notice anything weird at all."

"I guess that makes two of us," Grace said, still frowning.

"Don't beat yourself up," Penn said. "My password wasn't exactly strong. I made it easy on them."

"So whoever shot at you two probably was the one sending me these emails," Grace said.

"That's my guess," he said. "Seems like they wanted to pump you for as much information about Evie as possible."

"That's just so creepy." Grace hugged herself and shivered.

I glanced at Penn. "Let me guess, you think this was Hudson?"

"Might've crossed my mind."

A defense jumped to my lips, but nothing came out. Truthfully, I was running out of reasons why it *wasn't* Hudson. He'd already proved he liked communicating anonymously over the internet. And after the way Penn had gotten rough with Hudson at Last Call, it wouldn't be a leap to assume he was interested in me. Hudson certainly thought so, since he kept calling Penn my boyfriend.

"But Hudson told me where to find that letter. He helped."

"Did he?" Penn asked. "Or is he distracting you with a wild goose chase so he can kill you?"

"Scully," I muttered under my breath, like a curse.

"Hey, Pennington," the IT guy called from Penn's desk. We both walked over. "I tracked that IP address. Got a location where the emails were sent from."

"And?"

"Davenport Properties."

Penn turned to me and leaned in close. "*Told* you."

I tagged along on Penn's visit to the Davenport offices. If Hudson was indeed the culprit, I needed to see it firsthand. Besides, I didn't trust Penn not to fly off the handle.

Penn resisted rubbing it in my face any further, and the ride was mostly silent. We had almost arrived when Penn decided he wanted to discuss the very last thing I did. "So...you would've said yes?"

I'd been slumped in my seat, staring out the window, and his question startled me so badly I sat bolt upright. "What?"

"Earlier," he said, "you said if I had something to ask you, you'd say yes. And now I know what that something was."

Kill. Me. Now.

My cheeks were on fire. "Don't flatter yourself. So maybe I'd have dinner with you or something if you asked. Big deal."

I felt him looking at me. "We could have dinner," he said casually, like he didn't really care one way or the other. Not exactly the invitation I'd been expecting.

"You're just saying that because you feel weird. Seriously, it's fine. Let's forget about it."

"Okay," Penn said. "Never mind, then."

I watched him from the corner of my eye, attempting to discern if this suggestion was born out of pity, or if he'd actually like to have dinner with me, but again, he wore his unreadable detective expression.

"For the record, I didn't think the emails sounded like you," I said. "But Grace convinced me."

The corners of Penn's mouth twitched. "For the record, I wouldn't email your friend to find out how to ask you out. All I'd have to do is wait for you to show up at my house uninvited again. Easy."

"Ha, ha," I said dryly. "That doesn't mean you wouldn't have to put in any effort, though."

"Of course," he said, sounding surprised I'd suggest otherwise. "I'd lure you in with wine and some barbecue from that place down the street. And I'd probably have a fire going. I don't know, I'm just spitballing."

"You have a fireplace?" I asked, dreamy expression on my face as I pictured the scene he described. "That sounds perfect."

"Well, you know where to find me."

My heart kicked up again, but I didn't have the chance to ask Penn if that was a formal invitation because we arrived at Davenport Properties. He was so eager to nail Hudson he tried to open his door before unlocking the car, twice.

"Damn thing." He finally managed to get out.

"We still don't know it was Hudson," I reminded him as we walked through the sleek glass doors of the office building.

Penn ignored me and marched up to the receptionist, badge out. "I need to see your IT manager. Now."

The receptionist stared at his badge for a few seconds before reaching for the phone and dialing, a nervous expression on her face. "Uh, Dan? The police are here to see you."

Ten minutes later, Penn and I stood around IT manager Dan's desk as he pinned down the exact computer the emails were sent from.

"That IP address belongs to Hudson Davenport's computer."

"*Shit!*" I yelled, making Dan jump.

"Do you need me to show you where..." Dan trailed off when Penn abruptly left the room.

"Thanks, Dan, but we know where he is," I said with a wince.

I hurried after Penn. "I need you to promise that you're going to remain calm," I panted. He was really power-walking, and I almost had to jog to keep up.

"Evie, I think I know how to apprehend a suspect."

"A suspect who's responsible for your shooting *and* is trying to kill me?"

He shot me a look. "What, are you saying I'm some kind of brute who can't control his emotions?"

"Uh..."

Penn didn't have much time to be offended because we reached the small waiting area outside of Michael Davenport's office. Hudson, typing away at his desk next to Michael's admin, looked up at us. He flashed me a big smile, and even after noticing Penn, his expression remained serene—as always, not worried in the least.

"Hudson Davenport," Penn spat, pulling his cuffs off his belt, "you're under arrest for the attempted murder of Evie Hartley."

Hudson sighed and stood, compliantly placing his hands behind his back.

I exchanged a quick, nervous look with Penn, and I could tell he felt it, too—something was off. Nevertheless, Penn wrestled the cuffs onto Hudson.

The admin gaped at us, but as Penn started pushing Hudson towards the door, she snatched up her phone, surely to alert her boss.

"You're just wasting everyone's time," Hudson said.

"You have the right to remain silent," Penn reminded him gruffly.

Hudson shook his head. "Detective Pennington, with all due respect, you really are a complete idiot."

CHAPTER TWENTY-TWO

"Fuck!" Penn yelled. "Fuck, fuck, fuck!"

I stood a safe distance away in the dusky parking lot, bundled up tightly in my coat, as Penn continued to swear while pacing like a caged animal. After what had gone down in interrogation, I knew he'd lose it, but I had never seen him quite this upset before.

"Penn..." I said after the cursing came to a halt. He stopped his pacing and looked at me, anger still clear in his narrowed eyes. I opened my mouth but had no clue what to say.

"He's *guilty*, Evie." He resumed pacing. "And because of his goddamn lawyer and his rich daddy, we can't *prove* it."

"I know you think Hudson is behind all this, and I agree something's not right with him." I spoke slowly, trying not to say the wrong thing. "But if you don't cool it, you're gonna be in some serious shit."

Penn huffed, but he knew I was right. He'd gotten chewed out by his captain thanks to his hasty Hudson arrest, then had been threatened with a suspension if he continued to harass the Davenports.

When we'd walked into the station with a handcuffed-Hudson

hours earlier, Michael Davenport had been ten minutes behind us, lawyer in tow.

"This is over," Michael boldly declared as he and the lawyer burst into the interrogation room where Hudson was being held. "If you release my son now, I won't report you to your superior officer."

Penn laughed. "Your son is a suspect in a drive-by shooting. We have proof he hacked into my email account and posed as me to obtain information to help him *plan* said shooting." He paused to let it sink in. "Impersonating a police officer is a serious offense. Not as serious as attempted murder, though."

I smirked behind the mirror as this news registered on Michael's wrinkled face.

"You have proof these emails were sent from Hudson's personal computer?" Jonathan, the lawyer, asked.

Penn paused before saying, "His work computer."

"His work computer," Jonathan repeated. "Which anyone in the office could've accessed?"

Penn's jaw clenched. "His *password-protected* work computer."

"Everyone in IT has access to employee passwords," Michael said. "I don't see my entire tech department in handcuffs."

"As far as I know, none of your IT people have reason to want Evie Hartley dead," he shot back.

"This is ridiculous," Michael said with a shake of his head. "Hudson is always in meetings with me, away from his desk for long periods of time. Plenty of opportunity for someone else to log on unnoticed."

"I'd like to see the timestamps on these emails," Jonathan cut in. "I'm positive we can prove Hudson didn't send any of them."

An hour later, Jonathan had obtained security camera footage from the hallway outside Michael's office and waiting area, which Michael, Jonathan, Penn and I viewed together. While it didn't give us a view of Hudson's desk, we could see when he'd entered and exited the office. Sure enough, at least two of the emails were sent long after Hudson had been away from his desk.

Upon this revelation, Penn fumed while Michael and Jonathan shared equally smug smirks. But I was more fascinated with the people we *had* seen flitting into the office during our crucial windows of time.

There was Michael's admin, of course. A few other employees bearing folders had filtered in and out quickly. But Michael himself had been present—and so had his daughter.

"Does Samantha come to your office a lot?" I asked Michael innocently.

"Of course," he said. "She's in charge of interior design. She's been popping in constantly to get approval for decorations and furniture for the apartment common areas. My daughter works very hard."

I refrained from rolling my eyes. So Samantha got to play designer while Hudson was stuck as his dad's assistant. Certainly seemed to back up Hudson's claims he wasn't the favorite.

Unfortunately, I couldn't get any more information out of Michael because he and Jonathan stormed into Bristol PD Captain Charles Moreno's office and demanded Hudson's release. After a brief, but very loud, conversation with Penn, their wish was granted, and Michael led his son out of the police station by the scruff of his neck.

In the parking lot, Penn did another tight circle of pacing. "I hate this. I haven't gotten this worked up over a perp in a long time. I want to kill him."

I believed him. "You really need to calm down, Penn," I said, moving closer. "You're getting reckless. One more slip-up, and you'll get suspended, which will really mess things up."

Anger flashed in his eyes again, and this time I could tell it was directed towards me, not Hudson. "You mean it'll mess things up for *you*. Can't have your all-access pass to the investigation ripped away, right?"

"*Seriously?*" I looked up to the sky and put my hands on my hips. "Did you ever think that maybe I don't want you to get in trouble at work? I'm no detective, but it seems like getting suspended is a bad thing." And with that, I stalked across the parking lot towards the sidewalk.

"Wait. Evie!" He hustled after me.

I kept my eyes straight ahead, walking briskly through the cold night air.

"Where are you going?" Penn asked.

"Home."

"Well, let me drive you." He reached for my arm, but I shook him off. "Come on, it's three miles. You can't really intend to walk it."

I batted him away like a fly. "I've got my comfortable boots on. I'm good."

I picked up the pace even more, enjoying hearing him pant as he tried to keep up. Penn might've been all muscle-y under his shirt, but his cardio was no match for a furious woman. The rage propelled me forward—I barely noticed the shin splints.

I wondered how many blocks he'd follow me for, but I was forced to stop and wait for the cross signal at a busy intersection. Penn took the opportunity to block my path.

"Evie," he said softly. I felt him staring at me, so reluctantly, I met his gaze. Damn his sultry eyes.

"You have anger issues," I mumbled.

"I know."

"You need therapy," I went on, crossing my arms.

"I'm in therapy."

I blinked. "What?"

"Yeah. I started going after the..." The word "baby" hung in the air. He cleared his throat. "I was pretty depressed. It helped a little. Well, that, and the Zoloft."

I stood there, blown away by this confession. I'd pegged him as one of those classically angry men who kept everything bottled up and would rather die than talk about his feelings.

"Oh." The light changed, but I remained rooted to the spot.

Penn pointed to the Bristol Diner across the street. It was all lit up and looked nice and warm. "You hungry?"

"Yeah, kind of."

As we went inside and got seated, it hit me that Penn and I had sort of ended up getting our dinner date.

Maybe this disastrous day could be salvaged after all.

"What do you know about Michael?" I asked Penn after we'd gotten our food: a cheeseburger for me, a hot turkey sandwich for him, and a big basket of fries to split.

"I know he's a dick," he said.

I rolled my eyes. "Anything I don't already know?"

"He owns a lot of apartment complexes," Penn said as he cut into his sandwich. "Both here and over in Tennessee." He took a bite and swallowed. "I think he owns your building, actually."

"Not sure if I like that."

"He and his wife do a lot of charity work," Penn continued. "Volunteering, donating to the homeless shelter..."

"If he really wanted to help the homeless, he could offer them some of those brand-new apartments."

Penn snorted. "But then he might have one less giant pile of money to count."

"So Michael's just interested in a good photo op." I took a huge bite of my burger. "The Livingstons said the same thing when I asked about the reward he offered for information on Danielle."

"You know, if he killed Danielle, offering the reward would've been a smart move," Penn said. "Who'd suspect the guy who was offering a ton of cash to find the missing girl?"

"Michael would've had plenty of opportunities to use Hudson's computer too." I frowned as I remembered one major problem. "But it doesn't quite add up. Michael doesn't know either of us. How would he know..." I cleared my throat and grabbed a few fries, swirling one in ketchup, no clue how to phrase my question.

"How would Michael know to take the date angle?"

"Yes," I said, relieved Penn found the least awkward way to say that. I'd been thinking something along the lines of, "How would Michael know we're currently in a weird, flirty tension-filled situation?"

"That's a good question," he said. "You're right. It doesn't fit."

"Which leaves us with Samantha" I said.

"You're joking."

I shot him a look. "Why? Because she's a *girl,* and girls can't kill?"

"While I will say the statistics aren't on your side," Penn said, "I really meant that Samantha just doesn't seem like a killer to me. She's friendly with Audrey. I've met her a few times."

"People who don't seem like murderers end up killing people all the time. And meeting her a few times doesn't mean you know her."

"Okay, well, Audrey knows her," Penn said. "And clearly, she doesn't think she's a murderer."

I frowned and thought back to when Audrey told me, point-blank, she didn't think Samantha killed Danielle.

"Think about it," I said. "Samantha would have easy access to Hudson's computer too."

"What about the content of the emails?" he asked. "Samantha would be just as clueless as Michael."

I shifted uncomfortably in the booth. Penn noticed and raised an eyebrow, a silent question.

"It's...possible Samantha could know," I said.

"How?"

I toyed with my silverware, delaying the inevitable. "This is going to sound embarrassing."

Now Penn looked amused. "Just tell me."

Lord, help me now.

"Well, after Audrey and I met with Samantha for drinks, you sort of came up." I paused, and Penn stared at me. "And I don't know why she said this, but Audrey told me if I were interested in you, I had her blessing."

"Oh."

"Which is so ridiculous," I said hurriedly, once again, shooting myself in the foot. "But anyway, it's possible she could've mentioned us to Samantha, inspiring her to send those emails."

"I see." Penn shoved some fries into his mouth. Was he upset because I claimed to be uninterested in him? Or was he embarrassed that his ex-wife was trying to meddle in his love life?

"I mean, I think she's just convinced there's something going on because I quote you a lot in my stories," I continued, filling the heavy silence. "I haven't implied anything or..."

Jesus, Evie, stop talking!

Ignoring my nervous rambling, Penn said, "Say Samantha sent the emails. Yes, she could know or find out Hudson's computer password. But what about my email password?"

I thought for a minute. "What was your password?"

He cleared his throat. "Uh, well, I already mentioned how it wasn't that strong..."

"Please tell me it wasn't 'one, two, three, four.'"

"Of course not," he said, irritated. "It was my old dog's name. Archer."

I exhaled loudly. "Your dog's name. Which Samantha might know?"

Penn winced. "Yeah. She came to the house a few times over the years. She knew him."

"I'm convinced," I declared. "The emails were from Samantha. She's the one trying to kill me."

"Well, hang on," Penn said. "Just because she sent the emails, doesn't mean she's behind it all. The whole family could be in on it."

"That's exactly what Hudson said."

Penn huffed and shook his head. "If Samantha sent the emails, but didn't do anything else, that makes Hudson's alibis meaningless." I watched his fists clench more tightly around his fork and knife.

"Promise me you won't kill him," I joked.

Penn flopped back in the booth and gave me a begrudging, "I won't."

I wasn't convinced, but my buzzing phone distracted me. *Emma* popped up on the screen.

"Sorry, I'd better get this," I told Penn. He gave me a nod and polished off his sandwich.

"Hey, is everything okay?" I asked.

"I was calling to ask *you* that, silly," my sister yelled in my ear.

"Well, I'm fine."

"I don't like that you're down there all by yourself with this going on," Emma continued, still talking very loudly. I guessed she was drunk. "I'm with Elise, and we think we should come stay with you until this blows over."

"Hi, Evie!" Elise shouted from the background.

Yes. If Elise was there, so was booze.

"That's so sweet of you to offer," I said, shooting Penn a panicked look. "But it's not necessary. I'm safe."

"But you're all *alone*," Emma insisted.

"I'm not. Penn is keeping me company."

She gasped. "Is that the cop? Are you two—"

"No!" I said, stopping that train of thought. "We are not."

"Let me talk to him," she said.

I groaned. "I don't think..."

"As your big sister, it's my job to make sure you're safe. If you don't let me talk to him, we're coming *right now*."

She said it so loudly I had to pull the phone away from my ear. Penn raised an eyebrow, bemused smile on his face. I wanted to mention the irony of Emma worrying about my safety, when she'd been the one who helped me sneak out of the house to go on dates and gave me my first vodka cranberry when I was seventeen, but I refrained.

I held the phone out to Penn. "My sister would like to talk to you."

"Hello?" He listened to Emma babble for a while before chuckling and lowering the phone. "She just asked for my badge number."

"Of course she did."

Emma went on some more.

"Don't worry," Penn said, looking up at me again. "I'll keep an eye on Evie. You don't need to come all the way down here."

I gave him a grateful smile and mouthed, "Thank you."

The conversation lasted a bit longer. I couldn't make out what

Emma was saying, but when Penn said, "Uh, yeah, I'm single..." I snatched the phone out of his hand.

"You are ridiculous," I told her.

"Oh my God, Evie, do all the men there sound like that?" Emma asked dreamily. "If you don't want him..."

"I'm hanging up now."

"Wait!" Elise yelled from the background, making me pull the phone from my ear again. "I want to talk to the hot cop!"

"Goodbye!" I ended the call and tossed my phone into my purse. "Sorry about them," I told Penn with a wince. "They're embarrassing."

"This hot cop thinks they sound fun," Penn said with a giant grin.

I put my face in my hands. "Do you have a sister?"

"A brother." Penn paused. "Maybe we can set him up with Emma."

I almost died yesterday.

I sat cross-legged on my couch, staring at this one sentence on my laptop screen. I'd written a news piece on the drive-by, but I hadn't yet updated *Evie Investigates*. I normally found these easy to write, my fingers flying across the keyboard, but tonight, I was stuck.

Writing about my confrontation with Roger had been only mildly traumatizing—mostly, it'd been thrilling, like starring in my very own action movie.

This was entirely different. When I thought about the shooting, I still heard the bangs from the gun and pictured Penn's blood-stained shirt. It made me queasy to think about how I'd been inches away from dying, and if Penn hadn't been there, I *would've* died.

Drumming my fingers lightly on my keyboard, I willed the right words to come. I wanted to be honest with my readers, but I also didn't want to taunt the shooter into a follow-up attack. For my own peace of mind, I told myself they'd wanted to rattle me, nothing more. It'd been two days since the incident, with no signs of a second attempt on my life.

"I'm sure they won't come back," I said to Wally. "Right?"

He let out a short *meow*.

I leaned my head back against the couch and pondered who my would-be assassin might be. Despite what Penn thought, I knew it wasn't Hudson. He had not one, but two exonerating alibis. He'd have to be some sort of time-traveling criminal mastermind to pull that off.

In my mind, it was down to two. Michael and Samantha. But I still couldn't be sure which. I slowly managed to finish a few paragraphs.

I almost died yesterday. It's a weird thing to think about. Plenty of journalists put their lives on the line for their jobs, but I'm not reporting from a war-torn country or attempting to unravel a government conspiracy. I'm a crime beat reporter in Bristol, Virginia. Threats on my life shouldn't be an expected occupational hazard, and they weren't— until I started looking into Danielle Livingston's disappearance.

Something bad happened to Danielle, that much is clear now. And whoever was responsible wants me to stop looking for them. I won't allow myself to be terrorized.

I thought that was good enough for now, and I could flesh out the rest in the morning. It'd been a long, frustrating day, and I just wanted to crawl into bed. I even managed to sleep soundly, which made the buzzing of my phone the next morning all the more jarring.

"Hello?" I mumbled, eyes still not open.

"Evie?" I didn't immediately recognize the voice. "It's Tom Delaney."

"Tom?" I pushed myself up, my heart racing. Why was Delaney calling me at seven-thirty in the morning? "What's wrong?"

"There's something I need to talk to you about," Delaney said, voice all business. "Hudson Davenport came in this morning to report an assault. He's all beat up."

"*What?*"

Before I could fully panic, Delaney confirmed my worst fear. "Evie, he said it was Marcus. Hudson said Marcus attacked him."

CHAPTER TWENTY-THREE

"WHERE IS HE?"

I'd burst into the police station, out of breath as I wildly scanned the bullpen, looking for Penn. The only familiar face was Delaney's.

"He's in with Moreno now." He gestured down the hall towards the interrogation rooms.

"*What?*" Interrogation with the *captain* of the Bristol Police? "Is he under arrest?"

"Well, no." Delaney broke eye contact. "Right now, it's Hudson's word against his."

"He didn't do it...right?" I dreaded his response.

"That's what he says." Relief rushed through me. "But he's got no alibi. Marcus said he was home alone all night."

I cringed. "That's bad, isn't it?"

"Well, again, it's he said/he said, but it sure would help if someone could verify his whereabouts."

I didn't even think before blurting, "He was with me all night."

Delaney opened his mouth, closed it, then opened it again. "He was."

"Yep," I said. "He couldn't have attacked Hudson. He was with me all night, then left early this morning."

Delaney knew I was full of shit. "Why didn't Marcus mention that, then?"

"I don't know. He was probably embarrassed. You saw how he acted last time we got caught together."

Delaney considered this, and uncertainty spread across his round face.

"We had dinner at the diner last night." I fished out the receipt from the bottom of my purse and slapped it into Delaney's hand—my irrefutable proof, that only proved I had dinner with *someone*. "And then we went back to my place."

Delaney eyed the receipt, his forehead scrunched up. "And what did you do back at your place?" He spoke like he was humoring a child's active imagination.

"You want a diagram?" I huffed.

"Look, Evie, I know you want to help Marcus, and I do, too. But if you're lying, it's just going to make things worse."

"I'm not lying," I lied.

Delaney considered this, the frown still on his face. "Okay, then. I'll talk to Moreno."

He headed down the hall and waved Captain Moreno out of the interrogation room. They briefly conferred before heading towards the captain's office. I took the opportunity to slip into the room. Penn was hunched over the table, head propped up by his hand, but at the sound of my entrance, he sat up straight.

"What are you doing here?"

I ignored him. "Let me see your hands."

"What?"

I grabbed Penn's right hand off the metal table and examined it closely, tracing his knuckles with my fingertips, searching for any cracks in his skin or ugly purple bruising.

"I'm a lefty," he grumbled.

I dropped that hand and picked up his left. After performing a similar exam, I almost collapsed with relief.

"You didn't do it," I said. "Thank *God*."

Penn gaped at me. "Did you actually think I'd beat up Hudson?"

"I mean, you did threaten to kill him last night," I said. "I just had to make sure. I'm kind of sticking my neck out for you."

His jaw clenched. "What do you mean?"

"I'm your alibi," I said. "Delaney said you didn't have one, so I told him you stayed over at my place again."

"*Shit*, Evie, why would you do that?" he yelled.

I blinked at him. This wasn't the grateful how-can-I-ever-repay-you reaction I'd been expecting.

"Because I didn't want to see you in handcuffs! The Davenports obviously have it out for you now. This is bad."

"What's bad is that you lied to the police, and you just admitted it! I could arrest you."

"Oh, you wouldn't," I said, waving my hand dismissively.

"Jesus," he moaned, face in his hands again. "Delaney's going to think we're *together* now. He's still tormenting me about last time."

I narrowed my eyes. "Yes, it must be so embarrassing to have your buddy think you're getting laid."

While Penn tried to come up with a good retort, I noticed the photographs scattered across the table. I leaned down and stared at Hudson's face, somehow still smug despite his fresh injuries. He had a split lower lip, though really the injury just made his mouth look bee-stung and more kissable. One of his eyes was bruised and swollen half-shut, but otherwise, he looked a-okay.

"Son of a bitch! This is a total set-up." I held up the picture in front of Penn. "He probably took two little punches. He's practically *smiling*."

"Does this mean you're finally on the Hudson Did It train?" Penn asked.

I chewed on my lower lip. I didn't want to encourage Penn's Hudson obsession—and I also didn't want to admit he might be right.

Penn had been acting like a lunatic; I wasn't going to give him the satisfaction.

"I can see it in your eyes," Penn said. "Doubt. You think Hudson's been playing you. Distracting you."

I didn't have a chance to answer because the door burst open, Delaney and Moreno making their reentrance.

"Miss Hartley," Moreno said gruffly. "You're not supposed to be in here."

I straightened, coming to my full five feet, six inches. "Well, like I was telling Detective Delaney, there's been some terrible mistake. Detective Pennington was with me all night, so he couldn't have hurt Hudson."

Moreno studied me the same suspicious way Delaney had. "Yes, I heard." I waited for him to say more, but he didn't.

"That means you can let him go, right?" I asked.

Moreno frowned beneath his bushy mustache. He turned to Penn. "I'm sorry, Pennington, but until we get this sorted out, I'm suspending you."

Penn stood, and his voice came out as a low growl. "You can't be serious."

"Yesterday's stunt was bad enough," Moreno said. "And false accusation or not, I don't need the Davenports raising hell in the press." His eyes flicked back to me. "Not to mention, this case is obviously too personal for you. Not only were you shot, and refused to take recovery time, but you're involved with this perp's target. It's clouding your judgment."

Penn's jaw clenched and his lips parted, about to tell Moreno he and I were not involved—but that admission would conveniently destroy his alibi and get me in trouble. So he said nothing.

"Fine." He fumbled with the holster at his hip before slapping his gun onto the table. He reached into his pocket and did the same thing with his badge. Then he stormed out.

"Um..." I exchanged a bewildered look with Delaney. "Bye." And then I scurried after Penn, the heels of my boots clacking loudly on the asphalt of the parking lot. He'd almost made it to his car by the time I caught up to him.

"Stop following me. I'm fine," he yelled, not bothering to turn around.

"Really? You don't seem fine."

He wrenched open his car door and turned to look at me. I could see the hurt he was trying to mask with anger.

"Look, I know this sucks," I said gently. "But it'll get sorted out. Try not to get too upset."

"Like you'd be totally calm if you suddenly lost your blog," he said, still an edge to his voice.

"I wouldn't, but I wouldn't shut you out either." Cautiously, I reached out and grabbed Penn's hands. They were cold and a little shaky. "Come on. Let's go get coffee or something and figure out our next move."

He considered this, eyes avoiding mine, but he didn't try to pull away from my touch.

"You don't have to deal with this alone."

After a few more seconds, he shook his head and dropped my hands. "I do." He started to climb into his car.

"Penn, just—"

"Jesus, stop pestering me! Could you maybe take a hint and leave me alone for five minutes? Are you even capable of doing that?"

I blinked, and I imagined the hurt expression on my face was comparable to a kicked puppy. Stuffing those feelings down and narrowing my eyes, I said, "Fine. Call me when you're done with your little temper tantrum."

And then I stormed over to my car and sped off towards the *Daily News* building. How dare he get mad at me when he was the one who'd screwed everything up with his vendetta against Hudson? I was so sick of Penn's outbursts. Without fail, every time I felt us growing closer—his visits to my apartment, his chauffeuring me around, us getting dinner together—he would lash out and push me away again. It was maddening.

That didn't mean I was going to let Hudson get away with framing him, though.

He picked up on the second ring. "Evie! I figured I'd be hearing from you soon."

"What the hell is your problem?" I yelled into my phone. "You got Pennington suspended!"

"Really? That was fast."

"This isn't a *joke*, Hudson! Tell me one good reason I shouldn't think you killed Danielle. Because right now, it looks like you're trying to get rid of anyone looking into her disappearance. You've been bullshitting me this entire time, haven't you?"

"Okay, I get why you're upset," he said, "but Pennington was a necessary sacrifice. You'll see."

"A *necessary sacrifice*?" I sounded hysterical.

"Meet me for lunch and I'll explain. Twelve-thirty. The deli by the office."

I didn't respond.

"Come on, Evie. I'm on your side. Will you meet me?"

"Fine," I said, unable to resist the bait.

I could practically see the smile on his face. "It's a date."

The deli by the office turned out to be attached to Davenport Properties, and based on the number of sharply dressed, frowning people hustling around the eatery with trays of food, it was a popular lunch spot for Michael's employees.

I spotted Hudson at a small table by the display case filled with sandwiches. He looked just as put together as the other times I'd seen him in work attire—crisp, expensive-looking dress shirt and perfectly pressed trousers—but today, his appearance was slightly marred by his facial injuries. As I got closer, they looked even milder than in the photos taken at the police station. The swelling had gone down, and his bruised eye was now almost totally open.

I remained silent as I took the seat across from him.

"Not hungry?" Hudson asked when he saw I had no food.

"The line is crazy. And I'd rather just get what I came for."

"That sounds kind of dirty," he said with a grin. "But what do you want? I get to skip the line. Perks of being the boss's son and all."

I shook my head, frustrated. "Anything. I don't care."

"Hey, Noreen!" Hudson shouted to the woman behind the counter. "Can we get another turkey club over here for my friend?"

"Sure thing, sweetie," the older woman said with a genuine smile.

"Gross," I mumbled, though seconds later, a delicious-looking sandwich was set in front of me, along with a bag of chips, a pickle, and an iced tea.

"Huh," I said as I picked at the food. "Thanks."

"You know I'd love to have a nice long lunch with you, Evie, but unfortunately, I've only got fifteen minutes." Hudson checked his watch. "Actually, we're down to eleven now."

"You only get fifteen minutes for lunch? But you're the *boss's son*."

He laughed dryly. "Everyone gets fifteen minutes. Dad runs a tight ship." I looked around one more time at the bustling employees, packing away their food as quickly as Hudson was. Yeesh. Sometimes Grace and I would stretch lunches out to two hours, because if you weren't in the newsroom, Shelly assumed you were on assignment.

"It's amazing how quickly your face healed," I said, getting down to business. "Weird that Pennington went so easy on you considering he hates your guts."

Hudson smirked as best he could with his split lip. "Guess I'm just lucky."

I shook my head in disgust. "What really happened?"

"I might've picked a teensy fight with some drunk dude at Last Call," Hudson said as he took a small bite of his turkey club. "Guy had about fifty pounds on me, but a lousy right hook. I was worried I wouldn't bruise at all. What a waste that would've been."

"*Why* would you frame Pennington?" I asked. "He's only going to come after you harder now. He's *pissed*."

"Pissed, but suspended. That's important. He can't do anything meaningful without his badge."

"I thought you wanted justice for Danielle."

"I do," he insisted.

"Well, getting the cop on her case *canned* is a funny way to show it."

Hudson dropped his sandwich, his green eyes boring into mine. "Please, Evie. Just think for a minute. Dad got suspicious the second you turned up in his office to ask about Danielle. It only got worse when he found out I was Pennington's prime suspect in the shooting. He started to panic. And Dad is very good at damage control, if you know what I mean."

I stared at him for a moment. "So your dad wanted Pennington out of the way." I thought back to how a furious Michael Davenport stormed into Moreno's office to report Penn. I could picture him taking things too far to get even. A guy like that was used to getting what he wanted.

"He did," Hudson said. "And I think you can imagine how Dad might've tried to accomplish that if left to his own devices. So I came up with this idea." He pointed to his face. "I get to look like the loyal son, *and* I make sure your boyfriend stays alive. You really should be thanking me."

Damn it. *Damn* it. I had no idea what to believe. I normally had a good read on people; I could tell who was phony, or how to best pull a story out of them. But Hudson? My mind was blank. My gut told me he was dangerous, but so far, he'd helped me. More than once.

Sensing my hesitation, Hudson continued. "I swear, I'm not your enemy, Evie. But I can't be too obvious about helping you, or Dad will find out. Then I'm in a heap of trouble. Like, cut-out-of-the-will-or-turn-up-mysteriously-dead trouble." He paused as he polished off his chips. "Did you find the love letter?"

"I did. Though it's only signed 'M,' and Sharon Livingston won't confirm she had a relationship with Michael. Pennington said it's useless."

Hudson shrugged. "Not really my problem, is it? I did my part by telling you where to look. Now you're supposed to do your Nancy Drew thing."

I took a breath, struggling to maintain my patience. "The thing is, Hudson, you're helping...but not enough. And with Pennington sidelined, my police access is severely cut off. I'm grasping at straws here."

Glancing at his watch once more, Hudson leaned back in his seat, done with his lunch now. "Five minutes. Tell me exactly what you need, and I'll see what I can do."

I rolled my eyes, but nevertheless responded. "I need access to your family. I need to find the black car the shooter was driving—preferably, the gun they used too. I need straight answers from your father and sister about Danielle; I need to figure out if your mother played a role in any of this." I paused. "And I *really* need to find those DNA results so I can prove your dad is Danielle's too."

Hudson whistled. "That is a *tall* order, hon, I'm not gonna lie." A smile crept to his lips. "But you might be in luck. The annual Davenport holiday party is this Saturday. It'll be stuffy and insufferable as always—filled with Dad's corporate buddies all kissing each other's asses." He finished the dregs of his iced tea. "But it's always hosted at the Davenport house. My entire family will be there." His eyes flashed as they always did when he had an evil thought. Or, at least, that's what I told myself. "You could be my date, if you want."

I had a weird, sickly feeling in my stomach, but I ignored it. "Your date? Won't that look a bit suspicious? We want your dad to think you're *not* helping me."

"That's the beauty of it, though. If Dad thinks there's something going on between us, he'll assume I've turned you over to our side. I mean, who'd be crazy enough to go out with a murder suspect?"

"We are not *going out*," I said, shaking my head. "What exactly would being your date entail?"

"Nothing unsavory, I promise. I'll get to show up to this horrendous party with a gorgeous girl on my arm. That's all I need out of it."

"Well, good," I said, trying to inject confidence into my upcoming lie. "Because, as you know, I'm involved."

He laughed. "With Pennington? Yeah, right. It's obvious you aren't together. I can tell by the way he looks at you."

"How does he look at me?"

"Like he's a man dying of thirst, and you're a tall glass of ice-cold water he can't drink," Hudson said easily.

That was descriptive. My cheeks heated, but before I could come up with a witty response, Hudson jumped up from his chair.

"Sorry. Time's up." He gathered the trash onto his tray. "So was that a yes? Are you in?"

This was a bad idea; I could already tell. Every alarm bell was going off in my head—but the chance to spend an evening around the Davenports in their own home was too good to pass up.

"I'm in."

"Excellent. Pick you up at seven." And then with a wink, he vanished.

CHAPTER TWENTY-FOUR

"Evie? Did you hear a word I just said?"

I gave Grace a sheepish look over the top of my monitor. "I might've tuned out the last part a bit."

"Need I remind you that you're the one who asked me to give you a crash course on all things Davenport Properties?"

"I know, I know." I turned away from my computer and gave Grace my full attention. "I've just got a lot on my mind." My eyes darted to my phone. "Do you think I should check on Penn? It's been twenty-four hours now. I'm worried he might drink himself into a coma."

I was still upset by how he'd reacted after the suspension, and I was prepared to go full silent treatment on him, but I couldn't stop the worry from creeping in. He was already struggling with what had been going on in his personal life, and without his job to distract him, he might be in a dark place.

"I think he'll reach out when he's ready," Grace said. "He said he needed time alone, right? All you can do is give it to him."

I gave her a weak nod. This shouldn't affect me so much—we were barely even friends. Were we friends? It was hard to tell.

Gnat.

Leech.

Could you maybe take a hint and leave me alone?

"Okay, I'm focused," I said. "The Bristol Ridge apartments are Michael's fifth complex in the area."

"Yes. We've got Bristol Towers, Bristol Gardens, Bristol Hollow, and last but not least, your home sweet home, Bristol Hills."

I shuddered. "I *really* don't like that Michael owns my building."

"It gets creepier," Grace said, eyes trained on her computer. "Bristol Hills was the complex being built when Danielle went missing."

I sat up straighter. "That's right. David Livingston mentioned that he thought Michael offered the reward for Danielle to get some free press about the new apartments."

"Based on these old articles I dug up, Bristol Hills was Michael's big project," Grace said. "Before that, Davenport Properties was a lot smaller, and it focused on renovating old houses and renting them out. This was Michael's first apartment complex, and he had a lot invested in it. Bristol Hills basically turned DP into an empire."

"Someone needs to tell Emperor Davenport that his building has shitty water pressure," I said dryly.

"Imagine this. You're Michael Davenport. You've invested almost everything into this apartment complex. Things are going well. Then, a teenage girl comes out of the woodwork with DNA results proving you fathered her while happily married to your pregnant wife."

I raised my eyebrows. "I would do everything I could to make sure those results didn't see the light of day."

"Would you kill for it?"

"I wouldn't. But something tells me Michael Davenport might." I thought back to my conversation with Hudson at lunch—how he implied he'd done Penn a favor by getting him suspended. "Hudson made it seem like Michael is...dangerous."

"You sure this party is a good idea, then?" Grace asked, her forehead creased with worry. "What if Hudson's leading you into a trap?"

"I might be stupid, but I sort of trust Hudson."

"I thought you said he was creepy," Grace said.

"*Creepy*, as in he's always undressing me with his eyes. Not psychotic like a murderer."

"Well, that first one's not great either," she pointed out. "Be careful, okay?"

"I know how to handle guys like this. I can handle Hudson."

Sorry for the radio silence, folks, but unfortunately, my investigation has stalled a bit. Good news: No one's tried to kill me again. Bad news: The well of police information has run temporarily dry, due to some complicated circumstances which I can't get into.

Not to worry! I never stay down for long, and I always have a backup plan. I'll be going into sleuth-mode soon, meaning I might not be able to give out a lot of details about what I uncover—but I promise, it'll be worth the wait.

I put together a half-assed *Evie Investigates* post, to appease both Shelly and anxious readers bombarding me with tweets asking for an update, and finished getting ready. Staring at my reflection in the mirror, I took a few deep breaths, trying to calm my nerves. I picked up the mascara and swiped a few coats onto my light lashes, then applied a warm red lipstick—the perfect holiday shade.

I was decked out in my best festive attire—a velvet green dress, shimmery tights, and gold jingle-bell earrings. Going a little overboard couldn't hurt. I wanted Michael Davenport to see me as Nonthreatening Girl Reporter, and apparently that meant dressing as a Christmas ornament.

I was slipping on my shoes when my phone buzzed. Assuming it was Hudson, my heart sped up. Go time. I hobbled closer to my phone and almost tripped when I saw the screen.

"You're alive," I said cautiously, my heart still racing even though it wasn't Hudson.

"Hey. Yeah." A throat clearing. "Everything okay? No more death threats?"

"So far, so good. How are you holding up?"

Penn sighed. "I'm a little better. Delaney's keeping me in the loop, so that helps. Hudson dropped the charges, but Moreno still wants me to take some time."

"Hudson admitted he got into a bar fight. He claims getting you suspended was to save you from Michael's wrath—whatever that may be."

He snorted. "I'm sure. So you talked to Hudson?"

I cringed. "Well, I had to give him hell for falsely accusing you."

"I wish I had done it," he said. "Anyway. I'm sorry I snapped."

"It's okay." It wasn't really, but Penn didn't owe me anything. He wasn't my boyfriend; he wasn't my pal. We were colleagues, essentially —nothing more.

A few seconds of silence stretched between us. I opened my mouth to fill it, but my phone buzzed with a text.

Hey, baby, your date's here :)

"Hey, I have to go," I told Penn, my voice a little shaky. "I have plans. With Grace. Girls' night." I stood in agony for a few seconds, waiting for him to call out my lie. Going out socially in the middle of an investigation I've been obsessed with? A likely story.

"Oh, okay," he said. "Have fun."

We said our goodbyes, and I wrestled on my coat, the nerves coming back in a dizzying wave. Lying to Penn might've been a mistake, but I couldn't risk him barging into the Davenports' party, getting me kicked out *and* getting himself arrested for real.

The instant I set foot outside my building, I spotted Hudson. He was hard to miss in his cherry-red Jaguar, the engine purring loudly as he idled. Something about the sound felt eerily familiar. When he flicked his headlights, I realized I'd been staring for too long, so I clacked over to him and climbed into the passenger's seat.

Hudson let out a low whistle as I buckled up. "So your hair *does* come out of that ponytail. Can't wait until you ditch the coat."

I rolled my eyes. "Keep it up, and the coat won't be the only thing I'm ditching."

"Nah." Hudson put the car in drive. "You need me tonight, and you know it."

Unfortunately, I did need him. Instead of a snarky remark, I sat back and stayed quiet as Hudson zoomed down the street, the engine roaring whenever he accelerated.

"Nice car," I shouted. "Is this what all executive assistants drive?"

Hudson smiled. "Gift from Dad. This was after I tried to quit for the third—no, wait—*fourth* time."

"So Michael's strategy is to buy his kids' love."

"More like loyalty. Dad doesn't give a damn about love."

I filed away this information about Michael in my head, but the sound of the engine kept gnawing at me. "You know, this car sounds an awful lot like the one the shooter drove."

"You said that car was black. Last I checked, this one's red."

"How long has it been red?" I was already wondering if I could scrape off some paint to see if there was another color underneath.

Hudson looked at me and grinned. "Forever, Evie."

We settled into a comfortable silence for a few minutes, and I allowed myself to relax in my seat and enjoy the drive. I hated to admit that, besides the obnoxious engine, this was a *sweet* ride. It felt like we were gliding across the Bristol streets, which were typically a pothole minefield.

"You never told me where you were," I said, breaking the silence. "The night Danielle went missing."

"You still don't trust me, huh?"

"I trust you enough to get in a car with you," I pointed out.

"True. Say I *was* the one trying to kill you. I could easily do that right now." Hudson pressed the gas harder, and the glowing speedometer started inching towards sixty. "I could crash the car right now, speeding through that busy intersection."

The engine roared louder, and my heart dropped into my stomach as I looked through the windshield and saw a red light coming up, fast.

"Hudson, cut it out." I tried not to let my nervousness show.

"Though you'd likely survive that," he said, ignoring me. "The Jag's got a ton of airbags. And I wouldn't want to kill myself in the process, so my best bet would be you going through the windshield."

Lightning fast, Hudson reached across the console and hit the release button at my hip. My seatbelt slid across my body back into the side of the car. We were mere feet away from the intersection now, a steady stream of Saturday night traffic making it extremely likely we'd hit someone.

"What the *fuck* is wrong with you?" I fumbled to redo my seatbelt, but it was too late. We zoomed under the red light. I closed my eyes and braced for impact.

The deafening squeal of the brakes broke through the roar of the engine as we skidded to a halt. I pitched forward in my seat, my limp, unsecured seatbelt flapping around uselessly. I tried and failed to grab onto something, and right as I was positive I'd go slamming face-first into the dashboard, a strong arm shot out across my chest and pinned me back in my seat.

I slowly opened my scrunched-shut eyes. We'd ended up in the middle of the crosswalk—not the intersection. Entire body shaking, I turned to look at Hudson, who retracted his arm. My hand reached for the door handle, but it wouldn't budge.

"Let. Me. Out," I demanded, teeth clenched. "Right now."

"Lighten up, Evie." The light turned green, and he cruised through the intersection casually, like he hadn't just almost intentionally wrecked the car. "I wasn't going to let anything happen to you. I wanted to show you that you *can* trust me."

I scrambled to secure my seatbelt and placed my hand firmly over the button so he couldn't touch it again. "You could've *killed* me!"

"Yeah, and I didn't."

"You *bastard*." I hit him on the arm repeatedly. "I'm serious. Let me out of this car right now!"

"Don't get all hysterical on me. You know you're dying to go to the party." He let out a chuckle. "Ha. Dying."

"You're disgusting," I muttered, my heart still doing acrobatics in my chest.

Hudson scrubbed his hand over his face. "Well, we can't be showing up to the party in a fight. Our dating cover story won't look believable."

I crossed my arms and stared straight ahead at the road, determined to sit in silence.

"I was seeing some of my high school friends," Hudson said. "The night Danielle went missing. I was home on winter break and meeting up with the guys. Just hanging out, drinking. I lost track of time. Drank a lot. Danielle and I were supposed to meet at my house around eight. I was about an hour late. She'd been texting me to hurry." He swallowed audibly. "By the time I got home, she was gone. I didn't think much of it at first. And when she didn't respond to my texts, I just assumed she was pissed."

"So she could've opened the results without you."

"It'd be a good bet," he said. "I'm sure she was itching to open them."

"If Danielle read those results at your house..." My mind spun with all the possibilities. Danielle discovering Michael was her father in a house full of Davenports, sans her one true ally, could be a recipe for disaster.

"...it might've gotten ugly," Hudson said, knowing where my mind had gone.

Hudson took a turn down a quiet residential street. The gigantic, lit-up home at the end of the cul-de-sac had to be the Davenport house.

"When you got home that night, did you notice anything off?" I asked, knowing our chance to speak candidly was slipping away by the second. "Was everyone home?"

"Samantha was the only one home. I didn't even ask where Mom and Dad were—I was relieved they weren't there to catch me coming home drunk." Hudson turned into the driveway, a detached three-car garage straight ahead, in addition to the two-car one built into the side of the house. He hit a button, and the middle door on the detached began to open.

"I asked about Danielle, and Sam said she left not too long ago. So I just went upstairs and passed out in bed. I figured I'd make it up to her the next day."

As Hudson eased the Jaguar into the garage, my gaze was still locked on him. His eyes were doing that glittery, dancing thing again. I could feel him holding out on me—like he was preparing to drop a bomb.

"We're here," Hudson said with a big smile. "Stay put. I'll get your door."

"What a gentleman." I rolled my eyes, fidgeting in my seat as I waited for Hudson to come around. He opened my door with a flourish and a little bow, nearly making me crack a smile, but I held firm. Eyes looking everywhere except at him, I stepped out of the car.

And stood face to face with a Jaguar nearly identical to Hudson's.

"Whose car is that?" I asked, my voice high-pitched.

"This one?" He jabbed his thumb towards it. "Well, you remember how I said Samantha gets jealous. And when Dad bought me the Jag, she threw a fit about how unfair it was. So naturally, he got her the same exact car." He paused for dramatic effect. "Except Sam wanted black."

CHAPTER TWENTY-FIVE

"HUDSON, SOMETIMES I THINK YOU KNOW EXACTLY WHAT happened to Danielle, but you get some sick satisfaction out of watching me put the pieces together."

"Well, I'm certainly enjoying watching this," he said.

I glared at Hudson from the cold garage floor, where I was currently crawling around, snapping photos from every possible angle. I'd probably flashed him at some point, but I didn't care. This discovery had flooded me with adrenaline. Of course, there was no way to prove to the police this was the same black car the shooter drove, but I was convinced. There even was an M and 7 on the plate. This was the car.

When I'd finished with my pictures, I accepted Hudson's hand, and he helped me to my feet. I brushed off the dust and dirt on my knees, but my crawling had earned me a hole in my tights.

"When the police were questioning you about the shooting, you knew they were looking for a loud, black car," I said, annoyed. "And yet, you didn't share that your sister drove one?"

Hudson grinned. "Nobody asked. And hey, I'm no rat."

I shook my head. He was the rattiest rat I knew.

"I mean, I don't know her, but this car doesn't really scream Samantha." I put my hands on my hips. "It's kind of a guy's car."

Hudson put his arm around my shoulders and steered me outside into the cold night air. "Oh, she hates this car. Like I said, she only wanted it because I had it. That's why it collects dust in the garage. Dad takes it out every now and then."

I huffed. "So once again, anyone in your family could've driven it and shot at me?"

"Except me," he said. "Come on, let's go inside. Maybe by the end of the evening you'll figure out which of my fucked-up family members is the one whodunnit."

Hudson and I crossed the wide driveway towards the stone path leading to the front door, tiny lights in the lawn lighting our way. The party was in full swing inside—guests laughing, soft Christmas songs playing, the clanking of glasses and dishes.

We reached the grand entrance—a set of giant deep oak doors. Hudson put a hand on each knob and pushed inside, gesturing for me to enter first.

I took a few cautious steps onto the cream-colored marble floor, my shoe nearly sliding across the polished surface. In awe, my eyes scanned the gigantic foyer, taking in the equally massive marble staircase that curved up towards the second floor. From the eighteen-foot ceiling hung a crystal chandelier so huge I took a few sidesteps so I wasn't directly under it, almost running face-first into the ten-foot-tall Christmas tree tucked in the corner. My nose told me it was real, the sap-covered branches dusted with fake, sparkly snow. Pristinely wrapped gifts surrounded the trunk. How freaking perfect.

"Miss? May I take your coat and bag?"

I spun to my right and saw a well-groomed man in a suit, smile plastered onto his face.

"Uh, sure." I handed him my purse, then fumbled with the buttons on my coat, and the man gently pulled it off my shoulders without prompting. "Thank you."

"Thanks, Pete," Hudson said, tossing his own coat over the man's arm. He nodded and disappeared down the hallway.

"Whenever I had people over at my house growing up, we'd just throw everyone's coats on the guest room bed," I said.

"*Love* the dress, Evie." Hudson's eyes eagerly gave me several once-overs. "I was a little worried you were going to show up in jeans and a sweater."

Hudson was already on my last nerve, but I couldn't help checking him out too. He wore a charcoal suit that seemed to be custom-made for his tall, lean body, and his hair was neatly slicked back. If someone told me he was a movie star arriving at his own premiere, I'd believe it.

Suspects shouldn't be allowed to look this good.

"I need a drink."

No sooner had I uttered those words did a waiter appear with a silver tray of champagne flutes. I selected a glass with a pretty, perfect raspberry floating in the bubbly.

Hudson grabbed one for himself, clinked his flute against mine, then downed the contents in one go. He immediately swapped out his empty glass for a full one before the waiter could get away.

"You might want to pace yourself," I said as Hudson made quick work of his second glass of champagne. I wanted him sharp in case I needed his help or information.

"Me staying sober wasn't part of our deal, hon." His gaze darted towards the living room, from which the music and chatter emanated. "Shit. Let's get this over with."

Glancing through the scattered crowd of about two dozen guests, I zeroed in on what Hudson had seen—his parents. Michael had been chatting amiably with two people, but he must've felt eyes on him. Mouth still moving, he turned his head. The second he spotted Hudson and me, he froze mid-sentence, the muscle in his jaw tightening. Hudson raised his glass in his father's direction, snaked an arm around my waist, and pushed us closer.

"Act like you like me," he said out of the corner of his mouth.

I tried to relax, despite Michael's expression turning more hostile by the second.

"Hey, Dad," Hudson said with a forced smile. "You remember Evie, right?"

"How could I forget?" he said wearily. "I don't recall inviting the press tonight." Michael couldn't have been more displeased I was there, and his icy gaze sent a shiver down my spine.

"Oh, she's not here in an official capacity." Hudson's grip on my waist tightened. "We've been seeing each other."

Somehow, Michael's eyes narrowed even more. "Excuse me?"

"I just felt *so* bad," I told him. "With Hudson getting wrongfully accused in that shooting, I wanted to apologize in person. It's obvious Detective Pennington is a little..." I made the universal hand signal for crazy. "Anyway. Hudson and I talked, and we really hit it off."

"Hmm," was all Michael said.

"Mom," Hudson said to the blond woman standing a few feet away from Michael. She'd still been mingling and flinched at Hudson's interruption. She dramatically mouthed *"Excuse me"* to her guests and moved towards us.

"Mom, this is Evie," he said.

I put on the biggest, fakest smile I could muster and extended my hand. "Hi, Mrs. Davenport. It's nice to meet you." Finally. I'd been zoning in on Michael and Samantha as my prime suspects, but Georgina could've easily gotten roped into covering up her family member's crime. I needed to suss her out.

"Georgina, please," she said faintly, shaking my hand with about as much strength as a baby bird. She was a wisp of a woman, probably no more than a hundred pounds. Her bleached hair matched Samantha's, and she had the same green eyes as her son. Her wrinkled nose and pinched features made me wonder if she'd been dreading Hudson's appearance at the party, or if that was just her face.

"You have a beautiful home," I said after no one else said anything for a few seconds. Hudson seemed more focused on locating another traveling tray of drinks than making small talk with Mom and Dad.

"Thank you," Georgina said. I couldn't tell if something was distracting her, or if she just didn't like me.

"Evie's a reporter with *Bristol Daily News*," Michael added unenthusiastically.

"*Oh.*" Georgina seemed more interested. "Were you the one who wrote about the new complex? We're very excited about it. Our first luxury-style apartments—but still affordable!"

Thanks to Grace's articles, I happened to know those affordable apartments were anything but.

"My colleague was responsible for that story. I cover the crime beat. I'm actually writing about the ten-year anniversary of the disappearance of Danielle Livingston."

Georgina's pinched features went slack, and some of the color faded from her cheeks. "Oh. How awful. Danielle's disappearance was so tragic."

"The police are thinking murder now, actually." I took a sip of my champagne.

I could see Georgina worrying the inside of her lip with her teeth. "Really. And why's that?"

"As soon as I started asking around, someone tried to kill me," I said casually.

Hudson returned to the group, some kind of mixed drink in his hand. His arm slipped back around me. "What'd I miss?"

"Excuse me." Georgina's gaze flashed to her husband, then the exit. She hustled towards it, and after a few seconds, Michael followed.

"Yikes. What did you say?" Hudson asked.

"Just that the police are looking into Danielle's murder."

Hudson took a long gulp of his drink. "Evie, I thought the point was *not* to raise their suspicions."

"I had to see your mom's reaction." I gestured in the direction she went with my champagne flute. "And she knows something."

"They all know something." He looked over my shoulder and winced. "Oh, Jesus. Gird your loins."

"*What* did you say to Mom and Dad?" Samantha stormed over to us, heels clacking loudly and long, shiny hair swishing across her back. Based on the way she stumbled in her heels and the glass of melting ice in her hand, she had to be hammered. "I can hear them screaming at each other from all the way down the hall."

"And hello to you too, sis." Hudson leaned in and planted a kiss on her cheek, which Samantha dramatically wiped off with the back of her hand.

"To answer your question, I didn't say anything to Mom and Dad. That was all Evie."

Samantha hadn't even noticed me. She slowly turned, and it took a few seconds before her eyes flickered with recognition.

"Oh. Evie," she said, blinking a few times. "Hi. What are—what are you doing here?"

"She's here with me," Hudson said, as if it were obvious.

"With you," Samantha repeated. She turned to me for confirmation, and I gave her a cheery nod.

"But I thought..." Samantha's dark brows scrunched together. "Aren't you dating Audrey's ex? Marcus?"

"Uh, no." I tried to look as confused as possible. "I barely know him. Why would you think that?"

Samantha opened her mouth, then closed it, panic in her bloodshot eyes. "I..."

I waited for her to finish, but nothing more came.

Samantha *had* to be the one who'd tried to kill me. She thought there was something going on between Penn and me, hence the emails to Grace. And she must've seen us leaving my apartment together the morning of the shooting, presuming, like Delaney did, that we'd spent the night together; that it was turning into a full-blown relationship.

Hudson didn't seem to be making any of the connections I was—he was looking for drink number four.

"Could you point me to the bathroom?" I didn't want Samantha to know that I suspected her.

She looked immensely relieved. "Down the hall, across from the office," she said, pointing to the left.

"Hurry back, Evie." Hudson winked.

Pushing through the crowd, I almost slipped again on the polished marble in the foyer. In socks, it must be an ice rink.

I made my way down the long hallway, dodging more waiters with trays of drinks and appetizers. I snagged two mini quiches and stuffed them into my mouth when I realized I was starving. No more drinks for me.

When I found what I assumed was the powder room door, it was shut, a thin beam of light visible through the crack. This was fine by me, since I didn't actually have to use the facilities. I was far more interested in the fight between the Davenports that Samantha mentioned. And when my strained ears caught hushed, urgent tones coming from the room across the hall, I crept towards the closed door, going as far as to press my ear against it.

"...said you would handle this!" Georgina hissed. "That's what you always say, but big surprise, you didn't!"

"I've handled it for ten fucking years, haven't I?" Michael shot back.

"Then why are the police asking questions now, huh? Why has our son been dragged into that police station twice?"

"It's all because of that damn reporter. And *our son* is the one who brought her here tonight. You need to do a better job keeping Hudson in check, Georgina."

"*I* need to do a better job? You're the one who lets him run wild. Spoils him. Bribes him instead of laying down the law. You've always been a pushover when it comes to the kids. That's how we ended up in this mess in the first place!"

I'd held my breath for the entire exchange, scarcely daring to blink. The conversation lagged, and I was about to lurch away from the door to avoid being caught when there was a loud crash, followed by a thump. I pressed my ear closer against the wood of the door, desperately trying to figure out what was going on inside.

"Don't you ever...call me a pushover...again," Michael growled in a low, dangerous tone. I could practically see him pinning his wife to the wall, his face mere inches from hers. "I did what was best for my family. That's what I *always do*. I don't remember you complaining at the time."

"Get off of me, you *bastard*," Georgina said, followed by more shuffling. "As long as Hudson is with that reporter, we have to assume he's told her everything. He's the only one who could destroy us. You need to do something about your son, Michael."

Footsteps grew closer, and my heart jumped into my throat. Thankfully, the occupant of the powder room had exited—I dashed inside, managing to secure the lock as the office door swung open. I stood, back against the door, panting, as Michael and Georgina started down the hall.

"Don't worry," Michael murmured to his wife before they were out of earshot. "I'll take care of Hudson."

CHAPTER TWENTY-SIX

"I was starting to think you got lost."

On unsteady feet I made my way back to Hudson, replaying Michael and Georgina's fight in my head over and over. There was nothing but two mini quiches and a glass of champagne in my stomach, but I suddenly worried I might vomit.

"You don't look so good, Evie," Hudson said. "You eat anything? Here." Hudson waved over the nearest server, who was offering stuffed mushrooms. He relieved him of the entire tray.

"Thanks," I managed weakly, shoving a mushroom into my mouth. I hardly tasted it, but after I ate a few, I felt better.

"You going to tell me where you were?" he asked after I'd cleared the tray.

"I..." I didn't know where to start, and when I saw Michael, Georgina and Samantha lingering nearby, all combination of words escaped me. When the pianist launched into a jaunty rendition of "Have Yourself a Merry Little Christmas," I put the tray down on a nearby end table, grabbed Hudson's hand, and led him into the middle of the living room, where the furniture had been cleared for a makeshift dance floor. Two older couples, barely swaying, were our only company.

"Normally, I don't dance," Hudson said as I put one hand on his shoulder and laced my right one with his. "But you're in luck. You're just hot enough, and I'm just drunk enough."

"Hudson, I didn't want to dance with you. I needed to talk to you alone without it looking suspicious."

"Ah," he said, giving me a lopsided grin. "Clever move, Detective Hartley." Hudson's hand on my lower back urged me closer.

I acquiesced, not wanting to draw attention. "I overheard your parents fighting," I whispered.

Hudson laughed. "What else is new? That's practically a tradition at this thing. Last year it was because Dad got caught with his pants down. Literally." Hudson spun us 180 degrees and pointed to one of the waitresses circling the room. "I believe she was the not-so-lucky lady."

My jaw dropped. "Are you serious? Your dad openly cheats on your mom like that?"

"Are you surprised?" He furrowed his brow. "This whole mess got started because he probably knocked up Sharon Livingston, right?"

"Right."

Hudson and I continued our slow, swaying circles across the room. Every now and then I caught the rest of the Davenports in their huddle, their intense conversation occasionally interrupted by a smiling, clueless guest wanting to chat.

"Looks like there's a family meeting happening without you," I said.

Hudson glanced over his shoulder "*Again, what else is new?*"

My throat got dry as I tried to press forward. "I heard your parents arguing about you. It sounded bad, Hudson. It sounded like..."

He raised his eyebrows, urging me to continue.

"Your mom said your dad was a pushover and spoiled you too much." I tried to remember every word. "She was panicking that you told me everything. And your dad told her not to worry, and that he'd *take care of you.*"

Hudson silently considered this, his expression far calmer than I'd have expected.

"Why aren't you freaking out?" I asked. "It sounded like they're planning to whack you or something."

"Whack me?" Hudson tipped his head back and let out a deep laugh. "Evie, you're adorable. And your concern for me is truly touching. But Dad's idea of 'taking care of me' is a lot less dramatic than you're imagining."

The pianist transitioned into "I'll Be Home for Christmas," and Hudson took the opportunity to pull me even closer, pressing his body against mine.

"Dad's go-to negotiation tactic is bribery." Hudson's hand on my lower back inched dangerously downward. "Like the Jag, when I tried to quit. Another time, he paid for me and my buddies to take a boys' trip to Cabo. I'm sure after tonight, Dad will wave some more money in my face to get me to break up with you. Which—no offense—I'll accept. The end."

I was still unconvinced. "It sounded serious."

"Trust me, Evie. I know my parents. But thank you for the warning."

We danced for a few more minutes without speaking, but when his left hand slid even lower down my body, I couldn't stay silent.

"Your hand is on my ass," I said, teeth gritted in a fake smile. "Kindly remove it."

"I don't know, I think you're starting to like me." His eyes sparkled.

"Just because I don't want you dead doesn't mean I like you."

A smile twitched at his lips. "Come upstairs with me."

"You can't be serious," I said with a laugh. "If that's your go-to line, it needs work."

"You have a dirty mind," Hudson said, eyes wide and innocent. "I was simply wondering if you would want to poke around upstairs, where we might find my sister's high school diary, filled with all kinds of secrets."

I tensed in his arms. "What?"

"Yeah, it's probably in her old room somewhere."

"Then what are we still doing here dancing?" I tried to pull away and head for the door. "Let's go."

"Keep your panties on." Hudson snuck another look at his family. "We don't want to draw attention, right?"

I still wanted to bolt, but he was right. We continued to sway for the remainder of the song, and when it finally ended, we made our way across the dance floor towards the foyer.

"Sure, Evie, I'll give you that tour you asked for," Hudson announced loudly.

I peeked back at the Davenports and locked eyes with Samantha, but Hudson pulled me safely out of view. We ascended the curving, marble staircase slowly, Hudson going on and on about the architecture, really committing to this fake tour to disguise our true mission.

"...and I think these bannisters were imported from Italy. Actually, a lot—"

Hudson stopped his droning as my shoe slipped on the second to last step, and I flailed forward. He managed to grab me in time before I face-planted onto the stone floor.

"Jesus," I muttered as I righted myself. Hudson squeezed my arm tightly as we climbed the final step. "This marble is an accident waiting to happen."

"Lots of banged-up knees over the years. But homes aren't supposed to be warm and comfortable, right?"

I assessed Hudson with a sympathetic frown and softer eyes. I'd been a guest in his family's house for barely two hours, but I already couldn't stand the Davenports or their ridiculous mansion. It was hard to imagine a childhood here would be filled with a lot of love or joy. Add in a philandering, potentially abusive father and a cold, controlling mother, and it's no wonder Hudson turned out the way he did.

"Why are you looking at me like that?" he asked as we made our way down the hall.

"I just feel like I understand you a little better now, that's all."

Hudson gave me a bemused smile. "Don't even think about warming up to me, Evie. I'm still a snake." We stopped at the second door on the left. "Sam's room," he said as he turned the knob.

I followed him into the room, and darkness enveloped us before Hudson fumbled for the light switch on the wall. Soft, yellow light flooded the room, revealing a teenage girl's bedroom similar to Danielle's, but much more lavish.

While Danielle's decor looked more Target store-bought, Samantha's was ripped from the pages of a *Pottery Barn* catalog. The bed was layered with a lush duvet and coverlet, the sheets and pillows perfectly matching the periwinkle-and-cream color scheme. The dresser, nightstand and desk all matched the expensive, white-painted bed frame. Elegant wallpaper covered the walls with a subtle forget-me-not print.

"Whoa." I did a slow pass through the room. "My childhood bedroom did *not* look like this."

"Well, yeah, because you're normal," Hudson said.

"Professionally decorated?"

Hudson shook his head. "Nope. This was all Samantha. She gets off on this crap."

"Oh, right. She does interior design for the company." I took a few steps towards her desk, which was clean apart from an open laptop. It looked new. I also noticed a small overnight bag. Samantha must've been planning to stay over—a good idea considering how many drinks she'd had. My heart sped up as I realized we might not have much time.

"How did she end up getting that job?" I asked Hudson, who was distracted by some photos on the wall. "She go to design school?"

Hudson snorted. "Samantha traipsed around Europe during a supposed gap year before deciding college wasn't for her. So Dad just hired her straight away, while I was still finishing school."

I turned to look at him, eyes wide. "You're the one with an actual degree, but you're just the executive assistant?"

"It's almost like Samantha is the obvious favorite or something."

"Shit, Hudson, that sucks."

He shrugged. "Used to bother me more, but once I realized I hated my entire family, it made seeking their approval a lot less important. It was kind of freeing, actually."

I wandered over to where Hudson stood, examining the pictures on the wall. I pointed to a shot of three young kids at the beach. "You, Samantha, and Danielle?"

"Yeah. I think I was around nine there, so they'd be seven."

I stared at the messy hair and the sunburned cheeks, giant, toothy smiles on every child's face. Danielle was in the middle, an arm thrown around Hudson and Samantha's shoulders. With all their tiny heads pressed together, it was easy to see a resemblance.

"You really do look alike," I murmured, tracing my fingers over the faces. I turned to look at him. "Sharon said the adults were all friends— that your families would take trips together."

Hudson nodded.

"I just find it hard to believe your dad would spend that much time with his ex-mistress," I said. "Wouldn't that be dangerous? Risk the secret coming out at any moment?"

"Maybe they all knew about it and were cool with it. I can say that I didn't suspect a damn thing until Danielle came to me with the letter."

"Hmm." I glanced at the door again. "Okay, where would this diary be? Under the mattress?"

"Nah. Samantha's not that clever. Check the bookcases. I'll look in the desk."

I walked over to the tall built-ins, scanning the shelves of dusty books. Samantha had everything from *Jane Eyre* to *The Sisterhood of the Traveling Pants*. Neck aching, my eyes scanned the spines, looking for something more personalized. Nothing.

"Any luck?" I spun around and saw Hudson sitting at the desk, messing with Samantha's computer. I walked over. "Would it be on there? That laptop looks pretty new."

"Oh." Hudson quickly clicked out of something. "No, I'm just snooping." Eyes still glued to the screen, Hudson reached into the left drawer of the desk, produced a small, leather-bound journal, and handed it to me.

I scoffed. "You knew exactly where it was. Why do you always have to waste so much time?"

"Maybe I just want to prolong every second with you," he said with a smile. "Because I know the minute you solve this thing, I'll never see you again."

"Hudson..." I had no clue what to say to him, and he knew it. He waved me off and turned back to the laptop.

"Well, go on, start reading."

I wandered to the bed and perched myself on the edge. Taking a deep breath, I opened the diary. Looping cursive writing covered the front page, declaring, *Senior Year!*

I scanned the first entry of Samantha detailing the first-day senior breakfast where she met up with Danielle and a few other friends. The next few entries were similar, but also filled with complaints about schoolwork and a disinterest in college. I started skipping days and flipping through the pages, stopping when I got near the end of October.

"Hey, listen to this one."

Hudson got up from the desk chair and sat beside me as I read.

"Danielle cancelled on me. Again. We were supposed to go to Christina's party (where FINN was going to be!), but she totally bailed. And her lame-ass excuse? Working on the freaking college essay. The Essay. I feel like it needs to be capitalized, since it's causing so many damn problems. I told her that one Saturday night of fun wouldn't kill her, but then she somehow got mad at ME, saying I wasn't supportive. Seriously? So what if she doesn't get into UVA? (Though, Hudson goes there, so clearly they'll just let anyone in.)"

I paused and cringed at what I'd read, but Hudson chuckled, so I continued. "The point is, Danielle will get into some college, so she needs to just chill and enjoy her senior year before it's too late. I don't know how much more of this I can take."

"Told ya there was some trouble brewing between the girls," Hudson said.

I shook my head. "This is nuts. I mean, Samantha sounds like a real..."

"Bitch? This is exactly why I always preferred hanging out with Danielle."

I looked back to the diary and eagerly paged through, looking for any and all mentions of Danielle. I'd just spotted an interesting-looking entry when my ears perked up, the sound of heels on the marble hall floor growing closer.

I froze and looked to Hudson, eyes wide. Before I could ask what we should do, he lunged towards me, his mouth pressing against mine. I yelped, but it came out muffled. Hudson pushed me backwards onto Samantha's soft duvet cover, the diary now hidden between our bodies. He continued kissing me, and instinct made me kiss him back. Two seconds later, the bedroom door flew open.

"What the..."

I wrestled my lips away from Hudson and turned to see Samantha in the doorway, glaring at us. Hudson looked over at his sister, smirking.

"Sam, you're kind of interrupting something here."

"Are you *serious*? Get the hell out of my room! Jesus, Hudson, how gross can you be? Your room is right across the hall!"

"Yeah, but it's always more exciting to do it in someone else's bed," Hudson said with an eyebrow raise.

I glared at him on his sister's behalf. "I'm sorry," I told her quickly. "We'll get out of here."

"Yeah, sure, just give us a second." Hudson reached down and started fumbling with the diary, trying to shove it into his jacket pocket.

Samantha mistook the movements for something else. "*God*, I do not want to see that!" And she stalked off down the hall.

"Smooth," I said after she'd vanished.

Hudson brushed some hair off my face and smiled. "It's a classic diversion. And kissing you is definitely a bullet I was willing to take. Kind of felt like you enjoyed it too."

I rolled my eyes so Hudson wouldn't think he was a good kisser—which, unfortunately, he was. "You can get off me now."

"Remember what I said earlier about prolonging my time with you?"

I gave him a push, and he rolled onto his back with a soft thump. I got to my feet before Hudson could get any more ideas.

"Well, I hate to say it, but I think the party is over," he said as he sat up. "I need to get the hell out of here before Samantha tattles on me. Hope you got enough."

I trailed Hudson down the stairs, taking my time as to not slip again. In the foyer, he gestured to the man in a suit, and a few seconds later he reappeared with our coats and my purse.

"Should we say goodbye?" I asked after I'd buttoned up.

"Good one."

We walked out into the night air, my breath a steady cloud in front of my face. Neither Hudson nor I said a word until we were in the safety of the driveway. He reached into his pocket and put the diary in my hands.

"I hope there's something good in there," he murmured.

"This is very helpful," I said. "But the thing that would really seal the deal is those DNA results. Do you have any idea where they could be?"

"If Dad has them, they'd be in his office safe. It's where he keeps all his shit he doesn't want any of us to find." Hudson paused. "I can try and look, if I get the chance."

My heart started pounding. "Please do."

Hudson pulled out his phone. "Well, I'm too drunk to drive, but I'll call you an Uber."

Five minutes later, a car pulled up. I gripped the diary as if it might be taken away from me.

"Thanks, Hudson." I stood there for a moment, shifting awkwardly, then pushed onto my tiptoes and kissed him on the cheek.

"I knew you liked kissing me," he called after me as I started for the car.

With a last wave, I climbed into the backseat. I tried to page through the diary on the way home, but it was too dark to read. Instead, I texted Delaney.

Tom, I think I found the car the shooter drove. Sending you some pictures now.

CHAPTER TWENTY-SEVEN

I ASCENDED THE STAIRS TO MY APARTMENT SLOWLY, ATTEMPTING to text and walk at the same time. In between answering a barrage of texts from Delaney about the car and where I'd found it, a message from Grace came in.

Evie, I'm so sorry. Don't hate me! He caught me off guard, and everything just sort of spilled out. Warning—he's PISSED.

This made me stop on the landing and sigh. The text was confusing, but I could piece enough together to get an idea of what happened.

And the second I got to the top of the stairs, I saw Penn waiting outside my door, arms crossed, steam coming out of his ears. Damn it. I'd been hoping to gently break the news of the Davenport party to him. Now the story was going to come out all confused and frazzled.

"Hey, Penn." I extracted my keys from my purse, overtly aware of the presence of Samantha's diary. After the glimpse I got at the Davenports', I was dying to keep reading, but I couldn't now—and I didn't want to show Penn my evidence until I was sure it really *was* evidence. I had to prove my slightly reckless move had been worth it.

"Guess who I ran into at Food City?" His voice was cold, his eyes colder as he gave me a once-over, taking in the short hemline of my dress and my stockinged legs, the hole at my knee clearly noticeable.

"I'm going to guess Grace." I unlocked my door. I didn't invite him in, but Penn followed me anyway and slammed the door behind him. I put down my things and pulled off my coat, trying to act totally calm.

"Imagine my surprise," he continued, "since you told me y'all had plans. So I thought to myself, 'Why would Evie lie?' Well, she cleared that right up for me."

"I didn't tell you because I knew you'd get mad. Kind of like you are now." I crossed my arms, freezing in the sleeveless dress.

"I have good reason to be mad, Evie!" he shouted. "Hudson is a *murderer*, and you're going to parties with him like it's no big deal."

"This was my one chance to get close to Michael—to look for anything that might help us. And I don't believe Hudson did it. I think it might've been Michael. Maybe even Georgina, she's a piece of work too. I overheard a nasty argument between them. They're getting nervous. That means we're close to nailing them."

Desperate now, I was about to retrieve the diary from my purse when Penn's phone let out a loud buzz. He read the message, and his brow furrowed.

"'I got to her first.'" He looked up at me. "What the hell does that mean?"

I suddenly felt like I was at the top of a rollercoaster, the fifty-foot drop coming any moment now.

It came two seconds later when Penn's phone buzzed again. He stared at it for a long, long time before letting out a bark of humorless laughter.

"What about this, huh?" He flashed me the screen of his phone. "Was this part of your big plan to get close to *Michael*?"

My mouth went dry as I looked at the picture on the screen. It'd been taken in Samantha's bedroom—based on the angle, from the camera on the laptop that'd been on her desk. I was speechless as I stared at the still of Hudson on top of me on Samantha's bed, locked in what appeared to be a passionate kiss. Son of a *bitch*. That's what he'd been doing on the laptop—setting up a recording. It hit me that Hudson had planned on jumping me all night, whether Samantha barged in or not—and he couldn't resist setting this up, all for the added bonus of pissing off Penn.

I exhaled, pinching the bridge of my nose. "It's really not what it looks like. I can explain—"

"What's there to explain? Anything to get the goddamn story, right? I shouldn't be surprised. It's what you do."

I blinked and tilted my head, convinced I'd misinterpreted what he'd said. "Excuse me?"

"Hudson," he said, ticking off one finger. "That kid singer from The Ranch. Delaney. Me, the night we met. And let's not forget about that D.C. cop." Penn shook his head at the five fingers he held up. "You're incapable of accomplishing anything without offering yourself up as part of the deal." His eyes zoned in on my torn stockings again.

My jaw dropped, and my entire body heated. I was so angry my hands shook. I was stunned he'd thrown the D.C. cop back in my face. It felt like a punch to the gut. I'd confided in him, shared my lowest moment. I thought he understood, but he hadn't. He'd hung onto it as ammunition.

"You really think I'm a giant slut, don't you?" I hissed. "You have *no* right to judge me. You have it so fucking easy. But I don't have a dick, and I don't have a badge—so excuse me for trying to level the playing field with what I do have." I started to storm to my bedroom. "And maybe I wouldn't do what I do if it didn't *work* every damn time," I called over my shoulder. "You men are all the same!"

"Still doesn't make it okay to fuck a murder suspect," Penn yelled after me.

I froze, spun on my heels, and marched back towards him. "Nothing even happened, you *asshole!*" I placed my hands on his chest and gave him a hard shove. Caught off guard, Penn stumbled backwards.

"He kissed me for two seconds before I pushed him off," I continued. "Hudson's lying, as usual. He's trying to get under your skin, as usual. And, *as usual*, it's working—because it's so easy to push your buttons, because *everything* makes you *mad!*"

I took two deep, shaky breaths, fists clenched at my sides. "Now, if you'll excuse me, this giant slut would like to get out of her slutty dress."

I stormed out for good this time, slamming my bedroom door. It startled Wally, who sat on my bed, ears on high alert.

"Sorry." I managed to sink onto the bed before the tears started. My chest felt like it was going to explode as I held in the deep sobs, but I hadn't heard Penn leave yet. I didn't want him to know I was crying. So I bit my lip and let silent tears run down my cheeks as Wally tentatively stepped onto my lap. His claws dug into my legs a bit, further destroying my tights, but I appreciated the gesture.

After about ten minutes, I pulled myself together. I nudged Wally off my lap and reached around to yank down the zipper of my dress. Kicking off my shoes, I padded to my dresser, extracting my comfiest leggings, sweater, and fuzzy socks from the drawer. I felt better once I put them on. My makeup had been ruined, so I grabbed a wipe and scrubbed my face so hard it hurt. A few more deep breaths later, I decided enough time had passed. Penn must've left by now.

But he hadn't. As I emerged from my room, he was there, perched against the arm of the couch, head bent.

I wiped at my still-runny nose with my sleeve. "Why are you still here?"

Penn raised his head to look at me. "I...I didn't want to leave like that."

"Well, I really don't feel like getting ripped apart again, so..." I gestured at the door.

He exhaled loudly. "I'm sorry, Evie. I took things too far. I didn't mean any of that."

"I think you did." I headed to the couch. I sat at the opposite end, tucking my feet under me. "I can't even argue with you. I use my looks all the time to help me out. I've slept with sources. But I'm not going to apologize for it, and I'm not going to let you make me feel bad. If you've got an issue with it, then that's your problem, not mine."

Penn slid off the arm onto the couch. "I'm sorry I got so mad—that I get so mad. It makes me say horrible things sometimes. You know I'm working on my temper."

I snorted. He'd already played the therapy card once before when we fought. I wasn't letting him use it this time.

"When I saw that picture of you and Hudson," he said, voice softer, "it made me crazy."

I relaxed as it became clear Penn wasn't about to scream at me more. Turning towards him, I realized he actually might be on the cusp of a confession. I waited for him to go on, but he remained silent.

"Why did it make you crazy?" I asked, desperate to keep him talking.

Silence.

"Marcus."

His dark eyes flicked up to mine. Exhaling heavily, he raked a hand through his hair. "I don't want you kissing him."

Heat flooded my body as if the thermostat had been turned up twenty degrees. I fought a smile. "Yeah? How come?"

Penn leaned his head back against the couch. "You're really going to make me say it?"

I was only ninety-five percent sure of what was coming, so I said, "Yes, I am."

"Because *I* want to be the one kissing you."

The grin I'd been holding in broke out across my face, and my heart felt like it might take flight. "That wasn't so hard, was it?"

He shook his head and let out a laugh, covering his face with his hands.

"So if you want to kiss me, why haven't you?"

Penn pulled his hands away and looked at me like I had two heads. "I didn't want to get rejected again!"

I squinted, genuinely confused. "Again?"

"The night we met. At the bar. You shot me down."

"Oh, that doesn't count!" I whacked him on the arm. "I didn't even know you yet."

"Okay, well how about when I said you could come over anytime." He raised an eyebrow. "You didn't exactly jump at that. You didn't say anything at all, actually."

I threw my hands out in front of me. "I didn't know you were serious! I just thought you felt bad about the fake date emails."

"I was serious," he said. "I didn't think you were interested. I thought you wanted to keep it professional."

I almost laughed at the absurdity. I often worried I was far too clingy, too obsessive, too obvious that I was incredibly attracted to him —only now to discover he wasn't even sure I viewed him as more than a colleague.

I crossed my arms and lifted my chin defiantly. "Well, I am interested."

Penn opened his mouth, then closed it. "Then why didn't *you* make a move on me?"

I had the urge to strangle him. "You act like you can't stand me half the time! You're always mad at me. And 'gnat' and 'leech' aren't exactly terms of endearment, you know."

He laughed weakly and settled deeper into the couch. "Well, I did warn you I was a little rusty with this stuff."

I surveyed him, waiting for him to snap out of it and fix the mess we made—to finally make a move. But he just sat there like a dope.

I was going to have to take matters into my own hands.

With a heavy sigh, I climbed onto his lap, grabbed his face, and kissed him.

I sensed the initial shock, but Penn wasted no time wrapping his arms around me, kissing me back. After a few frantic seconds, I pulled away.

"Just to be clear," I breathed, "this is me making a move on you."

"Yeah, I got that." Penn's hand went to the back of my neck, and he dragged me back to him. I wrapped my arms around his neck and parted my lips, allowing his tongue to slide into my mouth. He let out a muffled moan as I shifted on his lap, trying to get even closer. Penn's left hand moved up my torso and cupped my breast through my sweater.

Our kisses turned hungrier, but neither of us began tugging at the other's clothes. The kiss itself had crossed one major boundary, and we were both hesitant to push another and risk ruining it.

Not wanting to spook him, my fingers fiddled with one of his shirt buttons until it popped out of the hole, which was enough to allow my hand access to his hard chest. Penn felt so warm and solid beneath my palm, and his heart raced as fast as mine. My small exploration sparked one of Penn's own, and his hand on my breast moved under the neckline of my sweater, eager for bare skin. He'd barely gotten his fingers beneath my bra when his phone went off, the ring deafening.

Penn yanked his hand away like he'd touched a hot stove. "Shit." He tore his lips away from mine and looked up at me, eyelids heavy. "Sorry, I should get that."

I nodded, unable to speak, and leaned back on his lap, allowing him to remove his phone from his pocket.

"Pennington," he answered, voice gruff. He cleared his throat as he listened to whoever was on the other line.

My face felt hot as the reality of what had happened sunk in. My earlier confidence evaporated, and I longed to get off him, but Penn's hand on the small of my back kept me in place.

"Okay, I'll be there soon." He hung up. "I'm sorry, I have to go. Delaney needs to see me. He says it's important."

"Oh. Alright." He probably wanted Penn to look at the pictures I sent. I'd forgotten all about those. And the party, and the diary. Pretty much anything not involving Penn's lips had been momentarily wiped from my mind.

We stared at each other for a few seconds. "Um..." Penn gave my hip a little pat.

"Right." Face burning, I dismounted, tumbling gracelessly back onto my side of the couch.

Penn stood, fingers racing to redo his shirt buttons, buttoning more than I'd undone.

"I'll give you a call later." He checked his watch then added, "Or maybe tomorrow. I might be late."

"Okay," I said, still dazed and frozen on the couch. Penn walked to the door and as he grabbed the knob, I finally found my voice. "We should've done that a while ago."

He laughed. "If you recall, I tried to make that happen night one." He opened the door. "Goodnight, Evie."

"Night." I continued to stare at my door until Wally jumped onto the coffee table and meowed.

"Holy crap, Wally!" I whispered. "What just happened?"

CHAPTER TWENTY-EIGHT

"Ooh, check this one out," Grace said from the couch. "November twenty-first. 'OMFG. I literally cannot believe what just happened. I was sitting in my room, minding my own business, when I heard laughter coming from Hudson's room. A *girl's* laughter. I snuck across the hall and opened the door just a crack, and what did I see? Freaking DANIELLE. In Hudson's room. Laughing. Literally, what the hell? My supposed best friend doesn't even tell me she's in my freaking house??? And she's giggling with my BROTHER, who she always said gave her the creeps? Thank God I didn't catch them making out or something, but it was even weirder than that. It looked like they were looking through some old photo album. So freaking weird. God. Honestly, I really hate Danielle lately.'"

"Good find." Spinning towards my open laptop, I scrolled through each diary entry—which I'd painstakingly scanned and uploaded onto my computer—until I located November twenty-first, and hit print. The machine whirred and then beeped, the low ink light flashing. I mumbled a curse under my breath, located my last cartridge, and switched them out. Finally, the printer spit out the page. I highlighted a few key sentences, then pinned it to my wall with the others Grace and I had pulled out.

"Okay, I think it's time for a break." Grace set the open diary on the coffee table. "Your breakfast is getting cold."

Part of me wanted to keep going, but right on cue, my stomach rumbled. I plopped down next to Grace and picked up the Styrofoam container of veggie omelet and home fries she'd brought me.

"So Hudson came through again," Grace said as we ate.

"He did. He even said he'd try to get into his dad's safe, to see if the DNA results were in there."

"Seems like he knows a hell of a lot more than he's letting on." She stabbed a piece of potato with her fork.

"Grace, I think he knows *everything*," I said. "Including what happened to Danielle, and which of his family members were responsible. What I can't figure out is why he's suddenly helping now. If Hudson's always hated his family like he claims, why didn't he rat them out ten years ago?"

"No clue," Grace said. "But that means he's hiding something from you. Maybe he had a part in this after all, which means he can't be trusted. I have to side with Pennington on this one. You should keep your distance from Hudson."

I froze mid-chew at the mention of Penn. It had been about twelve hours since the incident, and he hadn't called last night or this morning as promised. The wait was excruciating. That kiss had probably been the best of my life—and it'd been clear Penn had enjoyed it too—but I had no earthly idea what was next for us. While I wanted answers, the thought of discussing it made me mildly queasy.

Grace and I had just finished our omelets when someone knocked on the door. My blood went cold.

"Evie?"

"Speak of the devil," Grace said with an eyebrow raise.

I stared at the door, heart thumping.

"Aren't you going to get it?" When I didn't respond, Grace touched my shoulder. "Why do you look freaked out?"

"Penn and I made out last night," I whispered.

"*What?*" Grace's eyes looked comically large behind the lenses of her glasses. "Why didn't you tell me?"

"I don't know!" I hissed, my heart racing as it all came back to me. "It happened so fast. He came over to yell at me about the party, and we had a really bad fight, and then we sort of admitted feelings for each other, and then—"

Penn knocked on the door again, and I covered my eyes with my hands.

"What should I do?" Grace said. "I can climb down the fire escape if you need to be alone with him. Or better yet, I could hide in the closet so I can eavesdrop."

"Lord, no!" I took a deep breath and stood. "I'm not ready to talk to him about that yet, so you're staying *right there.*"

On wobbly legs I went to the door and pulled it open. Delaney stood next to Penn. Disappointment and relief simultaneously flooded through me. This wasn't a social visit.

"Oh. Hi, guys," I said.

Delaney gave me an easy smile, but Penn's was different. The way the one side of his mouth curved up more than the other looked both sexy and shy. My heart thrummed at the sight of it, thinking about how that mouth was on mine not too long ago.

"Morning, Evie. You busy?" Delaney asked. "We wanted to talk to you more about the car, and whatever else you might've found at the Davenports'. Marcus mentioned something about an argument you overheard."

"Yeah. Come in." I opened the door wider, and they shuffled inside, both pausing when they saw Grace on the couch.

"Hey, Grace," Penn said, his voice coming out a bit strained.

"Hi." Grace had a giant, knowing smile plastered onto her face. I shot her a subtle warning look.

"Oh, you two haven't met." I looked from Grace to Delaney. "Tom, this is my friend, Grace. She works at the paper too. Grace, Detective Tom Delaney."

"Pleasure," Delaney said enthusiastically, stepping forward to shake her hand. He had on the same expression he'd worn the first time we met at the station, eyes big and shiny.

"Here, sit down." I grabbed one of my kitchen chairs and set it in the living room. I sat next to Grace on the couch, and Delaney swooped in to take the armchair. Penn didn't seem to mind getting stuck with the kitchen chair though. He'd wandered over to the wall covered in the new diary entries and studied them.

"What's all this?" he asked.

"Samantha's diary. Written right around when Danielle went missing. I swiped it from the Davenports'."

He gave me an incredulous look. "Why didn't you mention it last night?"

"I was going to. But you were all mad. And then..." My face got hot, and I was overtly aware of everyone's eyes on me. "...I guess I got distracted."

He blinked, rattled by my reference to the kiss, then turned back to the entries. "Anything incriminating?"

"We haven't quite made it to the day of Danielle's disappearance," Grace said. "But this girl was building up a lot of resentment towards her best friend, which is an odd coincidence if Samantha had nothing to do with it."

"It confirms what Hudson told me from the beginning," I added. "Danielle was focused on getting into UVA, and Samantha didn't give a crap about college. It caused some major tension between them. It makes perfect sense to me that Danielle would confide in Hudson about Michael potentially being her father, instead of Samantha."

Penn nodded and sat with a grunt, looking tired. He and Delaney had probably had a late night.

Wally, who'd made a pitstop at his water bowl, padded into the living room to see what all the fuss was. I'd never had this many people in my apartment.

Delaney noticed him first. He bent over and called, "Here, kitty, kitty." Wally sat and stared at him for several seconds before trotting over to Penn and rubbing enthusiastically up against his legs, his purring very audible.

Delaney raised an eyebrow. "Been here a lot, huh, Marcus?"

"Shut up." Penn looked more embarrassed than I'd ever seen him.

Grace grabbed my wrist and gave it an excited squeeze.

"So I looked at the pictures of the car," Penn said, steering us back to business. He reached down and scooped up Wally, stopping his constant figure eights around his legs. I stared in shock as Wally stayed still, allowing Penn to hold him without putting up a struggle. "I think it could be it."

"I think so too," I said. "It technically belongs to Samantha, but Hudson says she barely drives it and leaves it in the Davenports' garage."

"So any of them could've used it to carry out the shooting," Delaney said.

"Yes, but I'm convinced it was Samantha. She had the means and opportunity to send those fake emails to Grace. Not to mention, she was shocked when I arrived as Hudson's date. She assumed Penn and I were dating, and when I denied it, she knew she'd revealed something she shouldn't have known."

"Maybe Samantha's behind it all, then," Delaney said. "You said there were issues between her and Danielle. They could've had a fight that night, then Samantha snapped and killed her."

"Maybe," I said, unconvinced. "But Michael and Georgina are at least in on it. They were terrified about me being there last night—worried about what Hudson might've told me. Georgina said, and I quote, 'Hudson's the only one who could destroy us.' She said they had to do something about Hudson, and Michael said he'd take care of him. I think he might be in trouble."

"Hudson will be fine," Penn said. Wally's patience finally wore thin, and when he made a warning chirp, Penn put him back on the floor. He bolted from the room.

"What now?" Grace asked.

I turned to Delaney. "Is the car enough to bring Samantha in?"

He frowned. "Normally, I'd say yes. But we have to be extremely careful. No offense, Marcus, but you kind of fucked things up by going after Hudson so hard. The next time we bring a Davenport in, we have to make damn sure we can nail them."

"How do we make damn sure then?" I asked.

"Clear motive. The car and clear motive can get us a warrant to search the house for the gun used in the shooting."

"Once we have the gun, it'll be easy to make an arrest for the shooting," Penn said. "And I'd bet my life the shooter would be willing to make a deal and spill whatever they know about Danielle."

"So we're back to the DNA results," I said. "Danielle got those results the night she disappeared, and we have both Samantha and Hudson corroborating she was at the Davenports'. If the results proved Michael was her father, it would make sense she was killed to keep her quiet."

"Michael had a *lot* to lose," Grace said. "Like I told Evie, he had everything riding on this apartment building opening without a hitch. A secret love child would've given him the wrong kind of press. Could've hurt business, *especially* if it caused his wife to divorce him. Davenport Properties would've been chopped up and sold for parts."

"And there's our clear motive," Delaney said. "Where are these results?"

"Hudson thinks his dad might've held onto them," I said. "He said he's going to look around for them for me."

"How generous," Penn said in that loathing tone reserved for Hudson.

"Penn, we get it. You hate him. But he's helping. He's the one who gave me the diary."

"Let me see this diary," Penn said, as if he doubted its existence now that he knew Hudson had something to do with it.

Grace handed it to Delaney who passed it to Penn.

Forehead crease very prominent, Penn paged through the diary, increasing the pace of his flipping the further into it he got. He was about smack dab in the middle of it when he frowned, went back a page, then forward again.

"Danielle disappeared on December seventeenth, right?"

"Yes." The date was ingrained in my brain clearer than my own birthday.

Penn looked up from the diary. "There's no entry for that date."

I exchanged a wide-eyed look with Grace. "Are you sure?"

"She wrote in that thing religiously, almost every day," Grace said. "That's why it was taking us so long to get through it."

Penn shook his head. "Nothing for December seventeenth." He began paging forward, past the day of Danielle's disappearance, his index finger tracing lines down the pages as he quickly scanned them. We were silent as we watched him make his way through the book, giving us the occasional head shake.

"No mention of Danielle. Nothing about Danielle going missing, nothing about being concerned or wondering where she was—" Penn swallowed hard. "After Danielle disappeared, Samantha never mentioned her again."

CHAPTER TWENTY-NINE

"I HATE THIS," I SAID, IN THE MIDDLE OF MONDAY AFTERNOON. I was supposed to be working on a piece about an accidental shooting—*Gun Discharged in Bristol Home, No One Hurt*—but I couldn't bring myself to do it. I couldn't sit still. I kept bouncing my right leg, making my chair squeak, which had to be driving Grace crazy.

"I mean, we're literally sitting here, waiting for something to happen," I continued. It made me insane that I was out of moves. I wanted to keep digging deeper, but I had nowhere left to dig. All I could do was pray Hudson came through with tracking down those results.

"I know it sucks, but we just have to wait, like you said." Grace paused. "You know, you could kill some time by talking to Pennington about that kiss."

"That is a terrible idea, Grace. He hasn't brought it up at all. In fact, I've barely heard from him since. That can't be good."

"He's *busy*," she said. "You know he is."

This was true. Penn and Delaney took Samantha's diary with them when they left yesterday and were copying and studying the whole thing from cover to cover. Penn was still technically suspended, but that didn't stop him from doing grunt work behind the scenes.

And while Penn and I hadn't had time for chit-chat, he'd sent me a few more diary entries which he and Delaney were using to build a motive.

Tried to hang out with Danielle again, but things are still the same. Nonstop chatter about UVA and how goddamn helpful Mrs. P is with her admissions essay. Major yawn. Can I please have my best friend back now? I keep telling myself it'll get better once the application is in, but I realized it won't. Danielle will spend months worrying about whether she'll get in (which I'll have to listen to and assure her a hundred times that she will), and then, whether she gets in or not, I'll never hear the end of that either.

I'm just...really not feeling college. Kara's thinking of traveling, Europe or something, which sounds amazing. Maybe I'll take a gap year, or maybe I won't go at all. Who gives a shit? Dad said he'd find a spot for me at the company regardless. He would've done the same for Hudson, but he was so dead set on making something of himself on his own. Ha. He'll come crawling back soon enough.

With this entry Penn had written, *More motive? Could Samantha's job have been threatened by Danielle and those results?*

To this I'd responded, *I like the way you think, Buster!!*

I didn't get a reply. That one was weird, even for me. This was exactly why we shouldn't talk about the kiss yet, because I was a bumbling mess.

While pondering my awkwardness, a text from Hudson appeared on my screen.

Come downstairs.

I got up and craned my neck, trying to get a look out the window. His red Jag stuck out like a sore thumb in the sea of Toyotas, Hondas, and Kias filling our lot. Heart already kicking up, I threw on my coat and hustled down the stairs.

"Hey, Evie." He stretched his arm across the back of my seat as I climbed in. "Been thinking about me a lot since Saturday?"

I burst out laughing. "Not at all, actually. What the hell is wrong with you, sending Pennington that picture?"

His smile fell, like he'd genuinely forgotten. "Right. Oops. The idea came to me around drink three or four. It's just so fun to push his buttons. Was he mad?"

"Yes, Hudson, he was mad," I said, shaking my head. "But your plan actually backfired—he was so mad, he kissed me. And guess what? It was a lot better than kissing you."

"*Ouch.*" He clutched his heart. "Just remember, I had the balls to do it first."

"Why are you here? Do you have the results?"

"Well, first of all, we have some unpleasant business to take care of," Hudson said, face grave. "You're a nice girl, Evie, but I think it's best if we stop seeing each other. Especially considering you've been kissing another man. I'm sorry."

"You're breaking my heart," I said dryly. "So Michael demanded you end things with me?"

"Yep. And he wrote me a check for ten thousand dollars for agreeing. I told you he was going to bribe me. Nothing to worry about."

"Okay. Guess I was wrong." Penn had been right. Hudson would be fine.

"So these mysterious DNA results," Hudson said. "I'm pretty positive they're in Dad's office safe. It's what would make the most sense. Problem is, I can't really look myself. My folks are already suspicious of me. If I get caught poking around, I'm toast." He stared, as if he was waiting for me to respond.

"Alright..."

"How bad do you want them?" His eyes glittered, and my stomach felt queasy.

"*Bad.* You know that."

"Does that mean you're willing to do something illegal?"

The queasiness worsened significantly. "How illegal?"

"Just a teensy bit of breaking and entering."

My eyebrows shot up. "*Me?* You want *me* to break into your dad's safe?"

"Think of it this way," Hudson said. "You'll be breaking into Davenport Properties, but with the permission of a Davenport."

"That doesn't make it sound any better! You don't own the company or the building. And if I get caught, I can't even say you let me in. Hudson, I could get *arrested*."

Hudson leveled me with a gaze. "You knew this wasn't going to be easy, Evie. If I get caught anywhere near that safe, Dad will destroy the results, and then we're really fucked. You're our best shot at getting them."

I thumped my head back against the head rest, chewing on my lower lip. I couldn't really do this, could I? Besides being illegal, it involved putting a lot of trust in Hudson, right after Grace and I agreed that was a bad idea. Not to mention, Penn's head would explode if he found out.

"I'm surprised," he said after I'd been silent for a while. "I thought you'd be jumping at this chance. We could end this. Tonight."

I looked him dead in the eye. "Tell me you aren't going to screw me over."

"I'm not going to screw you over," Hudson promised.

"Fine. I'm in. But don't you *dare* tell Pennington."

I parked my car on a side street two blocks away from Davenport Properties and hurried to the building, head down, hands shoved into my pockets. Downtown Bristol at eleven p.m. on a Monday wasn't exactly hopping, and every rustle of a bush or tree made me jump. I felt like I had a big sign hanging over my head that said, *This woman is about to commit a crime!*

Cautiously, I crept into the parking lot, light on my feet so my black Doc Martens made no noise. I stayed as far from the building as possible, hopefully out of view of any cameras.

"Boo."

I gasped and jumped, spinning so fast I made myself dizzy. "Don't *do* that." I hit Hudson on the chest.

"Sorry." He looked me up and down. "Love the outfit, Evie. Very cat-burglar chic."

Having no clue how to dress for my illicit operation, I figured black was a good idea. I'd chosen black jeans, a black long-sleeved top, the Doc Martens, black gloves, and a black hooded jacket. My hair was pulled back into a ponytail as usual, but with the addition of a black headband, in an attempt to keep unruly flyaways out of my face. I'd thought this through.

"Let's just get this over with." My hands shook, and my breathing was quick and shallow.

"You'll be fine," Hudson said. "Okay, here's the deal. I unlocked the door for you, but the alarm is still going to go off the second you walk inside."

My heart stopped. "*What?* You didn't say anything about an alarm!"

"It's okay," he said. "Breathe. You'll have five or ten minutes before the cops show up. If you're not out by then, I'll pop out and tell them I forgot something at my desk and tripped the alarm by accident. I'll get them to leave."

I took a few deep breaths. "Okay."

"Dad's safe is behind the cabinet in his desk. The combo, big surprise, is his favorite child's birthday. Five, seven, nine, four. You got that?"

"Five, seven, nine, four," I repeated. May 7th, 1994. May 7th, 1994.

"What about cameras?" I asked. "I know there's one in the hallway outside his office. Any inside his office?"

"No, just the hallway one. Keep your hood up and your head down. The footage doesn't get reviewed unless there's a reason to look at it. If all goes well, by the time Dad realizes the results are missing, it'll be too late."

I kept nodding, trying to make myself feel better. Hudson seemed confident. He sounded like he'd thought everything through. I had no other questions.

"Tell me again," I suddenly said, delaying the inevitable.

"Tell you what?"

"What I asked you to tell me earlier."

Hudson smiled, his eyes shining in the dull streetlight. "I'm not going to screw you over, Evie."

"Okay, good." I shot a nervous glance at the building.

"You want a kiss for luck?"

I glared at him. "No. Alright, going in."

Flipping up my hood, I jogged across the parking lot towards the front door. I tugged on the handle, and it easily swung open. As I stepped inside, I braced myself for the blare of an alarm, but none came. Somehow, the silence made it scarier.

Realizing precious seconds were ticking away, I sprinted to the stairs, knowing the way to Michael's office by heart. Remembering Hudson's words, I kept my head down and stared at my feet as I made my way down the hallway. I breezed through the waiting room, past the admin's and Hudson's desks, and burst into Michael's office, shutting the door behind me. I took another deep breath to steady myself, then moved behind the desk. Crouching in front of it, I saw a top cabinet and a bottom drawer on each side. With gloved fingers, I tried each handle.

"*Shit.*"

They were both locked. Hudson hadn't said anything about them being locked, and my stomach dropped.

Don't panic, Evie. Don't panic. You have time. Hudson will take care of the cops.

While my eyes scanned the surface of Michael's desk for something to pry the cabinet lock open with, I tugged on the drawer handles for good measure. Adrenaline slammed through me when the left drawer opened. I fumbled out my phone, turned on the flashlight, and my heart kicked up even more when I saw the tabs on the many file folders.

Bristol Ridge, Bristol Towers, Bristol Gardens, Bristol Hollow...and way in the back was a thick folder labeled *Bristol Hills.* I grabbed it.

My fingers trembled as I opened the folder. I didn't have time to read anything, and Michael would notice an entire file missing, so I began snapping quick pictures of everything. Page by page, I methodically flipped through. *Click, click, click.*

I couldn't help but notice what kind of documents I was photographing: blueprints, contracts, financial information, landscaping plans. I had no clue if any of this would be useful—and I doubted it would be incriminating, since it was located in an unlocked drawer—but I took pictures of everything. Just in case.

When I was done, I slid all the papers neatly into the folder and stuffed it back in the drawer. That's when I spotted the sharp letter opener sitting atop Michael's desk. I grabbed it triumphantly and knelt in front of the cabinets, trying the left one first.

I jammed the pointy tip of the letter opener into the tiny keyhole, jiggling and twisting, praying this would work. A cold sweat broke out at my hairline as thirty seconds ticked by with no results.

Then came the click.

Dropping the letter opener to the floor, I pulled on the cabinet handle and whispered a desperate, "Thank you," when I revealed the safe. I'd guessed correctly.

The celebration came to an abrupt end when blue and red light splashed through the blinds. Shit. The police.

Breathe, Evie. You knew this would happen. Nothing to worry about. Hudson will take care of it.

I punched in five, seven, nine, four. Relief rushed through me as the tiny screen lit up green, followed by the mechanical churn of the tumblers. The door popped open.

I heard nothing but the sound of my own heartbeat in my ears as I reached inside and pulled out a stack of papers. There was a lot of stuff in here. Trying not to let my frustration take over, I paged through them, not entirely sure of what type of document I was looking for.

About halfway through the stack, I heard something.

I froze and strained my ears. At first, I tried to convince myself it was just my imagination. But then it became unmistakable what the sound was. Footsteps, slow and steady—as if a cop were making his way methodically through the building, clearing each room.

My heart dropped to my feet, and my fingers started working faster, frantically flipping through the papers. Goddamn it, the footsteps were getting louder. Closer. What had happened outside? Why didn't Hudson call off the officer? Was it possible the footsteps belonged to Hudson, and he was coming in to tell me it was all clear?

One look at the window told me that was wishful thinking. The red and blue lights were still flashing. It wasn't clear. Not at all.

My heart continued to flip inside my chest. Where were these damn results? If I was about to get busted, I needed to make sure it'd been worth it.

Finally, my fingers connected with the pointy corner of an envelope. I yanked it out of the stack of papers. I wanted to cry when I saw who it was addressed to.

Danielle Livingston. In the top left corner, the return address told me it was from Richmond DNA Diagnostic Center. Holy shit, this was it.

I hurled the other papers back into the safe and shut the door and cabinet, getting to my feet so fast my vision went spotty.

That's when the beam from a flashlight shone through the crack of Michael's office door. I hadn't heard the cop's footsteps in the carpeted waiting room, but he was right outside—about to bust me. I couldn't open the results now. Feeling like I might throw up, I folded the envelope into thirds, then shoved it down my shirt, securing it inside my bra.

The door burst open, and the flashlight blinded me.

"Police! Show me your hands!"

Gasping, I threw my hands up.

"Come around the desk. *Slowly*," the cop commanded, both his gun and flashlight still aimed at me. As I did as he instructed, I noticed he was quite young. A rookie. And he looked as scared as I felt.

"I'm sorry, I'm sorry," I blurted.

"Put your hands on your head and get on your knees." His voice shook slightly.

"Okay." I did as he asked. After several long seconds, I heard him holster his gun and flashlight, and extract his handcuffs. Oh, God. I was actually being arrested.

"Look, I have permission to be here," I said desperately as he knelt and yanked my arms behind my back. "Hudson Davenport. He let me in. His dad owns the company, and..."

"Up," he instructed, hauling me to my feet. He led me out of Michael's office and towards the entrance.

"Please, you don't understand," I said. "This has been a terrible mistake. Hudson Davenport is right outside, and he can explain."

"Ma'am, there's no one outside," he told me as he grabbed the front door. The cold air hit me like a slap to the face. Panicked, I scanned the parking lot, looking for some sign of Hudson. But I knew. I'd known the second the cop had entered the building.

Hudson screwed me over after all.

"Hudson, you son of a bitch!" I shrieked wildly as the cop led me to his car. My voice echoed through the empty lot, slicing through the quiet of the night like a knife. "I swear, I'm going to get you for this!"

"Ma'am! You need to calm down."

"Fuck you, Hudson," I screamed as the officer shoved me into the backseat. "*Fuck! You!*"

Somehow, I knew he could hear me.

CHAPTER THIRTY

"WHAT ARE YOU IN FOR, HONEY?"

My heavy eyelids snapped open, and I turned my head to the right to look at the man speaking to me. He sat on the floor, forehead pressed up against the bars separating us, eyes glazed over. I could smell the booze on his breath all the way from my spot on the cot.

"Breaking and entering," I mumbled, leaning my head back against the hard cinderblock wall.

He let out a deep, short chuckle. "You don't seem like the type, honey."

I wished this drunk man would stop calling me honey. Being locked up in a Bristol PD holding cell was bad enough. I hadn't even considered I'd have unsavory company. Clearly, I didn't think *any* of this through.

"I got tricked into it by a guy," I said. "A bad guy."

"Aw, shit, I'm sorry, honey," he rasped. "It's always a bad guy, isn't it?"

"What can ya do?" Antsy, I jiggled my leg and snuck a peek at the young rookie who'd arrested me. It appeared he was on babysitting duty; he sat at a desk nearby, pretending to read something, but he kept glancing up every now and then to glare at me. His semi-watchful eye made it impossible for me to extract the results from my bra and look at them. When I'd been brought in, they'd taken my jacket and phone and patted me down, but the envelope went undetected. At least I had that going for me. Had to take the wins where I could get them.

The sound of the door flinging open made all of our heads turn, and the moment I heard the heavy, angry footsteps, I knew exactly who it'd be.

"Oh, no." I scrunched myself into a ball, as if making myself as small as possible would prevent Penn from noticing me.

"Um..." The rookie babysitter stood quickly and attempted to speak to Penn, but he breezed past him and stopped outside my cell, hands on his hips. I stared at him guiltily, waiting for him to say something, but he was silent.

"I told Grace not to call you," was the only thing I could say. She'd been my one phone call; I'd asked her to feed Wally if I wasn't home by morning. Part of me knew she'd ignore my request and call Penn anyway. Jeez. I couldn't imagine what he must think of me now. I'd never seen him *this* angry—so angry that even yelling alluded him.

"What were you thinking?"

His voice was calmer than I'd anticipated, and there was a softness behind his eyes. He looked sad, pitying. Oh, shit. Penn wasn't mad—he was *upset*. He looked utterly disappointed in me, which somehow stung even more.

"I wasn't," I said, voice soft. "I trusted Hudson, and I shouldn't have."

"Shit," he muttered under his breath. "Evie, you've been *arrested*. We can't get you bonded out until morning. You have to spend the night in a fucking *holding cell*."

"I realize that."

"They said you didn't take anything," Penn said. "Which means you pulled this stunt for nothing."

I shot a nervous glance at Officer Babysitter, got off the cot and walked up to the bars. "Come here." I waved Penn closer. He still glared at me but stepped as close as possible.

"Well, I found a ton of documents on my apartment complex," I whispered. "Not sure if there's anything useful, but there's a bunch of contracts and financials. Could help paint a picture of Michael's mindset right when Danielle went missing. I took pictures of everything on my phone."

"Jesus," Penn mumbled. "You need to stop telling me this stuff right now."

"I found the DNA results," I breathed, quieter than a whisper.

His body stiffened, and he was unable to resist the bait. "What did they say?"

"I don't know. I didn't get the chance to read them." I looked over at the rookie officer again, then moved to my right, so Penn's body blocked me from view.

Penn watched me, puzzled expression on his face, as I reached down my shirt and produced the folded envelope, holding it up triumphantly. He fought a smile for several seconds before letting out an incredulous chuckle.

"You do it." I offered him the envelope through the bars. Penn took it, carefully unfolding it. He examined the front, taking in Danielle's name and the diagnostic center's return address. Penn moved painfully slowly, and I couldn't stand it. I turned away and began pacing my cell in a tight circle. My drunk pal next door had fallen asleep.

Penn stared at the results for a long time, his eyes scanning the sheet more than once. My stomach clenched, the anticipation killing me.

"Evie..." Penn looked up, his eyes wide. "They're not a match."

I froze. "What?" I hardly recognized my own voice.

"Probability of familial match," he read straight from the paper. "Zero percent."

I marched over and reached between the bars, snatching the paper from his hands. "No, that can't be right. You're reading it wrong."

My eyes wildly scanned the paper, confusion flooding my brain as I attempted to decipher the columns of random letters and numbers. I focused on what made sense—Danielle's and Hudson's names were at the top of each column. And sure enough, summarized at the bottom of the sheet, was what Penn said:

Probability of familial match: 0%.

"No," I repeated, the letters and numbers all blurring together as my eyes teared up. "No, no, no."

"Evie..."

"No!" I shouted, more at the results than at Penn. I let out a frustrated scream, making both the drunk man and the rookie cop jump. My cheeks felt wet, and I realized I was full-on crying.

"*God!*" I gave the metal frame of my cot a swift, hard kick, and mumbled a curse as pain shot through my toes.

"Evie," Penn said. "Come here."

I turned to look at him, wiping at my eyes. "He knew. Hudson knew what these would say. You were right. He's been playing me this whole time, and I—" A little sob came out unexpectedly, followed by more tears. I raced to think of what could possibly be his angle, his reason for dragging me along on this wild goose chase, but I couldn't focus.

"I'm so *stupid.*"

"Come here," Penn insisted. Eyes focused on the ground, I walked back up to the bars, leaning my forehead against them. My breathing was shaky as I attempted to get the crying under control.

Penn stepped forward and put his arms through the bars, wrapping them around my waist. I reached out and grabbed a hold of his upper arms, squeezing tightly, allowing him to steady me. I wished with all my might we were anywhere else right now—that no bars stood between us, and I could feel him hold me properly; that I could bury my face into his shoulder and cry until I couldn't anymore; that this intimate moment wasn't marred by the presence of Officer Babysitter and the drunk guy who smelled faintly of urine.

"It's going to be okay." His hand moved up and down my back

reassuringly. "We'll figure this out. Everything will feel better in the morning."

"Okay," I said with a sniffle, smiling in spite of the horrible circumstances. Funny that a man who spent half the time yelling at me could be so comforting.

"I'll be right back," Penn whispered, pulling away. I reluctantly released his arms and dabbed at my eyes with my sleeve. He disappeared out of the holding room, only to reappear a few minutes later, two to-go cups in his hands. He passed me one through the bars.

"Tea," he said.

I took a grateful sip. "Thanks."

Penn let out a grunt as he lowered himself to the floor by the bars.

"What are you doing?" I asked.

He shrugged and sipped his tea. "Just sitting."

"Penn, you don't have to stay." I settled down on the floor beside him. "Seriously. Go home. I'll be fine."

"I'll just stay for a little bit," he mumbled, resting his head against the bars. He wore the same sleepy expression as the night he'd fallen asleep on my couch. I leaned my head against the bars too, and closed my aching eyes, his mere presence making me think everything might be okay after all.

"Well, isn't this adorable?"

I woke with a start, then winced as I tried to look up. My neck twinged in pain with every movement. Squinting, I took in my surroundings. Still in jail. Delaney stood outside my cell, grinning and staring at Penn and me. Wow. Penn stayed the whole night, and based on the groan he made as he tried to sit up, he'd screwed up his neck as badly as I had.

"I come bearing good news." Delaney produced a key from his pocket. "Evie, you're free to go."

My eyes bugged out. "What?"

"Michael isn't pressing charges." He unlocked the door, and it opened with a creak. "He saw the report—he knows Hudson let you in. Guess he wants to deal with that himself."

I grimaced. Hudson was in a shitload of trouble. Then I remembered his betrayal and realized I didn't give a damn what happened to him.

I stepped out of my cell, scarcely daring to believe my luck. By this point, Penn had managed to get to his feet. I threw myself at him.

"*Oof.*"

"Thank you for staying," I mumbled into his chest as I squeezed him. "I promise I'll never do anything illegal again."

"Um, okay." He awkwardly patted me on the back. This hug was nowhere near as satisfying as I'd hoped it would be, and I suspected Delaney's presence was the reason.

"Jeez, I'm the one who got you sprung," Delaney said.

I let go of Penn and turned to Delaney. "Thank you." I gave him a hug as well. At this rate, I probably would've hugged my drunk cell neighbor too.

"You want me to take you home?" Penn asked.

"No way. We need to get to the bottom of this." I pulled the crumpled results from my pocket. I was exhausted, starving, and had to pee really badly, but being free after a frightening eight hours as a criminal had reenergized me. Penn had been right—everything really did feel better now that it was morning.

"What's this?" Delaney snatched the results away from me. He scanned it and then looked up. "Well, shit. There goes our entire theory."

"Okay." Penn groaned, rubbing his face with his hands. "If we're sitting down and doing this now, I'm going to need food and coffee first."

A half hour later, I sat between Penn's and Delaney's desks, bladder empty, belly full of hot coffee and two Boston cream donuts. The caffeine and sugar had revived me, almost allowing me to forget I'd spent a very uncomfortable night in a jail cell.

"So if Michael Davenport's not Danielle's father, who the hell is?" Delaney asked.

"None of this makes any sense," I said, hearing desperation in my voice. "Samantha's diary never mentions Danielle again. That means she either did it, or at least knows what happened to her."

"We're back to Delaney's theory then," Penn said. "Samantha and Danielle were fighting for months. Danielle went over to see Samantha the night she disappeared, and things got out of hand. Samantha lied and said Danielle left on her own to cover her tracks."

I started shaking my head before he even finished talking. "Then *why* did Michael have these DNA results in his safe? You only hold onto something like this in case you need to deny it later. Which makes me think maybe he really is Danielle's father, and these are fake."

"Evie," Penn said, giving me a look.

"Think about it!" I sat up straighter in my chair and crossed my legs. "Hudson led me right to these. He wanted me to find them. He's covering someone's tracks, whether it be his own, his dad's, or his sister's. You were right all along, Penn. He's been leading me on a wild goose chase to distract us. I mean, *Jesus*, what if he *actually* did it?"

Horrified, I thought back to all the time I'd spent with Hudson—meeting him at Last Call, riding in the car he almost intentionally crashed, being his date to the party, kissing him...

I shuddered. I'd been canoodling with a psychopath. Even worse, this meant that beneath Penn's jealous Neanderthal act, he'd actually been *right* about Hudson.

"Well, I hate to say it," Delaney said with a grunt. "But we're back to square one."

"Wait." I suddenly remembered what else I'd found last night. "Those documents I took pictures of. We can look through them, see if anything jumps out."

I emailed every photo I snapped to Penn and Delaney, and we began the tedious process of sorting through everything. With every blueprint and typical contractor agreement we examined, my heart sunk lower. Of course, there was nothing incriminating in a conspicuous file folder in an unlocked desk drawer.

"Hmm," Penn said eventually, squinting as he scrolled through something on his computer screen.

"Find something?" The hope was palpable in my voice.

"Maybe." A frown began to form. "I'm sorting through a bunch of financial documents, and Georgina's name is coming up. A lot."

"Huh. She doesn't work for Davenport Properties, does she? I've never seen her there. Why's her name on everything?"

Penn did some more scrolling, then let out a little chuckle. "Well, my, my, my. I guess now we know who's holding the purse strings." Penn tilted his screen so Delaney and I could see. "Georgina signed off on *everything*. Contracts, checks for the builder. Michael even took out a loan to help build this complex, which Georgina co-signed."

"So before Bristol Hills," I said, "Michael didn't have any of his own money."

I recalled Hudson's tour of the sprawling Davenport mansion. He'd mentioned growing up there. They'd been in that house a lot longer than ten years. It must've been bought with Georgina's money.

"Okay, okay." I put my hands up. "So Georgina funded Michael's big project. Which means, ten years ago would've been *terrible* timing for Georgina to decide to divorce him."

"I know where you're going with this." Penn rubbed his face roughly.

I raised an eyebrow. "Where's that?"

"You're going to say that Danielle really was Michael's daughter. And her, and Georgina, finding this out right in the middle of construction would've been the end of Michael's marriage and business."

"Exactly," I said, adrenaline rushing through my body again. "Michael killed Danielle and held onto the doctored DNA results, just in case anyone ever put this together. Samantha, Hudson, Georgina— they all know about it, but Michael's been keeping the kids quiet with bribes all these years. They have a lot to lose at this point too. Samantha tried to scare me off with the note and the drive-by shooting. Hudson's been earning my trust, so he could lead me to the fake results." I took a breath. "It's a big, old fucked-up family secret, and they're all in on it."

Penn and Delaney remained silent as they considered all this.

"It's not a bad theory," Delaney finally said. "But we can't prove any of it."

"Yes, we can." I got to my feet. "We just have to get Sharon Livingston to come clean. I'm sure once we explain what's at stake, she'll be willing to testify that Michael is Danielle's father."

"Well, hold on a minute..."

"Penn, can you take me to my car?" I asked, pulling on my jacket. "I think I should try talking to Sharon alone; she might be more likely to tell me than you two."

Penn opened his mouth, I assumed to protest, but the sudden *whoop* of a police siren coming from the parking lot cut him off. We all turned to look out the window and saw a flurry of activity, two uniformed cops jumping into squad cars and peeling off towards the road.

"Hey." Penn grabbed another patrolman who'd been heading for the door. "What's going on?"

"One-car accident on Pleasant," the cop said. "A red Jaguar got totaled. Shame, huh? Sounds like the driver's in pretty bad shape too."

The cop continued towards the lot when Penn was too stunned to ask any follow-up questions. Penn turned to look at me, and I could tell we were both thinking the exact same thing.

This was no accident.

I swallowed hard. "Actually, I think we should go to the hospital instead."

CHAPTER THIRTY-ONE

"THANK YOU SO MUCH FOR LETTING US SPEAK TO HIM SO SOON," Penn told the nurse who'd looked up Hudson's room number. "We just really want to get to the bottom of what happened. We think someone tampered with his car."

"So horrible," she said with a solemn head shake. "Looks like he's in 206. He got lucky—no surgery. But his arm is broken, and he's got a concussion. We'll need to keep him for observation."

"Thanks, Heather. You're a lifesaver." Penn flashed her a smile. She returned it, her cheeks slightly pink. "Again, sorry for not having my badge on me. I can run back to the car to get it. I don't want to get you in trouble."

"Oh, don't worry about it," Heather said. "I think we can make an exception this time." Her eyes flicked to me before she returned her gaze to Penn. "Let me know if you need anything else."

"Will do," he said, smiling even wider.

I resisted the urge to roll my eyes, a little peeved that I'd seen him smile at this nurse more than he had at me in the entire time I'd known him.

"You were flirting with her," I said as we walked out of earshot.

"I guess I'm taking a page out of your book. And considering I'm still suspended, it was necessary."

I grunted in response.

He looked at me, amused. "You jealous, Evie? Because that's only a fraction of what I've had to deal with between you and Hudson."

"Please don't remind me. I might have to be shipped off to a nunnery after this."

"Well, that wouldn't be much fun for either of us," Penn said.

I stopped dead in my tracks, but Penn continued down the hallway and took a right into Hudson's room. This was the closest he'd come to acknowledging the kiss and moving forward romantically—and it gave me zero clarity. I hurried after him, more perturbed than ever that there wasn't time to discuss what the hell was going on between us.

Penn lingered in the doorway of room 206, taking in Hudson's condition. I pushed into the room to get a look for myself, and I couldn't help but let out a little gasp. It's not like I'd thought he'd been faking, but after he'd so easily dismissed my concerns at the party, it just didn't occur to me that something bad would actually happen to Hudson.

I stared at him lying in the bed, complexion pale, forehead bandaged, a few other stray cuts on the side of his face. His right arm was in a cast and sling, which added to his weak, disheveled appearance.

At the sound of our entry, Hudson began to stir, a strained expression on his face. His green eyes flickered open, and for once, they were dull.

"If it isn't Bristol's favorite crime-solving couple," he said, the joke falling flat when his smirk turned into a grimace of pain. Hudson let out a pathetic cough.

"You're a liar." My voice was low as the anger simmered inside me.

"Be mad all you want, Evie," Hudson said. "But you knew I was a liar from the beginning. I told you myself."

"What happened with your car?" Penn asked gruffly. He'd fully transitioned to his Hudson-loathing expression.

"A good question," he said. "Brakes stopped working. I swerved into that pole. Could've been a lot worse, I guess."

"You expect us to believe someone sabotaged your car?" I crossed my arms. "How do we know this isn't another one of your stunts?"

Hudson laughed, which turned into another cough. "Look at me, Evie. This would be a little extreme, even for me."

I still eyed him suspiciously, but Penn played along. "Fine, then. Someone screwed with your brakes. Any idea who?"

"Where were *you* this morning, Detective?" Hudson asked, eyes wide.

Penn scoffed, shook his head, then wandered over to a chair in the corner of the room. He sat and leaned back, getting comfortable. "Your turn," he told me, gesturing to Hudson.

"Hudson, I don't think you understand how thin my patience has worn with you," I said, approaching his bed. "Funny how a night in jail will do that."

He turned to Penn. "She's still a little upset that I dumped her."

I lunged for him, grabbed his injured arm, and squeezed.

"Ahhh!" Hudson's body tensed and his jaw clenched as he fought the pain. He tried to swat at me with his good arm, but couldn't get any decent hits in. After a few more torturous seconds, I released him.

"Jesus!" Hudson looked at Penn. "You seriously aren't going to do anything about that? That's assault."

Penn turned his palms up. "Not sure if you remember, but I'm suspended. Can't do anything, unfortunately."

"Let's try again," I said. "Who put you in the hospital?"

"Who do you think?" For the first time, I saw hostility in his eyes, and not one ounce of his usual friendliness towards me. "It was Dad. Punishing me for helping you break into the office last night."

"Helping me," I repeated with a laugh. "Is that what you call ditching me to take the fall?"

"Look, Evie, I had to. If I talked to that officer—if I identified myself—Dad would've definitely heard about it. So I bailed." Hudson gave me a rueful smile. "I didn't expect *you* to be the one to rat me out. I'm almost impressed. Really, it's your fault he came after me."

"You're the one who insisted your parents wouldn't hurt you," I said.

"Dad wanted to make a point I guess, since the cash didn't stop my meddling." He paused. "Did you find the results before the cop got you?"

I shot a glance at Penn, but his face offered no clues as to how I should proceed. He was letting me do this on my own.

"I did find them."

Hudson tilted his head, waiting for me to continue. He frowned when I didn't.

"And?"

"Shouldn't you already know what they say?"

He gave me the hint of a smirk. "I don't like when you use my tactics against me, Evie."

"Frustrating, isn't it?"

Irritation flashed across his face. "How would I know what the results say? Since, as I've told you, Danielle and I were supposed to open them together."

"*Liar.*"

"This was a lot more fun when you trusted me," Hudson said.

"Sorry you're not having *fun* anymore," I shouted. "You know what else isn't fun? Getting shot at. Spending the night in jail. Being led on a fucked-up, merry chase for your own enjoyment!"

"Whoa. You're really hot when you're angry. You should thank me for getting her all worked up, Pennington. I hear I'm some sort of aphrodisiac for you two."

I reached for his bandaged arm again, but he yanked it away before I could touch him.

"*Stop,*" he moaned through gritted teeth.

"Hudson, this whole time, you've known too much." I leaned in close. "I think you know everything. I think you could've helped the police solve this ten years ago, but you chose not to. And if you don't start leveling with me right now, you are getting *nailed* for this."

I stared him down, waiting for him to make a joke about getting "nailed," but he didn't.

Hudson took a breath and exhaled slowly.

"Like I told you, I didn't see the results myself. But I know they're negative," Hudson said, his voice almost a whisper.

Penn sat up straighter in his chair.

"Yes," I said. "So then *why* would your family kill Danielle? None of this makes any sense with negative results."

"Look..." Another sigh. "I had it bad for Danielle, okay? Ever since we were kids. So when she came to me with that love letter...I was disturbed, to say the least. The idea that we might've been related that whole time, and that all our parents were buddy-buddy like nothing was up..."

I leaned forward, captivated, wondering if I was finally about to get the truth out of him.

"I confronted Dad," Hudson continued. "I told him Danielle found that love letter and demanded to know if it were true. He denied it at first, but when I threatened to show Mom, he told me the truth. He told me he was Danielle's biological father. He'd had a brief affair with Sharon Livingston. They broke off all contact when she got pregnant, but then when Samantha and Danielle just so happened to become friends at school..."

"They acted like strangers," I said. "So no one sensed anything was off."

"Yep. And things really got sticky when Mom got on so well with the Livingstons. So Dad and Sharon were forced into this friendly foursome, all the while keeping this secret from all of us."

"Wait. If Michael *is* Danielle's father, what's up with these results? Did he doctor them?"

"No, those are the real results." Hudson reveled in my confusion for a few seconds. "When Danielle asked for DNA, I gave her some. Just not mine."

Of course. Even back then he was like this.

"Whose?"

"I got one of my buddies to do the cheek swab. Easy."

I exhaled and let out a humorless laugh. "Why would you do that, huh? I thought you wanted to help Danielle figure this out."

"I told you, Evie, I'm a snake," he said. "Sure, in a perfect world I would've helped Danielle expose my dad. He deserves it, after all the shit he's pulled. But I sold my soul to him instead."

I cocked an eyebrow, frustrated by how slowly this was coming out, but I wasn't going to risk pushing him. "What do you mean?"

"We made a deal," Hudson said. "If I got Danielle to drop this paternity thing, Dad would give me a job at the company. Something high up, like Junior Vice President, so by the time Dad wanted to retire, I'd be ready to take over."

My brow furrowed. "But you're just an executive assistant."

"The Davenports are liars," he recited with a smile. "Obviously, Dad didn't hold up his end of the bargain after Danielle died. But by then, it was all too late. I'd kept the secret for too long; going to the police would mean implicating myself."

"Wait, wait." I put my hands up. "If Danielle got these results and thought Michael wasn't her father, why would he kill her?"

"Something happened we didn't account for. Sharon came clean. Isn't that something? The night Danielle came over with the results, she already knew the truth because she'd confronted her mom."

The fight. The argument Sharon and Danielle had the night she went missing. Audrey had been right; it'd been about Danielle's father. And Sharon had finally admitted the truth.

"What happened?" I demanded.

"She came over, really upset. I tried to calm her down, but she just wanted one thing. To talk to Dad. She went upstairs. I could hear them arguing. And then..." He swallowed, and I swore I saw a few tears welling up. "I heard her fall. You saw those stairs, Evie."

"Oh..." A weird pain formed in my chest as I imagined Danielle tumbling down that marble staircase. She could've easily broken her neck or smashed her head on one of those stone steps.

"Dad swore it was an accident, that she slipped," Hudson went on. "But he said the cops would ask too many questions. They'd want to know what they were fighting about. And we couldn't prove she wasn't pushed and..."

"...you'd all get some really bad press, right before the grand opening."

"Dad said it would be better for us to handle it ourselves and not get tangled up in a complicated investigation. So he took care of things."

"Hold on." Penn leapt from his chair, something I guessed he'd been dying to do for a while now. He strode over to the bed. "Hudson, are you telling me that your father killed Danielle, then disposed of her body?"

Hudson nodded. "Sam and I cleaned up the blood, and we drove Danielle's car to the bus station. Mom and Dad took care of the body. I don't know what they did with it. I didn't want to. I figured the less I knew, the better."

I stared at Penn, stunned, my heart in my throat. I tried to figure out what the hell was going through his mind right now. He wore a different expression than he normally did around Hudson, but I had no idea whether he bought his story or not. I had no idea if *I* bought his story.

"Accident or not, you're an accessory, Hudson," Penn said. "And you withheld this information for ten years. These are serious charges. We would've gone a hell of a lot easier on you if you told us right away. You could've gotten a deal."

"Look, I know. I took the easy way out," he said. "I've felt horrible. But we're all mixed up in it. I didn't see a way for Dad to go down without dragging me with him." Hudson turned to look at me. "The second I saw you were looking into this, Evie, I knew I had to get a handle on it. Guide you towards my family but try to keep myself clean."

I shook my head in disgust. "You weren't just gunning for your dad, though. You encouraged my suspicions of Samantha, even though you and her had the exact same part in this. You didn't care who went down for it, huh? As long as it wasn't you?"

He gave me a weak smile. "As long as it wasn't me."

I glared at Hudson, lips parting to spew a few insults or expletives, but Penn put an arm around my shoulders and guided me into the hallway. We looked at each other for several long seconds without speaking.

"*Well?*" I asked. "What do you think?"

"I have no fucking idea," Penn said. "It makes sense, but I just can't believe a word that comes out of his mouth. We still don't have any concrete evidence. We bring in Michael, it'll be his word against Hudson's."

"I need to talk to Sharon, then. See if she'll confirm that she told Danielle who her father was the night she disappeared."

"No," Penn said quickly. "Things have changed now, Evie. We need an officer to get a statement from Sharon."

"A non-suspended one. You think Sharon is going to open up to Delaney about her biggest secret? This could be like the rape investigation all over again. Come on, I have rapport with her. I think she trusts me."

Penn knew I was right, but he wouldn't admit it. "It can't be you, Evie. Stay here, okay? Can you keep an eye on Hudson? Make sure he doesn't go anywhere. I need to report all this."

"Penn..."

He turned on his heel and left before I could protest. I blew out a lungful of air, cursed under my breath, and headed back into Hudson's room.

"Babysitting duty, huh?" he asked.

"This is ridiculous," I said as I collapsed into the chair Penn had occupied. I bounced my leg up and down and drummed my fingers on my knee.

"Face it, Evie, you got sidelined," Hudson said. "Might as well make the best of it. What should we do to kill all this time? I could probably think of a few things."

I barely heard him. I kept glancing at the door, then the clock, wondering how long it would take for Penn to explain everything Hudson had told us, how long it would take until an officer was sent to speak with Sharon. To speak with Michael. It could be hours. And what if Sharon wouldn't admit the truth about Danielle's paternity? Then it would take even longer.

"Evie..." Hudson said. "I know what you're thinking, and I can't believe I'm saying this, but I agree with Pennington. You should sit tight. Do this by the book."

I gave him a look. "You? Saying to do this by the book?"

We sat in silence for three more minutes before I jumped to my feet.

"Evie," Hudson warned.

"I have to talk to Sharon." I headed for the door. "I can't just sit here."

"Don't go," Hudson said, so adamantly it stopped me in my tracks. I turned back to look at him. His eyes looked bright. Sincere. And as always, a little dangerous. "Please, Evie. Stay with me."

"Sorry, Hudson. I'm done playing your game."

CHAPTER THIRTY-TWO

IT TOOK ME LONGER THAN I WOULD'VE LIKED TO GET TO THE Livingstons', due to having to walk to where I'd stashed my car near Davenport Properties. It was nearly sunset when I pulled up outside of the small house, looking for any signs of police visitors. All clear. I practically sprinted towards the front door, knowing they could arrive at any moment and haul me away.

"Oh...Evie. Hi." David had answered the door.

"Hi, David." I attempted a friendly smile despite the nerves shooting through my body. "I'm sorry to just drop by like this, but it's really important. Is Sharon home?"

"Um, yeah, she's here. Come in." He stepped aside and I walked into the living room, craning my neck, searching for her. David looked at me like I was crazy.

"David, is there someone..." Sharon entered the room from the kitchen, sleeves pushed up, dishtowel in her hands. When her eyes focused on me, she didn't glare, but she didn't smile either. I had the feeling she was still upset over my probing questions from my last visit —which meant me asking again might turn her openly hostile.

But I couldn't afford to worry about that now.

"Hi, Sharon," I said. "I really need to speak to you about Danielle."

"Okay..."

I shot a quick glance at David. "It might be better if we spoke alone."

Her face hardened and her lips flattened into a thin line. "Whatever you have to say, you can say in front of my husband."

Here goes nothing.

"Hudson Davenport claims his father is also Danielle's biological father," I said. The words hung in the air for several long seconds.

"Excuse me?" It was David who spoke first, his normally friendly eyes darkening with anger. Uh oh. He didn't know.

Sharon appeared too stunned to speak. "I'm sorry if this is a shock for you, David," I said. "But I believe Danielle was killed because she discovered Michael was her father."

"Evie," David said slowly, "do you really think my wife would have a child with a married man? That we would've been friendly with the Davenports all those years, lied to his wife's face constantly, if Michael was Danielle's father?"

"Um..." This stumped me a bit, because I'd been thinking the same thing in the hospital. If Sharon and Michael had had an affair that resulted in a love child he wanted nothing to do with, how could they possibly behave normally together for *years* in front of their spouses?

However, Sharon still hadn't spoken. No vehement denial like last time. In fact, it looked like she was beginning to tear up. She reached for the arm of the sofa and sunk down onto it.

David turned to his wife. "Honey?"

He sat beside her and took her hand. I felt awful—intrusive, like the gnat Penn says I am—for outing Sharon's big secret in front of her clueless husband, but I reminded myself it was necessary.

"I'm so sorry." I edged towards the armchair next to the couch and took a seat. "I didn't want to have to bring this up, but it's important. Hudson says his dad killed Danielle because he didn't want this to get out. We have no proof of her paternity, so we need you to confirm that Michael is her father."

Sharon cried openly now, and David put a comforting arm around her, whispering reassurances into her ear. I was touched by his reaction. He'd been lied to, as well. I'd expected shock, anger—but not this.

"I told you the last time you were here that Danielle's father was just an old boyfriend who passed away," Sharon said, wiping at her cheeks.

"But that's not true, is it?" I pushed gently. "I could tell you were lying, Sharon."

She took a shuddering breath. "Yes, I was lying."

My heart thrummed. Finally, I'd learn the truth from someone I could trust. Someone who could make a difference. We were going to nail Danielle's killer.

"But, Evie," Sharon said, making intense eye contact, "I swear to you, Michael Davenport is not Danielle's father. I have no clue why Hudson would say that. I didn't even meet Michael until Danielle and Samantha were in first grade."

My ears roared, and the room felt off-kilter. Time seemed to slow. I felt each rapid beat of my heart acutely, like it might pound out of my chest.

"I..." I had no words. I couldn't articulate just how much this one fact destroyed everything I thought I knew about Danielle's disappearance.

"Danielle's father is a man I was casually dating at the time." Sharon shifted on the couch, and David's arm remained securely around her. "We'd only gone on a few dates. I could tell he was much more interested in me than I was in him." She clasped her shaking hands together. "After our third date, I knew I wanted to break things off. But he clearly had other expectations for that night."

My stomach dropped, and I braced myself for what was coming.

"He forced himself on me," Sharon said, her voice a whisper. "I never heard from him again after that. Not that I wanted to. I have no clue where he is now."

"Sharon...I'm so sorry."

"This is why we didn't tell Danielle about her biological father," David said. "How do you tell a child that? We knew she'd struggle with it, no matter how old she was."

I nodded, feeling numb. I couldn't even attempt to process what this new information meant for the case.

"Danielle was writing an essay about wanting to find out her father's identity," I said. "Did you know this?"

Sharon nodded. "That's why we'd been fighting so much those months before. She kept asking, and every time it got harder to avoid the subject. The day she disappeared, she asked me one last time, and I...I lost it. I told her the truth, but not in the way I should've. I was upset, yelling. It came out wrong." She took a few breaths. "Obviously, Danielle didn't react well. She stormed out. And that was the last time I saw her."

I sat there for what felt like a long while, information bouncing around my head. The love letter from "M" hadn't been Michael. It'd either been from someone else, or a complete fake. Jesus, Hudson could've hidden it under Danielle's mattress himself, then led me right to it. I never even imagined Michael could've been Danielle's father until Hudson planted that idea in my head.

Hudson. Of fucking course.

Don't trust the Davenports!

"Evie. Evie?"

David's voice broke through the fog in my brain. I looked over to him, his face fuzzy as my eyes refused to focus.

"Is there something you're not telling us? Why would Michael kill Danielle then?"

And the answer to David's question, of course, was that he wouldn't. Michael didn't kill Danielle. And there was only one reason Hudson would lie about that.

I stood on unsteady legs. "I'm so sorry for making you tell me that," I told Sharon. "But I think you just helped me figure this out. I'm sorry, I have to go now."

"Wait, what do you mean you figured it out?" Sharon got to her feet. "Evie, what happened to Danielle?"

I darted for the door. "There's no time to explain, I'm sorry. I need to go to the police." I sprinted down the walkway to my car. "Detective Delaney or Pennington will be in touch!"

"Evie," David yelled after me again, but I ignored him. I felt bad for dropping that bomb and taking off, but I'd just learned I left a killer unattended in his hospital room. Shit! Penn had put me in charge of Hudson, and what did I do? Gave him the perfect opportunity to slip away.

Don't go. Please, Evie. Stay with me. Hudson hadn't wanted me to speak with Sharon—because he knew I'd get the truth out of her, and the jig would be up.

As I sped down the street, I fumbled my phone out of my purse. I dialed Penn but got his voicemail. The same thing happened with Delaney. I left them both messages, but who knew when they'd have the chance to listen.

"Damn it," I yelled as I was forced to stop for a red light. My nails dug into my steering wheel as I willed the light to change. The second it turned green I hit the gas, hurtling towards my destination. The police station was only five minutes away.

My phone buzzed, and I grabbed it, not bothering to look at the screen. "Hello?"

"Evie, hi. It's...It's Samantha Davenport."

I inadvertently slammed on the brakes.

"Samantha?" I pulled the car onto the shoulder, heart racing even more than it already was. What could she possibly have to say to me now?

"I...Can you meet me? I'm on site at the new complex, finishing up a few things."

"Uh..."

"Look, I haven't been honest with you about Danielle," Samantha said. "And I'm tired of lying. I need to tell someone what happened. You need to know the truth about Hudson. He needs to pay for what he did."

I hesitated a moment before saying, "I'll be there in ten."

I pulled a U-turn and headed towards the apartments. I should've told Penn first, but he had his hands full already. And if Samantha was ready to turn on Hudson, we'd have more than enough to arrest him for Danielle's murder.

I easily found a spot in the giant, vacant lot at Bristol Ridge, the strong smell of fresh asphalt hitting me as I got out of my car. Bright "Opening soon!" banners flapped against the stone buildings, with a phone number for interested renters to call.

I scanned the lot, cold wind whipping against my face, searching for Samantha. Across the lot I spotted the black Jaguar, and a chill went through me that didn't come from the weather. I reached for my phone in my coat pocket and hit record, then double checked the phone was concealed. If she was about to implicate Hudson, I wanted to make damn sure I got it on tape.

"Samantha?" I called, boot heels echoing ominously as I made my way to the car. The driver's side door opened, and she stepped out. I should've been relieved, but I couldn't relax. The empty lot, the looming, vacant apartment building...I hadn't realized how secluded it was. And while it was only half past six, it was dark as the middle of the night.

"Thanks for coming, Evie," she said, meeting me halfway between our cars.

"You wanted to talk about Hudson?" I asked, wanting to get this done as quickly as possible.

"Yeah, I do."

As I waited for her to elaborate, I sensed someone come up behind me. I didn't even have a chance to spin around before a strong hand clamped a cloth over my face.

I tried to bolt, to scream, but the person's grip on me was iron as they held me against them. Feeling faint, I shot a desperate glance at Samantha, who stood there, watching. Completely unaffected.

And then everything went black.

CHAPTER THIRTY-THREE

"Are you really not going to help me at all? This is going to take *forever*."

"Sam, my fucking arm is broken!"

"How convenient."

I heard the voices first. I tried to open my eyes, but they seemed glued shut. It felt like I was desperately trying to pull myself out of a nightmare that wasn't over yet. I tried to move, but my limbs felt heavy, as if they were asleep.

But I must've shifted some because the voices stopped for a moment.

"Shit, she's waking up!"

Finally, I won the battle with my heavy eyelids and found myself staring up at the night sky, only a sliver of the moon visible. The top half of Hudson's face came into view as he looked down at me.

"Hey, Evie."

"Hubsom," I mumbled, my lips not working properly. My slurring amused him.

"Sorry about that," he said with a small smile. "Believe it or not, I really didn't want to do it. You should've listened to me, Evie. You should've stayed with me in the hospital like a good little girl."

I rolled to my side, able to bend my legs a bit. I needed to get up. Putting my hands on the cold ground, I attempted to push myself up, but my arms instantly collapsed, and I fell back into the grass.

Hudson laughed at my attempt. "It's strong stuff, Evie. You might want to stop before you hurt yourself."

Frustrated, I did the only thing I could do—take in my surroundings. My vision had mostly cleared now, and I saw grass and dirt and trees. We had to be in the vast swath of land behind the apartment building.

I noticed a sound in the background—repetitive and methodical. To my left was Samantha, about ten feet away, standing in fresh dirt. I could hear the occasional grunt and pant, and when I caught the glint of moonlight off something metal, I realized what the sound was. A shovel in dirt. Over and over again. Terror rippled through me as I put together that Samantha was digging a grave. Mine.

I raced through my limited options as I remained semi-paralyzed on the ground. My phone was within reach, right in my pocket, but I could barely move my fingers. Hudson would notice me trying to make a call. Plus, I still had the recording going—it'd take even longer to back out of that and dial someone.

My lack of strength also meant I couldn't attempt to fight back. I eyed Samantha as she continued to huff and puff, exhausted from the digging. Judging from the number of times she brushed hair out of her face and stumbled as her stiletto-heeled boots sunk into the dirt, I guessed she wasn't used to things like manual labor. I could probably take her.

Normally, I'd be no match for Hudson, but as he'd just pointed out, his arm was broken. Heather the nurse mentioned he had a concussion too. If whatever they drugged me with wore off quickly enough, I might have a shot at overpowering Hudson.

That was a lot of ifs, but it gave me some hope. I just had to stop them from killing me before I could fight them off.

"You killed Danielle," I said to Hudson, drawing his attention back to me.

He grinned and got to his knees, sitting beside me. That was when I noticed the gun clutched in his left hand.

"When did you figure that out?" he asked. "Because it looked like you bought my story in the hospital. Did you?"

"It sounded really good. It made sense. Even Pennington thought so. But after all the shit you pulled, I couldn't take your word for it anymore. You know, fool me once..."

He exhaled and dropped his shoulders. "Which is why you ran to talk to Sharon. You just couldn't help yourself. If you hadn't done that, Evie, we wouldn't be here right now. But I know you, and I know you wouldn't have let this go."

He was right. If I'd listened to Penn, Hudson would still be in the hospital, unable to run—and I wouldn't have learned the crucial piece of information that ruined everything for him.

"So what was your plan exactly?" I clenched and unclenched my fists as I slowly regained more mobility. "If I hadn't gone to Sharon to ask, the cops would've. Then everyone would know you lied about that."

"When Sharon would deny Dad was Danielle's father, I'd say she was lying," Hudson said. "My word against hers and Dad's. It'd force them to hold Dad while doing the DNA test to check. In the meantime, since I spilled the beans, Dad would crack and admit he helped cover up Danielle's death—which he did, by the way. Then I'd claim that Danielle fell down the stairs by accident, and Dad forced Sam and me to stay quiet all these years. Our rich, evil father forced us to cover up a death as to not jeopardize his business. It's a great story."

"It is." I flexed the arm Hudson couldn't see. "So tell me. What actually happened to her? Was it an accident?"

"Eh, kind of," he said. "I pushed her harder than I meant to. But I knew we were near the stairs. I knew she'd get hurt."

Disgust roiled inside me over how casually Hudson admitted what he'd done. He killed Danielle, stayed silent all these years, then manipulated my entire investigation to cast the blame on his family members—made himself look like the victim in all this.

"What happened that night?" I asked, confusion momentarily replacing fear. It didn't add up.

Hudson leaned back, using his good arm to support himself. I eyed the gun, on which Hudson only rested his fingertips.

"Some of what I told you in the hospital was true," he admitted. "I was in love with Danielle. But, as you know, she wasn't really interested."

"Ha!" Samantha paused her grave-digging. "She thought you were a creep, Hudson. And you *are*."

"Shut up, Sam." He rolled his eyes. "Anyway, I got excited when she reached out to me that fall. She wanted to go to UVA, so she asked me all about it. We started texting. A lot. I could tell she was warming up to me."

I raised my eyebrows, urging Hudson to continue. I now had complete control over my arms. The legs still felt heavy.

"So Danielle starts telling me about her essay, about wanting to find her real father," he went on. "And I saw my opening. If I could act like I wanted to help her out, she might finally realize she had feelings for me. All I had to do was act like a nice, caring friend instead of the 'creep' she thought I was. Which was when I forged the love letter."

I sighed. "Of course it wasn't real."

"It was just vague enough to intrigue, right?" He grinned off into the distance, impressed with himself. "I was pretty proud of it. I practiced Dad's handwriting for a while to make it look legit. Then I told Danielle I found it in his things—a letter he never worked up the nerve to send. Once she got her hands on that, she was unstoppable. Wouldn't let it go."

"You must've panicked when she asked for the DNA test," I said.

"I did at first," he said. "But I thought we'd built a strong enough friendship by that point. I could end the ruse. Danielle would see the results, see we weren't related, and then realize how close we'd gotten. She'd realize she had feelings for me."

"I don't know," I said. "If I were her, I'd be pissed about the forged letter. About you purposely leading me on. Trust me, I know how that feels."

Hudson chuckled. "You know what, you and Danielle are a lot alike, Evie. Maybe that's why I liked you so much. But yeah, she reacted badly when I came clean about the letter. She was acting crazy when she came over that night."

"Maybe she was *acting crazy* because she'd just found out her real father was a rapist."

"Well, regardless, she was furious. It didn't go the way I'd been expecting." Any hint of his trademark smirk had vanished, and a darkness came over Hudson's face that I hadn't seen before.

"She stormed out on me. I went after her," he said, jaw clenched. "I caught up to her on the stairs, apologizing, begging for another chance. She laughed in my face when I told her I loved her. That's when she called me a 'desperate creep'...and I lost it. I shoved her. She tumbled down the stairs. And that was it."

"Everyone was home," Samantha said, leaning against the shovel. "We all saw it."

"Did you even care? Did you even care that your brother just killed your best friend?"

"Of course, I cared!" Samantha shouted back. "But Mom and Dad took charge right away. They didn't want their precious son going to jail for this—not to mention the bad press."

"Precious son?" I said. "Hudson, I thought you were the black sheep?"

"Is that what he told you?" Samantha asked, amusement in her voice. "Ha! Growing up, Hudson could do no wrong! The Davenport golden boy. It wasn't until he killed Danielle that Mom and Dad realized they created a monster by letting him get away with everything."

I thought back to what Georgina had told Michael at the party. *You're the one who lets him run wild. That's how we ended up in this mess in the first place!*

"We were all horrified," Samantha said. "But Mom and Dad couldn't resist cleaning up another one of Hudson's messes. I was pissed, but once Dad involved himself, I had to go along with it. I needed him."

"To give you your cushy job, right? Because you couldn't be bothered to get something on your own."

Samantha scoffed at me, then turned to Hudson. "Is it time to kill her yet?"

I tried to wiggle my legs. They seemed to be working. I pressed at my thighs with my index fingers and felt every hard poke.

"Samantha, I don't understand why you're helping him." I was desperate to get through to her. Surely, she couldn't be as cold-blooded as her brother. Maybe she could still put a stop to this. "You didn't kill Danielle. You could come clean, get some kind of deal with the police."

"It's too late for that." I could hear the conviction in her voice. "Hudson convinced me to help early on. I mean, if Dad went to jail, my entire future at DP would be up in the air." Samantha paused. "I fucked up when I shot Marcus. I was just trying to scare you; I didn't know he'd jump in front of you so fast."

"Yeah, shooting a cop is kind of a big deal, sis." Hudson turned to me. "So now Sam's stuck on damage control duty with me. Works out for both of us if the cops think Dad did everything."

"This is the last fucking time I'm helping you, Hudson," Samantha warned.

"You do realize killing me will just make everything worse," I said. "Your plan to make your dad take the fall might work, but when I go missing, you know Pennington won't stop until he finds out what happened."

"A suspended detective with a history of harassing me, who's personally involved with the missing person? Yeah, I don't think that'll be too hard to deal with. He'll go berserk and do stupid things, as usual. Maybe get fired this time."

"Come on, Hudson, let's get this over with." Samantha tossed the shovel aside and hobbled out of the dirt. Apparently, she deemed my grave deep enough. I had to try and fight now, whether my body was ready or not.

Hudson looked at me with big, sad eyes. "Oh, Evie. We really could've been something, you know? If you weren't so obsessed with your do-gooder macho man, things could've been so different. If only you would've just believed me."

"Hudson," I said, "you really are a desperate fucking creep."

And with that, I pushed myself up and lunged at him. He yelped as I tackled him to the ground. I still felt a bit sluggish, but between his injuries and the element of surprise, I had the advantage.

I darted for the gun as Hudson's fingers desperately tried to grasp it. He got hold of the gun, so I pressed down, hard, on his broken arm. Hudson's scream pierced the dark, quiet night. I wrestled the gun from his limp hand as he groaned in pain. I'd just managed to grasp it in my right hand when Hudson suddenly pushed against me with surprising strength and rolled us over.

Despite his broken arm, Hudson had me pinned, trapping my hand with the gun between our bodies. I kicked and flailed, but I couldn't get him off of me.

"You really are a pain in the ass," he growled, wrapping his left hand around my neck. He leaned up to put more pressure against my throat, which gave me the room I needed. I turned the gun up, pressed it against his abdomen, and fired.

Samantha gasped as the sound of the gunshot echoed around us. Hudson's face tensed, and his mouth fell open, emitting a quiet wheeze. I pushed him as hard as I could, and he flopped off me, hand clutching his stomach.

Gun still in my hand, I struggled to get to my feet, stumbling twice as I rose to my full height.

"You shot my brother!" Samantha screamed at me. She grabbed the shovel and charged towards me.

"Seriously?" I raised the gun at her. "Gun beats shovel."

This stopped her in her tracks. We stood there, locked in a staring contest for a long time, until sirens filled the air.

"Oh, thank Jesus," I muttered, tilting my head back and looking at the sky. Within a matter of seconds, the sirens grew louder until the police cars squealed into the parking lot. Red and blue lights splashed against the empty, stone building.

"Down here!" I yelled as car doors slammed. Half a dozen cops started jogging towards us, weapons drawn.

"Put the gun down!" One shouted at me.

"Ah!" I quickly dropped it, having forgotten I'd been holding it. Samantha threw down her shovel too.

"They both tried to kill me," I said to the officer, pointing to Samantha and Hudson, still moaning on the ground. His eyes darted to the shallow, crooked grave Samantha had dug.

"Evie?" The voice was distant, coming from the parking lot, but I recognized it.

"Penn?"

I craned my neck, trying to see past the officer approaching me. Two men hurried down the small hill towards us. One was moving much faster than the other.

"Evie?" he called again, the concern in his voice clear.

"Penn!" I dodged the cop in front of me and ran on my jelly-like legs. Penn rushed to me, and as my legs gave out, and I stumbled forward, he managed to catch me.

"Are you alright?" he asked as I threw my arms around him. I opened my mouth to say yes, but all that came out was a little sob.

"It's okay, I've got you." He hugged me tightly.

"They tried to kill me," I mumbled into his chest. "I *hate* Hudson."

"Me too," he said, his hand rubbing my back again. Man, that felt good. Finally, I was getting the amazing hug I'd been dreaming of since our lock-up embrace.

I reluctantly pulled away. "How'd you know I'd be here?"

"I didn't. I saw your car in the lot just now. But I knew something was wrong when I got your messages, and you never showed up at the station." He paused. "We found out Hudson's story was bullshit pretty quick. I checked out the accident report, and nothing was wrong with

Hudson's car. He must've crashed it on his own to frame Michael. When we brought Michael in and told him about Hudson's accusation, he told us everything. I guess when it came down to it, he wasn't willing to take the blame for his son's crime."

I nodded. "I went to Sharon's and she confirmed Michael wasn't Danielle's father." I reached into my pocket and pulled out my phone, which was still recording. I stopped it and showed it to Penn. "I also got Hudson's entire confession, so that's something."

Penn put his disappointed dad face back on. "I explicitly told you not to go to Sharon's."

"Yeah, well, I think we're past that now."

"We are *not* past that." Penn pointed a finger at me. "You and I are going to have a talk about your listening skills later."

I fought a smile. He was adorable when he got all stern. "Whatever you say."

"Anyway, once Michael confessed, we went to round up the whole family," Penn said. "Michael told us Samantha had been working here today, so we came to get her. Never thought we'd find this." He gestured to the scene in front of us. "But of *course* you'd be here, in mortal danger. You just can't help yourself, can you?"

He wouldn't be Penn if he didn't scold me after I nearly died.

"No, I can't." That reminded me of something else. I took out my phone again and opened the Notes app, thumbs poised to type. "Oh, do you want to give me a quote for all this now, or later?"

He laughed out loud—a deep, hearty laugh—then wrapped an arm around my shoulders and kissed me on the forehead. "Darlin', I'm taking you home now."

CHAPTER THIRTY-FOUR

No one really noticed what was going on when the police arrived bright and early, but by ten a.m., quite the crowd had gathered around my apartment complex, pushing as close as they could to the yellow crime scene tape secured around our backyard.

"Oh, thanks, Evie," Grace said as I offered her a cup from the cardboard carrier. Once she took her coffee, I moved down the line and held out the remaining cups to Sharon and David. They both took one, but neither drank. Their eyes were locked on the scene in front of us.

A dozen or so cops were scattered across the lawn, some marking various areas with spray paint while the others dug in the designated spots. Penn was one of the diggers, and despite the cold December wind, he stopped to wipe sweat from his brow every now and then. He had to be exhausted. They'd been digging for hours.

The night I almost died had been chaotic. Samantha was hysterical, Hudson was rushed back to the hospital in critical condition, and I was formally questioned since I'd fired the gun—the same gun that had been used in the drive-by shooting. My recording cleared me of any wrongdoing quickly, and Hudson pulled through. I was happy about that. I despised him, but I didn't want to be a killer. Besides, Hudson deserved to face every single consequence he had coming to him.

Despite Michael's initial cooperativeness, he wouldn't say where he and Georgina had hidden Danielle's body. Samantha and Hudson both said zilch on that front too. We all knew why they didn't want us to find her. If we had a body—well, bones at this point—a forensic anthropologist might very well be able to tell if Danielle had simply fallen down the stairs, or if she'd been thrown.

Unfortunately for the Davenports, we had a damn good guess where she'd ended up.

After my ordeal, Shelly had given me a week off from work to recover. I appreciated the gesture, but I didn't want a break. All I wanted to do was write up my blog posts and wrap up the mystery of Danielle Livingston's disappearance for my readers. The loose end of her body was driving me crazy. Penn had told me not to worry about it too much, that we had plenty to nail each and every Davenport for their part in Danielle's death, but I wasn't satisfied. I'd embarked on this case because I wanted to find a missing girl, and I still hadn't done that.

So I pored through everything. My days off were filled with more obsessive case behavior, taping things to my wall, color-coded highlighting, and memorizing every official statement from Michael, Georgina, Samantha, and Hudson. I was looking for any clues— anything that stood out. Getting increasingly desperate, I even went through those Bristol Hills documents I'd taken photos of during my break-in.

And I'd finally found something, in a landscaping receipt of all things. Michael had signed off on the planting of a slew of new trees and shrubberies on December eighteenth—the day after Danielle's disappearance. The timing was weird. Upon further digging through the landscaping plans, I'd found that the work initially hadn't been scheduled until after the holidays. For some reason, Michael wanted all that fresh dirt covered with greenery. Fast.

That's where Danielle had to be. I was convinced—especially

considering Hudson and Samantha had planned to bury me on the property of the latest Davenport complex. They'd probably chosen that because it worked so well the first time around.

Penn agreed my findings were enough to warrant a search. But after three hours of digging, I'd started to get discouraged.

"She's gotta be here," I whispered to Grace.

"They're going to find her," she said, her voice reassuring. "I have a feeling."

I gave her an uncertain look, but nevertheless sipped my coffee and let the police work. Every now and then, I cast a glance over to the Livingstons, who'd hardly uttered one word since they'd arrived.

I'd almost finished my coffee when one of the diggers waved a few others over. They spoke in hushed tones, and I couldn't make anything out. Two knelt to the ground and began digging with small garden trowels. I grabbed Grace's arm. After a few agonizing minutes, Penn stood and turned. He locked eyes with me and offered me a nod. They'd found her.

My eyes welled up, both from relief and a deep swell of emotion. I thought about how upset I'd been when I ended up in Bristol two years ago—how I'd mourned the old, fabulous life I thought I'd had, how I'd been furious with myself for destroying my career. At the time, I couldn't think of anything worse than being a reporter for a small-town paper no one read.

But as the team began to excavate Danielle's remains, I was struck with the intense feeling I'd ended up exactly where I was supposed to be—and it was no coincidence that this entire time, Danielle Livingston had been in my backyard, waiting for me to find her.

"Evening, Penn!"

He let out a little laugh as he stepped onto his front porch, squinting into the darkness. "What are you doing out here?"

"Oh, you know, just my usual stalker thing. Took you long enough to notice me."

He crossed the lawn, shoving his hands into his pockets as he walked towards me. I pulled my coat more tightly around myself and shivered in a dramatic fashion.

"Jeez, how long have you been out here? It's freezing."

"I know," I said, shuddering again. Penn took the hint and wrapped his arms around me.

"To what do I owe this visit?" He grinned and held me against his warm body.

"Well, I was thinking about what you said would happen the next time I showed up uninvited," I said. "Something about wine and barbecue and a fire."

"Hmm..." Penn pretended to mull it over. "That can be arranged."

"Just a warning, though." I looked up at him. "All that might just encourage future stalking."

Penn moved in closer, his face mere inches from mine. "I think I'll take my chances."

I closed the distance and kissed him, putting my arms around his waist. Penn leaned into me, pressing me against the side of my car. I sure didn't need the fire to warm me up anymore. After a while I pulled away, overcome with a fit of giggles.

"Remember when you said you never wanted to speak to me again?"

He laughed and ran his thumb across my lower lip. "Ironic, considering now I want to do all kinds of things with you."

I suppressed an excited squeal by giving him another quick kiss. "Marcus, are you going to invite me in, or not?"

Penn took my hand and marched across the lawn, leading me up his front porch steps. He opened the door and made a long, sweeping gesture inside.

"Darlin', come on in."

Thank you for reading! Did you enjoy? Please add your review because nothing helps an author more and encourages readers to take a chance on a book than a review.

And don't miss more from Rachel Mucha available now! Turn the page for a sneak peek of Another Day, Another Partner!

Also be sure to sign up for the City Owl Press newsletter to receive notice of all book releases!

SNEAK PEEK OF ANOTHER DAY, ANOTHER PARTNER

Have you ever heard someone's name and immediately knew they were going to be trouble? You haven't spoken to them yet — maybe you haven't even seen them — but you can already tell, just by their name, exactly what they'll be like?

This has happened to me several times throughout my life — most notably, in the eleventh grade when Grant Hunter showed up as the new kid in school. Grant Hunter. Now that's a name. And as Mrs. Pearson told us that he would be joining our English class, I immediately knew everything I needed to know about Grant Hunter. He'd be good looking, obviously, with a name like that. His parents had to have money — Grant is a family name if I ever heard one. And good looking plus money always equals playboy. Grant Hunter, I already knew, was going to be one smooth, charming S.O.B., on a mission to sweet-talk himself into as many girls' pants as possible.

So when Grant Hunter finally entered our classroom and was directed to the empty desk beside me, I silently congratulated myself on a job well done. It was already apparent that two of my deductions had been correct. Grant Hunter was tall and lean, with a great head of dark hair and a very attractive acne-free face. He wore neatly pressed chinos and Sperry boat shoes, and as he sat down, I got a big whiff of Polo by Ralph Lauren. Definitely rich.

My third deduction, the one about him being a sweet-talking S.O.B., was confirmed a few weeks later when he charmed me out of my virginity in the backseat of his dad's BMW.

Shakespeare didn't know what he was talking about with that 'What's in a name?' speech. A name can say a lot about a person.

Just take a look at mine. Luciana Martinelli. I know, right? In my opinion, it's borderline child abuse. But, nevertheless, it tells a story. One, it tells people that my parents are too Italian for their own good, and thought that honoring their heritage was more important than giving their daughter a name that could fit on those standardized test Scantron forms — though, I will admit that my sister, Valentina, has it just as bad as me.

Two, it lets you know that I'm no pushover, since growing up with a name like that in small-town Rhode Island, which isn't known for its high Italian population, would've led to a lot of teasing — and, naturally, some toughening up.

And three, the number of syllables alone suggests that I definitely have a nickname for this atrocity, and if you call me Luciana, you're likely getting a fist to the face.

Names, man. I'm telling you.

So, anyway, I found myself having one of those moments where I jump to all sorts of conclusions about someone based on their name when I heard I was getting a new partner. And not just any partner. A partner named *Dominic Delgado*.

Seriously. I think I might've rolled my eyes, which is pretty rude to do to your police captain, but I couldn't help it.

"Drop the attitude, young lady!"

Did I mention that my captain is also my father?

"Dad, I don't need a partner," I said, pretending the eye roll was about a partner in general and not one named *Dominic Delgado*. "I work better alone."

He let out a frustrated sigh. "You need someone watching your back out there, Lulu."

I held in a wince at the childhood nickname only my family was permitted to use. For everyone else, it was Lucy. I mean, a cop named Lulu? Have you ever heard of a more ridiculous thing?

"Need I remind you about the incident with Mrs. Webber?"

"That was a fluke thing," I insisted. "Plus, my hair's almost done growing back in."

"If she hadn't had a pool, you'd be dead right now." My dad jabbed a finger at me.

This sounds weird out of context, so I'll explain. We work out of a tiny police department in Portsmouth, Rhode Island. Portsmouth is your typical little charming New England hamlet, and with a population of just around seventeen thousand, not a whole heck of a lot of crime happens. Most of the calls I go on involve drunk fishermen, domestic tiffs, or teenagers trying to shoplift a twelve-pack from the grocery store.

Being such a close-knit community, you really get to know the locals as you're cruising around every day. And Pamela Webber was one local that every cop at the Portsmouth Police Department knew quite well.

The lady is bananas. I realize there are probably kinder terms for her condition, but after what she did to me, I don't owe her any favors.

I'd gotten the call last summer. One of Pamela's neighbors complained, again, that her TV was on too loud. This might sound like a petty complaint on the neighbor's part, but I'd dealt with this exact situation before, and let me tell you — Pamela, who's practically deaf, watches her TV so loudly it'd curdle your blood if you were in the room with her. And, she left it on 24/7. Imagine living next door to that.

I'd just gone over there to kindly ask her to turn it down. That's all. It shouldn't have been a big deal.

But Pamela was in a particularly nasty — i.e., drunk — mood that day. She wouldn't turn it down and she wouldn't let me inside the house, either. I stood on her porch, my ears already screaming for relief, so I did what anyone in my position would've done. I punched a hole through the flimsy mesh of her screen door, let myself in, dove for the remote, and turned the volume the hell down.

Well, Pamela didn't like that one bit. She'd been in the kitchen cooking something, and the second the TV was shut off, she started screaming every expletive in the book at me.

"Don't make me come back here again," I yelled, already turning for the door.

Pamela must've been really fired up that day, because she came bursting out of the kitchen with a butcher's knife. A butcher's knife! I was in such a state of shock that it didn't occur to me to pull my gun on her. I mean, I never took the thing out of its holster; never had reason to. And to pull it on Pamela, Portsmouth's resident crazy drunk lady? The thought just never crossed my mind.

In the interest of full disclosure, I should mention I might've been off my game due to the one-two punch of my recent breakup and the resignation of the only partner I'd ever had.

"Why can't you just leave me alone!" Pamela screamed as she chased me around the living room with the knife. Being much younger and more agile than her, it wasn't that tough to dodge her futile jabs, but admittedly, I was nervous. She blocked the door I came in, so I darted towards the kitchen, hoping to escape out the back. I was almost home free until my foot got caught on the leg of a kitchen chair and I fell over. Pamela caught up to me and stood over me with this crazy look in her eye. I scrambled to my feet, and she backed me into a corner by the stove. The water she'd been boiling for her mac and cheese was spilling over the sides of the pot.

"Mrs. Webber! You need to drop the knife, *now*," I said in the most calm, stern voice I could muster. In an acrobatic-like move, I leaned backwards as far as I could to get maximum distance between myself and the knife, my head dangerously close to that rapidly boiling pot of water.

With my mind focused on Pamela, it took me a while to notice what had happened. But suddenly, her angry, narrowed eyes grew wide and her jaw dropped.

"You're on fire!" She lowered the knife. It took me a few more seconds for her words to register. And then I smelled it. You probably know the smell — burned-hair-on-the-flat-iron smell. That unmistakable, stale, burnt odor instantly let me know that my hair had brushed over the lit burner on the stove and caught fire. But by the time

I realized this, my long ponytail had brushed against my shirt sleeve, to which the flames had quickly spread.

"You're on fire!" Pamela yelled, looking surprisingly concerned. This, I thought, was hilarious, given the fact that she'd been waving a knife at me ten seconds ago.

The intense pain on my upper arm stopped any laughter in its tracks. I started to panic, especially since it was clear that Pamela would be no help. I caught a glimpse of the pool in my peripheral vision and made a beeline for it. Which is how, a few seconds later, I found myself standing in Pamela's shallow end, soaked, with first degree burns on my shoulder and half my hair singed off.

Back at the station, my dad freaked out, though I was more concerned about my long, beautiful chestnut-brown hair going up in smoke. Fortunately, the flames hadn't reached my scalp, so my appearance could be salvaged with a very blunt bob. Roughly one year later, my curly hair finally reached my shoulders again, which I actually preferred to my length before the incident. I'd been cursed — or blessed, depending how you look at it — with a round baby face, so the shorter hair made me look a lot more mature.

See? A silver lining.

"You're working with Dominic, Lulu," my father said. "End of story."

I sighed. It was times like this when I wondered what I was thinking, voluntarily taking a job in which my father could boss me around. I was twenty-six years old, yet Captain John Martinelli always had the ability to make me feel like little Lulu again.

"Who is this guy?" I asked. "I don't know any Delgados in town."

"Just moved here." My father glanced down at what I assumed was Dominic Delgado's personnel file on his desk. "He was a detective at Boston PD for five years."

"What's a city detective doing here?" I tilted my head. "This is a major step down. You think a guy who's solved murders and hit-and-runs is going to be happy dealing with the Mrs. Webbers of Portsmouth?"

"Maybe he wanted a change of pace, Lulu." My father massaged his temples. "That's something you can ask him while you're spending your time together."

I suppressed another groan. I know I sounded like a brat, but traditionally, partners and me just didn't mix. Greg had been grumpy, old, and by the book, and never would have approved of punching a hole through Pamela Webber's screen door. After a few months with me, he decided to retire a year early. Linda had been a skittish young woman who had no business even being a cop in the first place, which I helped her figure out pretty quickly. And Rob...

I don't want to talk about what happened with Rob.

The point is, each of my previous partners had left after being paired up with yours truly, which is why I often go long stretches working alone. I like it that way — it's just *easier*. No awkward small talk. No messy eaters getting crumbs all over my squad car.

No chance of getting my heart crushed.

I'd been hoping I was in the clear on the partner front, because it'd been almost three months since Greg hit the road — a new solo record for me. But, unfortunately, my father is just as stubborn as me. Despite all the resignations, he's never wavered on this partner thing once. And, apparently, he wasn't afraid to risk the employment status of his newest recruit to try it again. It's like he *wanted* Dominic Delgado to go running back to Boston. Then it hit me.

Of course! I'll just annoy the hell out of Dominic Delgado, like I had with everyone else, and he'd be gone in no time. Maybe then my dad-boss would finally give up on his quest to find me a permanent partner and see I was born to fly solo.

"Okay." I flashed my dad a smile. "I'll give Dominic a shot."

He eyed me suspiciously. "Really?"

I nodded. "Sure. I just hope he's not too bored around here. After a week on the job, I wouldn't be surprised if he threw in the towel and ran for the nearest city."

I'd said this in a very casual, innocent tone, but obviously, my father knows me too well to be fooled.

"I know what you're thinking, and you need to stop it right now," my father said, finger pointed at me. "You will not intentionally try to get rid of him."

My forced smile fell and I got up from my chair.

"Seriously, Lulu, don't waste your time," Dad said. "I got the impression that this guy doesn't scare easily."

Of course Dominic Delgado doesn't scare easily, I thought to myself as I exited my father's office. Someone named Dominic Delgado wouldn't be intimidated by someone like me. Dominic Delgado was probably pretty slick. Probably pretty arrogant. Definitely a fast talker. With an alliterative name like Dominic Delgado, he'd likely been blessed with the gift of gab. Great. Just what I needed. Not only a partner I didn't want, but a *chatty* one to boot.

I'd been lost in my own thoughts, wondering if I could convince Dominic Delgado that I only spoke limited English and therefore it'd be best if we didn't try to communicate, when I realized I'd forgotten to make two very important assumptions about someone named Dominic Delgado. And my omission became glaringly obvious as I walked toward my desk and saw a tall, young man standing beside it, seemingly waiting for me.

The first important assumption was, of course, that someone named Dominic Delgado would be exceedingly, incredibly hot.

And the second? He was definitely going to be trouble.

Don't stop now. Keep reading with your copy of ANOTHER DAY, ANOTHER PARTNER.

And find more from Rachel Mucha at rachelmuchabooks.com

Want even more from Rachel Mucha? Read ANOTHER DAY, ANOTHER PARTNER and be sure to receive all the news and updates at rachelmuchabooks.com

Officer Luciana "Lulu" Martinelli prefers to work alone. Who wouldn't, after falling in love with their partner, only to have him up and leave? Unfortunately, her captain, who's also her father, is determined to pair her with someone. His latest recruit, former Boston detective Dominic Delgado, is turning out to be harder to shake than the others. Dom's as talented at his job as he is gorgeous, and the worst part is...he knows it.

Lulu can't understand why a big-city cop would want to work for a small Rhode Island police department—until he's brutally attacked after his first day on the job. Dom didn't exactly give up his old life by choice, and some pretty terrifying bad guys want him dead. Things only get stickier when Lulu's ex-boyfriend Rob resurfaces with a far-fetched explanation for leaving her, and an interesting connection to Dom.

Forced to team up with the man who shattered her heart, her dangerously charming new partner, and even her bored teenage sister home on summer break, Lulu discovers her little town isn't as crime-free as she thought — and that maybe, just maybe, having a partner to watch her back isn't the worst thing in the world.

All reviews are **welcome** and **appreciated**. Please consider leaving one on your favorite social media and book buying sites.

Escape Your World. Get Lost in Ours! City Owl Press at www.cityowlpress.com.

ACKNOWLEDGMENTS

I've made it no secret that this book is my favorite thing I've written so far, and I am so incredibly excited and thankful to have it out in the world. Once again, I have to thank my agent, Susan Nystoriak. She is always so enthusiastic about everything I send her, and *Bad Press* was no exception. She loved Evie and Penn as much as I do, and she helped shape them into perfection. You're awesome, Susan, and I know my characters are always safe in your hands.

Thanks again to my editor, Mary Cain. You are a dream to work with, and I love all the brainstorming we do. I wanted to thank the amazing City Owl team for the continued support -- I love having my books published with you!

Thank you to all my family and friends, who have been so supportive. The amount of people who read my debut and had such kind words is overwhelming in the best way. I truly appreciate all of you, and hope you enjoyed this one. Thanks again to my parents, who always want to know everything about what I'm working on. Thanks to Jess White, friend/beta reader extraordinaire, who may be a bigger #Penvie shipper than I am. Allysson, Elizabeth, Lauren and Skylar -- you're the most supportive and enthusiastic friends I can ask for, and I love you all!

Finally, thank you to the readers! And if you picked up *Bad Press* because you liked *Another Day, Another Partner*, thanks so much for coming on this journey with me. I hope you'll stick around, because I have some big plans for your favorite characters.

ABOUT THE AUTHOR

RACHEL MUCHA has been writing all her life, whether it be short stories or satire articles. A graduate of Ithaca College, Rachel currently writes business and HR articles by day, and mystery novels by night. Her fascination with crime-solving started at a young age with Nancy Drew books, and carried into adulthood with  countless detective shows and novels. Rachel currently resides in the Philadelphia suburbs, where you're just as likely to find her wrapped up in a dark police procedural as a mushy romantic comedy. When she's not reading or writing, Rachel enjoys mixing up fancy cocktails and traveling to new states.

rachelmuchabooks.com

 twitter.com/rachmucha
instagram.com/rachmucha

ABOUT THE PUBLISHER

City Owl Press is a cutting edge indie publishing company, bringing the world of romance and speculative fiction to discerning readers.

Escape Your World. Get Lost in Ours!

www.cityowlpress.com

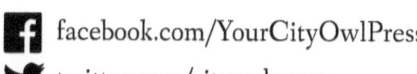

facebook.com/YourCityOwlPress

twitter.com/cityowlpress

instagram.com/cityowlbooks

pinterest.com/cityowlpress